BUDDY
&
THE JACK

A Novel

W. Bryan Smith

AmErica House
Baltimore

First printing

ISBN: 1-59129-224-7
PUBLISHED BY AMERICA HOUSE BOOK PUBLISHERS
www.publishamerica.com
Baltimore

Printed in the United States of America

For Corky II & Tycho: your muddy paws, shedding, and doggie breath… I could not live without them.

For Beanie, Pepper, Max, Corky I, Sparky & Barney: rest now, gentle friends.

ACKNOWLEDGMENTS

There are many people who have helped contribute in the writing of this novel.

First and foremost, the Danville Pennwriters: Pam Chappen Oren, Dave Freas, Laurie Creasey, and Marta Johnson – all great writers in their own right. Thank you for teaching me the craft of writing. I am proud to be among your ranks.

My friends and coworkers at Encompass Insurance, especially the M Unit: Lea Frank (the world's greatest boss), Karen Stauffer, Carolyn Ciesielski, Tammy Ruth, Kevin Hoss, & Terri Anton. Many thanks for reading the book in its various stages and for all your support. You are family to me.

Special thanks go to my publisher, PublishAmerica, for believing in me. Thank you for taking a chance on an unknown writer.

For the many teachers and professors over the years who have taught me the fine art of writing and an appreciation for literature. Thank you.

Bob Doyle: thanks for all your advice, on and off the golf course. And I assure you, I will not try to become the "Homer of Mount Carmel."

Amybeth Forbes: this book could not have been written without you. You were with me from the first sentence to the last word. Thank you for inspiring me and opening my eyes to the mistreatment of animals. I only regret I could not have written a better ending for us.

And finally I want to thank my family, particularly my mother and grandmother. Thank you for always being there for me, for all your encouragement, and your love. Although I've never said it, I want you to know, I love you very much.

There… I said it.

We are two travellers, Roger and I.
Roger's my dog – come here, you scamp!
Jump for the gentleman – mind your eye!
Over the table,– look out for the lamp!
The rogue is growing a little old;
Five years we've tramped through wind and weather,
And slept out-doors when nights were cold,
And ate and drank and starved together.

– John T. Trowbridge, *The Vagabonds*

I. A Dark Journey

So where have we come to now, Antigone, my child,
this blind old man and you–
what people and what town?
And who today will dole out charity
to Oedipus the vagabond?

– Sophocles, *Oedipus at Colonus*

There was a stranger in the alleyway.

The mongrel sampled the air. The scent was faint like a whisper, but still discernable through the light rain – familiar, yet foreign. It was another dog, but the mongrel did not know him.

A German shepherd perhaps? One with plenty to eat at home – an animal with no need to eat from the trash. Or maybe he was a Scottish terrier, a beloved clown prince from a doting human family, clever enough to free himself from the safe confines of his backyard. He could even be a stray mongrel, much like himself, but having a much better go of life on the streets. In the end though, the stranger's breeding really didn't matter. Whoever he was, he was competition – and a trespasser.

The mongrel had claimed this alley days ago, claimed it with a squirt of urine on every lamppost, his signature on every tree.

Keep away, the mongrel bemoaned. *Stay back*. The sound of tires contacting the wet roadway fizzled over the mongrel's warning. He had been coming to these same trashcans for over a week. He wasn't about to forfeit his right to them now.

Ker-click-click! The mongrel recoiled. The sound of their umbrellas deploying startled him. Several children raced by him, their rubber shoes scuffing along the sidewalk. Trembling, he cowered behind a stack of discarded boxes until their footsteps faded in the distance. The rain drummed scornfully on his back.

It seemed as though it had been raining forever.

The Jack Russell terrier carelessly ripped through the thin trash bag. Meringue leaked from a gaping hole and oozed its way onto the street. He lapped it up with delight, already anticipating his next mouthful. It was sweet on his tongue and rolled easily down his throat.

Oh, that raccoon! God bless his fat, old heart! He remembered watching that *fat, old* raccoon, keeping his distance – raccoons can be very nasty creatures – watching him work his magic on those trashcans. Standing up on his hind legs, using his fore paws to totter the trashcan, to knock it over. The lid came off – exploded off, really – and all that wonderful food came out. The Jack watched him do it a half-dozen times that night, just to be sure.

The white fur of his muzzle already stained with marinara sauce, the Jack added a considerable amount of meringue to his nose. He was so delighted with himself, he howled. He wouldn't have to eat for a whole week. The Jack moved without hesitation from the meringue to a half-eaten tin of lasagna. Gulping, snorting, he paused only long enough to breathe.

The Jack was a short, athletic dog whose usually white fur had a brownish tinge from a lack of proper grooming. He had a patch of brown fur over his right ear that extended well below his right eye, and a short cotton swab for a tail. He wore a simple nylon collar that proudly displayed his expired license.

He finished up the remainder of the lasagna and then busied himself with another trash bag.

In the distance, the mongrel waited. The coupling of his parents had produced a quite large dog and his thick brown coat hinted at collie somewhere in his bloodline. But his fur was knotted, even missing in patches, reminders of his bout with mange and a difficult initiation into stray life.

A long time ago, he had been named Buddy. When he was Buddy, he had patrolled a fair-sized yard and kept it free of squirrels and cats and mice and burglars and any other thing the master cared not to have around. The master said Buddy had a good *sniffer*. He'd use his *sniffer* to blow away the top layer of leaves and catch a field mouse in a conspiratorial pose. His *sniffer* was also useful to follow the trail of the neighbor's cat who'd climbed up the master's apple tree again, or to seek out a jerky treat the master had always kept in the pocket of his field coat. Buddy had a good *sniffer*.

This rainy October afternoon, as the soggy, fallen leaves squished between the pads of his paws, his *sniffer* proved its worth once more. It told him there was a scoundrel in his midst – a Jack Russell terrier to be exact.

The notion raised Buddy's hackles. He growled – a hoarse, strangled growl. This stranger was not welcome; this stranger was uninvited.

Buddy stumbled closer.

The Jack succeeded in opening another bag. A thousand exotic smells emerged from the trash bag and bombarded his nose like a swarm of honey bees: partially eaten pizza crusts; refried beans; sweet and sour chicken; even pierogies, a potato-filled ravioli which was a staple in this region of the state. For a stray dog, it was like virtually winning the lottery to stumble upon such a treasure of discarded goodies. His tail beat at the air.

Buddy used the cover of the fragrant trash as a stealth to get within inches of the dog. As the stranger gorged himself, Buddy instinctively located the terrier's hind quarters and conducted an inquiry. His *sniffer* told him the stranger was a youthful, confident male who was free of illness and new to these parts. He had not smelled his markings anywhere near the alleyway prior to that day.

Buddy knew he had his work cut out for him. He took the offensive. He found the stranger's tail and bit him. A shrill cry reported to Buddy that he had scored a direct hit.

The Jack's tail throbbed. He pulled his ass down, abandoned the trash and sought neutral ground some fifty feet away. Once he felt he was far enough from the danger at hand, he faced his attacker. His gaze fell upon a large, monstrous dog, frantically sniffing the mild breeze for any sign of the Jack. A sharp, steady pain in the Jack's tail testified to the might of the mongrel's jaws.

The mongrel cast a tremendous shadow. *What a horrid sight!* The Jack had never seen anything like him. The mongrel's one ear was gnarled and hung limply from the side of his head, and the tip of his tail was also missing. He looked like a ragged, though strangely magnificent, monster. A giant canine warrior, scarred by many battles, he easily towered over the diminutive Jack. But there was something not right about this animal. *Its eyes* – it had none.

It could not see him.

The Jack was right. Buddy was blind. Two dark holes marked his face like empty graves where there once had been eyes – keen, inquisitive eyes – eyes which in his puppyhood could have traced the flight of a hawk as it skirted the peak of some far off mountaintop.

Now there was nothing – no partial vision, no murky sight, no clouded, dead eyes that seem to stare off at nothing in particular. No light penetrated his world. Even the sun, when it made an appearance, failed to warm him. If the eyes were truly the windows to the soul, Buddy's empty sockets were the portals to a ghost ship. He was hollow – a spent cocoon.

Almost.

Buddy was still in there somewhere – the old Buddy – haunting the corridors of memory in a land of endless night. In those dark passages of his mind, the mongrel roamed, pawing blindly for what he had lost: a home; his sight; a life.

The Jack stalked toward the mongrel whose ears pricked at the return of the smaller dog's scent. Again, the larger dog's hair raised on its back, exaggerating its enormity even more. But the Jack was no longer fooled. *He can't see me*, the Jack reassured himself.

The mongrel's tail was plastered between its legs. His show of aggression was a facade. He was hiding a secret from the Jack's inquiring nose. He was concealing his fear and weakened condition from him.

Suddenly frightened and fearful that his size alone may not scare away this invader, Buddy began haphazardly biting at the air in a desperate effort to put another bite on the stranger. *Keep away*, he warned. *Stay back*.

But the Jack was too quick. He took full advantage of the mongrel's handicap and stayed behind the larger dog, moving when he did. It was working! The larger dog was confused. He kept turning in the direction of the Jack's scent – too late to catch the wily Jack. Every once and a while, the Jack would nip at Buddy's tail for good measure. *You can't see me*, he barked.

The Jack had discovered a new game! Playfully, he nipped under the mongrel's chin.

Buddy again turned too late and stumbled. He was slow to realize what was happening. The smaller dog wasn't attacking at all: he was playing. Surely, this dog was fresh from his mother's teat, no more than a pup, and most certainly at the height of his playing days. Buddy relaxed his tail and his good ear perked.

He was playing! Buddy remembered those days, not so long ago, playing in his master's backyard with the other dog, the one his master called Angus. He barked at the Jack as if to say, *I get it now! We're playing!*

He found the Jack's muzzle and placed a friendly nip of his own under the terrier's chin. He felt some of the old Buddy returning. *Playing! My God, after all this time!* Oh, how he loved to grab on to the end of a stick, Angus hanging on to the other side, pulling, tugging, growling, a rollicking game of tug o' war. Oh, those warm, sunny afternoons, lying on his back in the soft grass… staring up at the fuzzy, white cloud wisps rolling lazily overhead. Buddy remembered the unusual shapes the clouds would form as they scooted along the sky. He loved watching the clouds. Why, he was playing in the backyard on the day the strange man came – Buddy shivered. He didn't like to think about that day.

Suddenly, he stopped playing with the Jack and stood motionless in the alleyway, his muzzle tilted off at nothing in the distance. That was the last day he ever saw Angus and his master and the fuzzy, white clouds. That was the last day he ever saw anything.

The terrier was curious about Buddy's sudden lack of play. He sniffed at the mongrel's mouth.

Buddy dismissed him with a snarl. He didn't want to play anymore. He didn't want to do anything.

But the Jack didn't understand. This new game, this new friend, was so much fun. He placed another light nip under the mongrel's chin. The mongrel responded by biting the Jack much harder on the nose.

The Jack retreated. He'd gotten the message. The game was finished. The big dog didn't want to play anymore.

Dejected, he padded off. But before leaving, he looked back at the mongrel and sighed. Darkness shrouded the mongrel. It was black and opaque, and it lay over him like a funeral pall.

There was darkness *inside* the mongrel, too. The Jack's young heart ached as he watched the mongrel hover greedily over the scattered rubbish, protecting it from an invisible enemy.

But for all the mongrel's wretchedness, there was an air of nobility about him. He had been something once, the Jack was sure. There were secrets beyond his woeful appearance, past that face devoid of eyes. There was muscle beneath that ailing coat, and power hiding inside those chiseled canines.

But there was something else lurking too: a specter, a scent. The mongrel smelled of death.

The Jack shuddered. He suddenly felt the miserable dampness in his bones as if it had just found an opening in his skin and had all come rushing in at once. He yearned for a warm, dry bed, somewhere to shake off the mongrel's contagious moroseness. Heavyhearted, the Jack withdrew for such a place.

After the stranger's scent could no longer be detected from the host of other smells swirling about the alleyway, Buddy returned to the business at hand:

securing another meal from the trash. Why, for a minute there, he'd lost his head. *Playing? That was for dogs with masters and fenced yards, and kibble that makes its own gravy.* Stray dogs weren't allowed to play, especially a blind one who displeased his master so much, he called a strange man to come and take him away and pull his eyes from his head. *Playing? Ha! That terrier will see. He won't last very long if he continues to play with every stray dog he meets.*

At least the strange Jack had done him the courtesy of ripping the bags open. As he nosed through the garbage, tin cans rattling, plastic trash bag crinkling, the sound of his teeth chomping, Buddy failed to notice he was not alone once more.

Yellow eyes burned through the shadows – eyes that knew no master – wild eyes. It wasn't the friendly Jack, there were far too many. Buddy was too taken with feeding himself to hear them.

One by one, they materialized from the angular shadows. By the time their intrinsic scent reached his nose, it was already too late.

II. Cave Canem

Sir William De Tracy.-(I) Haunts Woolacombe Sands and Braunton Burrows, spinning ropes of sand. When nearly complete, a black dog appears with a ball of fire in his mouth and breaks the cord, so that the penance (for the murder of St Thomas Becket) is recommenced. (2) Many years ago a ferryman of Appledore heard someone hailing from Braunton and rowed across. There was only a black dog there, which jumped into the boat. The man rowed back, but as he neared Appledore the dog swamped the boat, swam ashore, and vanished over Northam Burrows.

– Theo Brown, from 'The Black Dog in Devon,'
Transactions of the Devonshire Association, Vol. 91, 1959

The ferals surrounded Buddy.

The pack, mostly made up of what the locals called "bush dogs," inasmuch as they lived in the nearby woods, had been making their fair share of news lately. Despite the efforts of local law enforcement and animal control, the dogs were causing quite a stir on the east side of town. Overturning trashcans, terrorizing children at the bus stop, not to mention barking and howling at all hours of the night, the ferals were a complete and utter menace.

Their presence was felt all the way from West Broadway Street where Old Lady Haversham's toy poodle was attacked and left for dead in her own yard, to Railroad Avenue and Chestnut Street where the dogs put the bite on a third grader waiting for the school bus.

To the residents of this community, they were the canine equivalent of Hell's Angels.

The alpha male, a muscular Rottweiller and Bull Mastiff mix, which isn't a friendly mix at all, stepped forward. He was an athletic dog whose lustrous coat resembled a velvet robe fit for the monarch of some netherworld kingdom. His dark eyes masked any sign of compassion or fear. Buddy could see none of this, of course. But what his eyes couldn't tell him, his nose certainly could.

There were many of them, more than he could count. Their coats smelled of rain and dander and wild places – and blood. Not their own blood, though.

It was old, encrusted blood – blood of smaller animals – blood stinking with fear; the blood of animals who were killed and knew very well they *would* be killed.

Buddy felt their fetid, hot breath on his muzzle. Their growling drifted on the dampness like a sinister, deadly song. His hind legs trembled.

The Alpha attacked. The aggression was so swift it easily knocked him to the ground. Buddy was disoriented. He snapped his powerful jaws at the air around him in an effort to ward off the attack.

But the Alpha was a seasoned fighter. Cunning and savage, he was too experienced in the ways of combat to fall victim to a blind dog's random bites. The Alpha placed a second, more savage attack on his bad ear. A kaleidoscope of pain exploded inside Buddy's head and he cried out in agony.

Some blocks away, that shrill cry reached the Jack's alert ears. He recognized it and started running. *It's the blind dog! He's in trouble!*

The Alpha pinned Buddy to the ground, ripping chunks of his diseased hair from his torso. Other dogs had joined the frenzy, stealing nips in his defenseless posture.

The torment was too much for Buddy, who had already endured having his eyes plucked from his head. He cried out one last time, a plea for mercy. But that was too much to ask.

He was about to die, and he'd made peace with it. There was nothing more to it. He merely lay on his side and awaited death. He remembered his master and Angus, and the fuzzy white clouds floating overhead. A nonsensical song played in his brain:

Oh, I was a dog named Buddy
strong and brave and wise.
Until the day
the strange man came
and took away my eyes.

The white clouds spun wildly in his mind. They came together, fused, then separated once more. They swelled with darkness; then rained blood. He clawed at the ground, anchoring himself against the storm.

But instead of more pain, relief washed over him. His heavy breathing, bordering on choking, echoed in his ears. The attack had ceased. Above his labored panting, Buddy heard the growling of a stranger.

The Jack found Buddy lying on his side as if dead. His great, pink tongue stretched out over his teeth and spilled onto the ground. Only his tremendous chest rising and falling like a tired, old machine gave the Jack an indication he was still alive. Surrounding the fallen dog was a dangerous looking pack of feral creatures – creatures with burning, yellow eyes – eyes that have seen no kindness. Their implacable stares showed the Jack no sign they were capable of offering it, either.

The Jack stared back at them, though uneasily. He was quite overmatched, and he didn't expect much help from the blind dog, who looked as though he might die at any moment.

The Jack was a young dog and quite inexperienced in the ways of fighting. He'd been in a few scrapes in his short time on the streets. An old Schnauzer who'd gotten loose from his yard, an alley cat full of piss and vinegar, and that rather nasty raccoon protecting its share of an overturned trashcan – all were opponents the Jack had gotten the better of. But none of those animals matched the degree of difficulty presented by this pack of wild dogs. Turning tail now and running was a viable option. He was certain he could outrun them. He looked at Buddy lying at their feet. But then they'd go back to killing *him*.

It was true he really didn't know the blind dog, but they had made a connection back there. For a fleeting trice, something in the mongrel had shone through. And it was enough for the Jack to put his life on the line to preserve it.

He singled out a large black dog standing over Buddy, its muscles rippling beneath its shining coat.

It was the Alpha.

He looked like the strongest of the bunch. *Better to fight him first*, the Jack reasoned. *Better to fight him when I'm at my strongest*.

He curled his lip, exposing just enough of his pointed canines. The Alpha grinned back at him. It was a grin of self-assurance – of malice and anticipation. The message was clear to the Jack: this creature did not intend to lose. The Jack's timing would have to be just right.

With the agility of an acrobat, he vaulted onto the Alpha's back. He found the scruff of the Alpha's neck and sank his teeth into it. If he'd hurt the Alpha at all, the dog didn't show it. The act of aggression evoked an angry roar from the Alpha and nearly sent the much smaller Jack off and running again. But the Jack had great amounts of bravery to more than make up for his lack of size, and his keen intelligence placed him on the higher end of the canine IQ scale. But the size and strength of the feral was intimidating.

With the nails of both front paws dug securely into the sides of the Alpha, the Jack shook the creature's scruff with every ounce of strength in his eighteen-pound body. The Alpha twisted and turned his head in an effort to reach him. But The Jack had gained an excellent position. It prevented the feral from using his fatally strong jaws.

Buddy struggled to his feet. Slowly he regained his senses and noted with surprise a familiar scent on the air. It was – the Jack? The little dog was his rescuer? Buddy sniffed his way toward the commotion.

One of the other ferals came at him from the side. He sensed the offensive, guessed right, and bit the smaller dog on the nose. The counterattack sent the feral whimpering away.

He pushed his way through the other ferals to the Alpha. He zeroed in on the Alpha's frustrated growling and found his throat. Buddy opened his own tremendous jaws and closed them on the Alpha's neck.

Like Cerberus, the two-headed hound that guards the gates of hell, Buddy and the Jack attacked the Alpha from front and back, drawing blood in more than one place.

Above them, the morning sun broke through the rain clouds and momentarily cast the town awash in color.

Mrs. Elsie Pendleton was inspecting the remains of her summer perennials, humming show tunes from *Oklahoma!* when the unmistakable sounds of fighting dogs reached her ears. The horrid noise called her to the alleyway. A small, fiery dog had mounted a larger dog's back, while a mangy mongrel, apparently blind, ripped at its throat.

She'd closely followed the story of the feral dogs in the newspaper, so when she happened upon them practically in her own back yard, she took immediate action. Brandishing her ever-ready garden hose, she turned on the pressure and pulled the hose to the end of her yard.

The two strays continued to attack the larger dog, and she knew without a doubt they intended to kill it.

Recalling the tragedy of the Haversham toy poodle, Mrs. Pendleton sprung into action. She directed a torrent of water at the small white dog hanging savagely from the back of the bigger one. The blast knocked the smaller dog clear off the larger one and into a mound of rubbish where he lay upon his back, apparently dazed. The cold spray sent the other ferals off and running in all directions.

Next, she turned the stream of raging water on the mongrel that held the black dog's throat in its jaws. With a thrust of her hose she scored a direct hit on the mongrel's muzzle. The dog relaxed his grip on the muscular dog's throat and ran. He found the smaller white dog and grasped his fur in his teeth. The white dog then led the larger dog away.

It was like nothing she had ever seen before: a dog with a seeing-eye dog. Elsie Pendleton rubbed her eyes in disbelief.

Meanwhile, the muscular dog raised the hair on his back and bared his teeth at Mrs. Pendleton. Frightened, she let loose with a cold blast of water right in the dog's face. The water had no effect on the beast. He advanced boldly on her.

Although a high white picket fence separated her from the wild dog, Mrs. Pendleton was not taking any chances.

"*Cave canem*," she uttered to herself, remembering her days in high school Latin class. "*Cave canem*." Beware of the dog.

She dropped the garden hose and ran as fast as her 73-year-old legs could carry her, her flannel housecoat fluttering behind her like a cape in the wind.

Even though the dog was bleeding in spots, he easily leaped the fence and pursued her. He bounded along Mrs. Pendleton's stone path, past her garden gnome and through her once-burgeoning Black-eyed Susans. In an instant, he was at the heels of her slippers.

Mrs. Pendleton peeked over her shoulder as she reached the steps of her back porch. The wretched beast was right behind her. His eyes burned red with rage and aggression. At that moment, Mrs. Pendleton believed he was Old Scratch himself.

Nostrils flaring, teeth bared, he lunged for her, his mouth gaping wide open. Mrs. Pendleton climbed the steps, two at a time, something she hadn't done in twenty years. Did she have the strength to fight off this hound from hell? She thought of pulling off her slipper and hitting the dog across his nose. It nearly made her laugh. She was losing her mind.

She turned and faced her pursuer. He was in mid flight, his razor-sharp claws reaching out at her. Her legs melted like butter on the porch steps. Mrs. Pendleton saw her garden, then the sky, then the fiberglass canopy over her porch where her wind chimes tinkled in the breeze.

Then all light was eclipsed by the black behemoth flying above her as she lay on her back. *Funny*, she thought. *He must be the devil. He flies, too.*

But instead of pouncing on her and ripping out her delicate throat, he flew right into her house, denting her aluminum siding.

I wonder if my insurance will cover that, she thought.

The beast hit the wall, whimpered, and fell on his side.

Mrs. Pendleton didn't remember what happened next, but she soon found herself inside her home. She clutched her heart and bolted the door. Then she peered outside the window.

The dog looked up at her from the porch, his muzzle twisted in a sinister grin. The damned dog was grinning at her! Appalled, She drew close the curtains and backed away from the window.

The dog lingered for a moment on her back porch, then turned and skulked off. Seemingly without effort, he jumped her fence and was gone.

The nerve of that dog, she thought. *And after I saved his life, too.*

A burning in her chest signaled she'd had enough excitement for one morning. She found her nitro tablets and placed one under her tongue.

Something had to be done about these dogs.

She picked up the phone and called a number that had been quite busy recently.

"Byron Brady? It's Elsie Pendleton. I've just been attacked by a feral."

III. The Chocolate Chip Cookie Situation

"I haven't lived a good life," she cried. "I've been bad – worse than you could know – but I'm not all bad. Look at me, Mr. Spade. You know I'm not all bad, don't you? You can see that, can't you?"
– Dashiell Hammett, *The Maltese Falcon*

Byron Brady, Animal Control Officer for Anthracite County, Pennsylvania, peered out the dirty second-floor window of his office in the Courthouse Annex Building, preparing to eat his cinnamon-raisin bagel.

He scratched at the two-day growth of stubble on his square chin as he contemplated cramming the entire bagel in his mouth. To his dismay, Rita, the counter-person in the cafeteria, had forgotten the strawberry jelly again. Using his index finger, he scraped a generous amount of cream cheese from the inside of the bagel, wiped it on the wax paper, and deposited it in a tightly wrapped ball in his wastebasket.

He downed the bagel and began hammering away on his word-processor, readying a report on an alleged case of animal abuse while the remains of his breakfast moved tirelessly to his awaiting stomach. His position as Chief Animal Control Officer afforded no breaks.

At twenty-eight, Brady was the top dog (no pun intended) of his two-man office which included his own personal secretary, Rita the counter-person (available after 10:00 AM).

As an elected official, it was Brady's job to ensure the streets of his county were free of any and all unwanted strays who roamed about, creating civil unrest. This also included dealing with the weekly "House O' Filth" as they were coined by local media, usually a house fallen in disrepair, inhabited by an elderly woman and her forty dogs and cats who used the entire home as their personal bathroom.

Usually, the woman was a kindhearted soul who invited local strays into her home despite her fixed income. The woman would be relegated to standing to the side and merely watching as Brady and his assistant, Felix Mortimer, would bring the animals out, one by one, and place them into the truck. Sometimes, the smell from the mess inside the house was so overpowering, Brady and Mortimer would be forced to wear gas masks Mortimer had found in a long forgotten fallout shelter beneath the courthouse. In most cases, the woman would then be cited by local law enforcement and prompt the gossips downtown to comment on the shame another person has wrought on their fine community. Stately, restored Victorians drew record numbers of tourists to the historic district each year, and their dollars fueled the local economy. An unkempt home was an eyesore and potential monkey wrench in the gears of the tourist industry.

Such a house was becoming a regular occurrence in the county, so much so, a special meeting of the county commissioners was called that very morning to discuss a solution. Brady shuddered at the thought.

As Chief Animal Control Officer, his presence at the meeting was mandatory. That meant three-plus hours of white haired commissioners disagreeing while Brady fell asleep with his head resting on the table in a puddle of his own saliva.

The annual Fall Foliage Festival was only days away. It was Mount Canaan's biggest event, and it could not be jeopardized by marauding ferals or scandalous, dirty houses.

As Brady pondered the situation, Mindy McGovern stepped in from the street, carrying a tin of chocolate chip cookies tied neatly with red ribbon.

"Hello Byron," she said, sheepishly.

"Huh? Oh, hello Mindy," Brady replied without looking up.

Mindy silently moved to the front of his desk where she stood patiently holding the cookies in front of her.

"Ahem..." Mindy said, attempting to gain Brady's attention; however, Brady seemed not to notice and continued right on typing.

"I baked you– " she started, but was interrupted by the telephone.

"Excuse me," Brady said, picking up the handset. "Animal Control, Byron Brady speaking." It was Elsie Pendleton. "Yes, Elsie. What can I do for you?"

He listened as Mrs. Pendleton recounted her story. "Ferals again? That's terrible."

Mindy, still holding the cookies, tried to muster a concerned look. She stared dreamily at Brady, a mildly handsome man with short dark hair and a perpetual cowlick, and sighed. Seemingly, the entire county, except for Brady, knew she had a crush on him.

"He chased you right up to your back porch? You don't say?" He turned his back to Mindy and faced the window behind him. "I agree totally, Mrs. Pendleton. Something's got to be done."

Mindy looked at her own reflection in Brady's dirty window. What didn't he see in her? She was pretty. At least her mother said so. Shoulder-length strawberry-blond hair, pink skin, nice figure, button nose, emerald green eyes, tortoise-shell glasses... Ugh! My glasses! She slipped them off her nose, holding the tin against her body with one hand, and placed her glasses inside her jacket pocket.

Byron Brady and his desk and everything around it suddenly became a blurred kaleidoscope of colorful blobs of light and movement. The reflection of the pretty girl with the tortoise-shell glasses who, a moment ago, she'd been admiring in Brady's window, vanished. In her place was an empty void where depth and objects could not be determined without first reaching out a probing hand.

"Uh-huh, Mrs. Pendleton... You bet," she heard a pulsating mass of pink light say on one side of a telephone conversation. "I'll get right on it."

The mass whom she knew as Byron Brady seemed to reach out to her. The cookies! He wants my cookies! Without hesitation, she extended the container of cookies in front of her and released it from her grip into what she thought was Brady's awaiting hands. Brady, however, was still facing the window, his back to Mindy, staring out into the park below.

The cookies, with no where else to go, decided simply to fall straight down onto Brady's desk, where they proceeded to start an unlikely chain of events.

Brady, startled by the sudden thump behind him, stopped talking and immediately turned his swivel chair 180 degrees to face Mindy. Mindy, however, had felt the tin full of cookies slip from her hands and freefall to an unknown fate.

Instinctively, she leaped forward to save the freshly baked cookies, which claimed two and one-half hours of her life to make from scratch from her Grandma Ruth's family recipe. But since she was not wearing her glasses, she didn't perceive the close proximity of Brady's desk and toppled over it.

The cookies had problems of their own. It seems in Mindy's haste to deliver the cookies to Brady while still warm from the oven, when the cookies are soft and the chocolate chips are still chewy, she did not secure the lid tightly enough on the container. The ribbon easily became undone, prompting the lid to explode from the container, and freeing the entire twenty-three cookies (Mindy ate one), which leaped from the tin, still soft and chewy, and rained down atop Brady's nearly always cluttered desk.

Mindy, in mid-flight, flipped head-first over the desk top, knocking over a photograph of Brady's mother and a picture of himself and his first dog, Skippy, taken when he was seven years-old and missing his front teeth, and all the paperwork which seem to rest permanently on his desk.

Brady dropped the phone and leaned forward in a knee-jerk reaction to save the photograph of himself and Skippy. He clunked heads with the plummeting Mindy, and blacked out.

Mindy landed on the desk, atop the soft and chewy cookies that soiled her favorite blue dress she wore especially to catch Brady's eye.

But physics wasn't finished with Mindy yet.

Mindy and fifteen of the twenty-three mashed cookies fell into Brady's lap. Like a pretty, blue parachute dotted with chocolate chips, Mindy's frilly skirt fluttered silently over her and the head of the unconscious Brady. And there Mindy McGovern lay over Brady's knee, her head on the floor, her face pressed against Brady's gleaming Florsheim shoes, her supple bottom pointing skyward, and her skirt covering Brady's head. Inside Mindy's jacket pocket, her tortoise-shell glasses made a peculiar sound that only broken glass and plastic can make when mixed together and jostled. Mindy began to cry.

Felix Mortimer sauntered lazily into the office. His gaunt frame, which barely filled his baggy uniform, stopped short of Brady's desk, and a bony hand passed through his long, greying hair.

Mortimer was the biggest gossip in Anthracite County. So, it was Mindy's and Brady's misfortune to have him walk in and catch them in this somewhat compromising position with Mindy's rear-end, clad only in her favorite blue cotton underwear – the ones with the yellow smiley faces – exposed for the entire county to see.

"Oh my word!" Mortimer exclaimed, his usual cigarette dangling from his lips. Then Mortimer turned and shouted into the hall.

"Hey, everybody…" Mindy heard him begin. But she didn't hear the rest. Her crying drowned out the remainder of his words. She didn't even care that Felix Mortimer could see her near-naked butt.

"Hello? Brady? Hello?" Elsie Pendleton's voice called out unanswered from the dangling handset. "About those ferals…"

IV. The Lair of The Jack

Here we are all, by day; by night, we're hurled
By dreams, each one into a separate world
– Robert Herrick, *Dreams*

With Buddy's teeth clenched steadfastly to the Jack's collar, the dogs hurried into the cover of the nearby woods.

Strange scents and unfamiliar sounds overloaded Buddy's senses: exotic plants and flowers; the queer calls of unknown animals; the sound of the mysterious Jack's panting. He wasn't sure where the Jack was leading him nor was he certain he could trust him.

Buddy's faith had been shaken by his time on the streets. Trust was a luxury a stray could not afford; however, if he let go of the Jack's scruff now, out in the middle of this alien world, surely it would be his end.

His paws ached and his bleeding wounds didn't feel much better. Reluctantly, Buddy held tightly to the Jack's collar and pressed on.

The Jack was happy.

He was a very social animal and appreciated the company of a good dog. His time as a stray had been a particularly lonely time, and the companionship of another dog, even a blind one, was most welcome to him. He was a dog who was most content when he had a job to do. Whether it was keeping the mailman away from his master's house or chauffeuring around a blind dog, the Jack approached the task with tremendous zeal.

The Jack led Buddy onto an uneven dirt road away from the town and, more importantly, far away from the strays. A dog's mile along the road, the Jack abruptly veered right onto a narrow trail, over an embankment, between two large mounds of black rock, and into an abandoned wooden shed.

The door had fallen off the shed long before the Jack had ever discovered this hiding place.

Inside, he shook free of Buddy's grip, circled twice and then lay in one corner of the rectangular room.

Buddy was rigid and he dared not move from the place the Jack had left him. There had been too many twists and turns en route to this destination –

wherever it was – and he could not be sure how far they had traveled. His tail remained between his legs. He sniffed the air for any threat of danger.

The Jack was nearby. He heard him break into a scratching fit, no doubt one of the damned fleas or ticks that infested these woods. Like yawning, scratching is contagious, and Buddy's skin soon yearned to be scratched, too. It felt like his flesh was covered by a thousand creepy crawlers – feasting on him, drinking his blood.

Oh, to give in, to surrender to its lure. But he couldn't. He had to keep alert, to guard against sudden attack. He weathered it out.

The stranger's tired panting filled up the silence between them. Buddy found comfort in this sound. It was better than the quiet. Buddy despised silence. Silence was nothing more than blindness to the ears. Besides, as long as the Jack was panting heavily, he knew the stranger would be too tired to pull any tricks.

Buddy relaxed a bit. He didn't think this dog meant to harm him in any way. He certainly didn't have to bring him all the way here if that was his intent. He could have left those ferals finish him off. They were doing a pretty competent job of it.

Cautiously, he lowered himself to the ground. The rain beat steadier against the shed.

Suddenly, the Jack's panting ceased. Buddy grew still – listening. He could hear the other dog moving – drawing closer. *Keep away*, Buddy growled. *Stay back.*

Buddy tensed. He could feel the Jack standing over him. He flashed the Jack a glimpse of sharp, white teeth. *Keep away. Stay back.* But his warning had no effect.

Keep away, Buddy growled again. *Stay–*

Something soft and wet glided across his bad ear. It left a hot sensation, a trail of soothing warmth. It was the Jack's tongue.

Buddy sighed. The Jack was cleaning his wound. *Keep away*, he groaned once more. But there was no threat in it. The Jack's caress, gentle and deliberate, brought back a feeling Buddy had not experienced in some time: acceptance. He rested his head on the ground. He imagined the Jack as a ball, a white, bouncing ball, always bouncing.

The Jack continued to clean his bites, removing all debris and with it, threats of infection. Buddy felt somewhat ashamed he'd mistrusted him. This Jack was a good dog.

He whimpered. Such kindness Buddy had not been shown in quite a while. He repaid the Jack with a lick across his muzzle.

This seemed to satisfy the Jack, and he lowered himself to the ground beside Buddy. Within minutes, Buddy could hear the relaxed breathing of the Jack, interrupted now and then by a casual snort, and he soon sensed the dog was asleep. Calmed by the other animal's rhythmic breathing, Buddy soon found himself asleep as well.

Buddy loved to sleep – and dream. In his dreams, he could still see Angus and his master, be with them, in his old house, patrolling his old yard. He could watch for his master limping down the garden walkway, leaning on his cane, or see the sunlight gleaming off of Angus's gray coat. But on this day, he dreamed neither of his master or Angus.

Instead, he dreamed he was in a moonlit plateau, the full moon rising above him. A hundred yards before him, he saw a large game bird with magnificent, flowing feathers break from the edge of some tall grass and fly upward into the night sky. But instead of pursuing him, as every dog's chase instinct tempts him to do, he just stood there, watching the bird fly away. He watched it fly for some time, until it was merely a graceful shape on a midnight blue canvas. Then he howled at it to return, to take him with it, high above the clouds, where no man or beast could ever harm him again.

Lying beside Buddy, the Jack was dreaming, too. And like Buddy, he also often dreamed of his old master. Specifically, he dreamed of the family's youngest daughter, Ginny, and of her pigtails bouncing as she walked. She used to let him sleep in her bed, and he'd kick the covers off himself every time she tried to tuck him in.

He dreamed of her for some time, playing with her on the living room floor. But gradually, that dream gave way to a simpler kind of dream – a dream that young dogs dream.

Round and round in a circle, the Jack chased his tail. But as soon as he'd catch it in his strong, full teeth, the furry snake would slip his grasp, only to have him give chase again. He growled at it in his sleep.

As the rain lessened to a mere pitter-pattering on the tin roof of the shed, the Jack stirred slightly.

Buddy, sensing his new friend's movement, licked the Jack lightly on the ear. Then both dogs nuzzled in the darkness and were soon dreaming once more in a world where blindness and hunger were mere annoyances solved with a gentle wash of the tongue.

V. Canis Mors

"Ah, my lord Arthur, what shall become of me, now ye go from me and leave me here alone among mine enemies?"

"Comfort thyself," said the King, "and do as well as thou mayest, for in me is no trust for to trust in. For I must into the vale of Avilion to heal me of my grievous wound. And if thou hear nevermore of me, pray for my soul."

– Sir Thomas Mallory, *Morte D'Arthur*

Josephine McGillis hugged the sun-bleached, threadbare blanket against her plump frame and fought back her tears. The old Jeep Cherokee seemed to find every bump in the road, every pothole, despite the best efforts of her husband Jim, to avoid them. Balled up in her clenched fist, she squeezed something Dr. Ketchum thought would help her grief. Josephine doubted anything could.

She didn't know if she'd ever feel the same again. After fourteen and a half years, she said goodbye to her best friend, Barney. He was just a mutt, a Schnauzer and terrier mix, nothing extraordinary. He never pulled anyone from a burning house, or saved his family from a grizzly bear, he was just a house pet; a damn fine house pet.

His only flaw was growing old, giving in to that burglar we all try to protect against. Old age snuck up on poor Barney when he was asleep and stole away his hearing and sight. For the last few months of his life, he bumped around Josephine's house, trapped inside his own head.

She wondered what he thought about, marooned in that dark, silent world. Did he think she'd abandoned him? Surely he could still smell her? Surely he could still recognize her gentle touch?

Not being able to hear himself – not being able to *hear* – he'd whimper, pacing circles on her Persian rug. Was she being selfish keeping him alive? Was she being cruel?

Many thought so. But he was her best friend. What would she do without him?

Dr. Ketchum, a dedicated veterinarian with large but gentle hands – she always admired his hands – assured her Barney was suffering, and his quality of life would only continue to deteriorate. She'd always trusted this man with

Barney's welfare, so she made that fateful decision. She surrendered her friend's life.

One swift and painless needle administered by Dr. Ketchum's hands would put an end to the suffering. When it was all over, that is what she would remember: those large hands. One large hand brandishing the needle, the other stroking Barney's ears, coaxing him into that final sleep.

Josephine held Barney through it all, wrapped in his favorite blanket. She felt the instant he was gone. She felt that wearied head against her bosom suddenly relax, that whimpering muzzle suddenly grow silent.

Her husband Jim, a tall, burly man with a full head of black hair and a lumberjack's beard, held his grieving wife's hand and battled back his own tears as well. He loved the dog nearly as much as she did. And because the couple was unable to have children, he thought of Barney as almost a son.

He'd sneak the dog a little something from the dinner table when Josie wasn't looking, and take him for rides in the old Cherokee, just Jim and the dog. How ironic that he'd drive him this last time, a one-way trip, with no return ticket home.

Jim and the dog were close, but make no mistakes about it: Barney was Josephine's dog. She'd raised him since a pup, she did, that tiny, gray ball of fur she'd picked out of seven similar yipping balls of fur. From the moment she'd held him in her hand, she'd felt a bond with the dog that transcended species and time. So many instances, in moments of grief, he'd sensed her pain and comforted her with a gentle kiss of his tongue.

She remembered especially the time after her mum died. Her emotions all knotted up inside her, she brooded in her sitting room, staring numbly at the walls. No one could reach her then, not even Jim. No one could take away the loneliness and despair – no one except Barney.

Named after her kindly uncle who had always bought her ice cream as a child and made her laugh, the small dog had marched into the sitting room and flopped down before her on the rug. Unnoticed by Josephine, whose mind had drifted to a dark place, Barney barked. It was a strong, heartfelt bark – strong enough to find her – and it drew her back.

Startled, she turned to face him sitting there, wagging his clipped tail, staring back at her with all the understanding a roomful of mourners failed to muster. He knew – he understood. She patted her lap and he was atop her, unleashing a barrage of wet kisses. He had burrowed through the darkness and found her.

He had loosened the knot.

Holding the blanket in her arms now, much in the same way she held Barney that day, Josephine kept her tears in check. Jim soon had the Jeep parked in front of their brownstone on Broadway.

Past the corner of the kitchen where the dog had made his bed she went. She stumbled past the mantel and fireplace where he'd pass away the dark, winter evenings, dreaming of things only dogs dream about. She reached the worn, familiar easy chair. It was still lightly coated with Barney's fur.

As if she could not go another step, Josephine collapsed upon it. He had been here just an hour before, walking in circles, crying. Her eyes passed over a spot on the rug. His weakened bladder had emptied itself there and she had scrubbed it clean with Pine-Sol. The smell still dominated the room. It didn't make sense: he was gone but his fur and the stain still remained.

She lowered her chin to her chest and let her long, dark hair fall over her face.

Jim knew at moments like this, he was no use to her. He was a man with rough, work-hardened hands, not a man of words, and he knew none that would comfort his wife. So he said nothing. Grieving himself, he sought solace in what he knew best: he retrieved his tools from the basement and headed for their garden – their secret garden, Josephine called it – where the wooden gate had fallen into disrepair. *It'll do me some good*, he thought, surrounded by his wife's colorful dahlias, begonias, and ferns. The tiny yard, which faced the rock wall of the mountainside behind the house, had the overgrown look of a British garden, which was Josephine's intent. Jim cared not what style it was, he was only too grateful to cast his thoughts elsewhere, and the light rain felt nice on his face.

Inside the house and alone at last, Josephine's heart exploded within. Her eyes clouded, heavy and gray, and the tears rained down. The fourteen and a half years she'd shared with her dog were not long enough, and she recalled them now as if on a train, watching places and time flash past the window.

What a cruel trick! Allowing animals into human lives, animals that lived only a fraction of a person's time on Earth. She thought bitterly of some people she'd known who didn't have a tenth of the moral fiber her Barney had, and questioned why they had the good fortune to be born human. Funny how pets can work their way into the fabric of everyday life and become as common as a person's own shadow. One moment they're puppies, wide-eyed and curious, chasing their tails in circles on the floor. The next moment, they're blind and deaf, retracing those circles, retracing those steps back to puppyhood.

Dr. Ketchum worked his way into her thoughts, his hands beating back the dark like the wings of a dove. He placed one hand on her shoulder, and squeezed her own hand with the other. His warmth enfolded her hand, consoled it.

"Here," he whispered, slipping a folded sheet of paper in her hand. "Read it when you're alone. It'll make you feel better."

He smiled.

Josephine opened her hand and looked at the crumpled paper she still grasped. Her hands trembled, but she managed to unfold it.

It read:

Canis Mors

For nearly fifteen years he served man loyally. Now his time had come. His small, broken body shook slightly under the blanket he knew as home. His paws moved, his ears twitched, and a small, muffled bark filtered through his once strong and plentiful teeth. He was dreaming.

He was a pup again, his legs mighty, his eyes clear, his ears alert. He was chasing the dogs, the dogs he had always known in his dreams. Sleek, mystical dogs who were free of man. Their coats were shiny in the blinding sun and their eyes glowed with a fierceness no creature in his world had known. He could almost see through them. Like ghosts, they'd disappear into the mist, leaving him alone in an unknown meadow. He'd cry out to them, but they wouldn't return. Slowly, the darkness swallowed him up, and once again he'd find himself in the blanket. Sometimes, in the midst of the long nights, he'd hear their call, shrill howling from deep in the lungs of these ancient beasts which penetrated his ears and shook him from his sleep. Now they were returning.

It was his time to take his place among this celestial pack. He had given all he could to this world and to his master, now he had barely the strength to dream. His master had conceded his life, fifteen years was long enough, and now he was granted his freedom. Ahead of him lay this land of endless full moons, interminable hunts, and limitless valleys.

There was a place in the pack reserved for him, as there is for all dogs who have ever lived or will ever live, since the dawn of time. No masters or fenced yards, just this canine world cast beneath an infinite sky and a majestic blue moon. The moon bathed and cleansed him in its nocturnal light. Soon he'd be a pup again, free of the ills that plagued him and bound him in this crippled shell. Soon the bark of a powerful hunter would spring from his new lungs and echo into the night. Out of the darkness they'd come, their paws running silently beneath them.

He could smell their scent. It surrounded him in the thick night air. Some he recognized, brothers and sisters who had fallen before him. And his mother. Fifteen years after he'd been taken from her, he'd never forgotten her. The warmth of her body had pressed against him, sheltering him from the darkest and coldest nights. Now she was there to welcome him into this new, yet familiar world that every dog has seen in his dreams.

The strength he had known long ago returned to him. As he lay his head down one last time, he remembered the faces of men who had shown him kindness in his lifetime, his human family who had cared for him all these years.

Then he surrendered his blanket, closed his eyes, and set out to gain the acceptance of the mysterious creatures who haunted his dreams. His paws moved him along in magnificent strides as he glided across the meadow.

The pack wouldn't escape him again. They nipped at him playfully as he rejoiced in this new-found vigor. In an instant, a blinding light revealed to him the knowledge all dogs must know. Suddenly, he possessed the ancient secrets of this land that, until now, only existed in the dark recesses of his mind. Now he was one of them, a four-legged warrior roaming the mist-laden corridors of a land promised to him long before he even took his first breath. Finally, he was one of the dream creatures he had chased all his life, one of the creatures other dogs chase into the mist of their own dreams.

Josephine carefully folded the paper and pressed it against her heart. No more circles. Barney had finally caught his tail. He had found where he was going.

"Go bravely," she said aloud. "No man nor beast can harm you now, my little friend. Joy will be the very air you breathe and pain and hunger a mere faded remembrance dreamed of long ago by some other creature than you." She breathed in deeply. "Though you are gone from my sight and side, you will be remembered and loved all the same. For I called you my friend, and that you will always be."

VI. Feast of All Saints…

The guests were not disappointed: they had a very pleasant feast, in fact an engrossing entertainment: rich, abundant, varied, and prolonged.

– J.R.R. Tolkien, *The Fellowship of the Ring*

Early evening brought a respite from the rain, and Buddy and the Jack seized the opportunity to seek out some dinner. A natural hunter, the Jack had caught a rabbit not far from their shed, as well as two rats and a field mouse. However, he had acquired a taste for the sweet, sticky refuse in people's trash and soon learned it was much easier to rip open a trash bag than to expend all his energy chasing a mouse which, in the end, failed to satisfy the protests of his hungry belly anyway.

So the Jack, with Buddy in tow, made his way into Mount Canaan to seek out the savory scraps discarded after the people of the town had finished their dinner. Following along the Anthracite River, the dogs made their way not to the new side of town, where they encountered the ferals in the morning, but to the historic district, where many old Victorian homes lined its streets.

The whistle of the vintage steam locomotive signaled another sightseeing excursion was under way.

Cautiously, the Jack made his way across the old railroad tracks. He'd narrowly escaped being struck by the train on a previous visit, and he was determined not to make that same mistake again. He waited until the last of the train cars was tugged along the horseshoe curve and out of sight. Then, he, like a small, white locomotive, led Buddy onto the old, splintering ties, over the humming iron rails, and along the shoulder of the road.

Buddy, his teeth clenched to the Jack's collar, his tail plastered firmly between his legs, inched along behind his smaller comrade, halting at the clamor of each passing automobile.

Buddy didn't like cars. He didn't even like riding in them. The sound of their engines and the smell of their exhaust reminded him of the day he was taken away from his master and Angus. Why did the stranger take him away? What had he done that was so terrible it prompted his master to order him away?

They happened upon a fresh road-kill, no more than a day old at best. It was a raccoon – a fat, old raccoon – half of him on the road, and half of him on the shoulder.

He'd almost made it. His eyes were still open, icy and black, but there was no shine in them. A narrow pink, serpentine tongue had leaked out from his mouth. He lay on his side, crumpled, a discarded piece of want-not. Disposable life, left to rot on the hot asphalt, the once living, breathing – thinking animal, was reduced to a mere weigh station for flies.

Was it the same fat, old raccoon? *No – he was too smart to die like that.* The Jack shuddered. No animal deserved to die like that – no raccoon, certainly no dog, especially not himself or his friend. Though the evening was mild, the Jack turned suddenly cold.

It spread to his friend.

Sensing Buddy's fear, the Jack made for the historic district with all the more urgency. He padded along the loose gravel, putting distance between them and the rotting carcass. They followed the busy highway to the old train station.

There, in the tiny park outside the station, the dogs sought the sheltering shade of the tall oaks, the oldest living things in Mount Canaan.

Buddy sniffed the air around them, picking up the scents of tourists from strange places, who sought the refreshing detour of this quaint, little town. He was uncomfortable with so many people about, and he voiced his displeasure with a hoarse, barely audible snarl. *Keep away*, he growled his mantra. *Stay back.* The result was a low, guttural chant.

The fall brought many tourists to the little town, some on day trips from the nearby Poconos, while others just liked to browse the quaint shops and art galleries which brought the town a resurgence in the 1970s. Many enjoyed dinner, a stout pint of ale and some good conversation at one of the many inns, while others took in a show at the old Mt. Canaan Opera House.

An elderly couple from Edison, New Jersey, who had exited the station with literature on the Fall Foliage Festival, stopped abruptly when they saw the dogs lying beneath a park bench.

"Clyde," the woman said to her husband. "Look at the dogs. Isn't that white one so cute?" She approached them cautiously as they regarded her from the shadows.

"Martha, I wouldn't get too close." Clyde warned his wife.

"Nonsense! Why, that white one, I could just eat him right up!"

"What about the big one there? He don't look none too friendly."

"Here, boy," she called, ignoring her husband. She knelt down on the sidewalk, no more than ten feet away, and removed a handful of sunflower seeds from her purse. “Yum-yums… I have yum-yums.” She held out her hand to the Jack, who was the closer of the two dogs.

Buddy, whose fear had repressed his urge to break into an all-out, snarling defense, continued his chant. *Keep away. Stay back.* He pointed his muzzle away from the direction of the woman’s voice. Even though he had no eyes, he was careful not to appear he was making eye contact with the stranger. A frightened or passive dog will not stare down his enemy.

But the Jack was neither frightened nor passive, and he returned the woman’s gaze without so much as a blink. He pushed a low, ominous *grrrr* from his lungs that aroused Buddy and brought him to his feet.

The woman clutched the front of her blouse, as if she held her own heart rigidly in her hand. “Clyde, my God… It has no eyes! The poor thing has no eyes!”

The fear in the woman’s voice raised concern inside the Jack and he now also stood in defense of his friend.

“Now, Martha, you just slowly back away, do you hear?” Martha instinctively raised to her feet, withdrew her hand with the sunflower seeds still gripped tightly in her fist, and slowly backed toward her husband.

“Nice doggie,” Clyde said, in a soothing voice. “That’s right, no one wants to hurt the nice doggie.” Within seconds, Martha backed into her husband’s arms. He continued to talk softly to the dogs.

The Jack, well aware now of the woman’s nervousness, barked out an alarm to all who would listen. He and his friend were under siege. The terrier’s uneven, hyper barking soon brought the attention of other passersby.

Suddenly, tourists walking by the park stopped to gawk at the two dogs causing all the commotion.

“No eyes, Clyde,” The woman said of the mongrel. “Who could do that to such a pitiful creature? What can we do? We can’t just leave a blind dog walk around the town. He wouldn’t last a day.”

“We can let the local law know, that’s for sure. It ain’t safe for them to be running around like that. Someone’s going to get bit.” He stomped his feet loudly and shouted at the Jack, “Get on now! Git! You hear?”

Frightened, the Jack backed away.

Buddy, startled at the loud stomping, quickly found the Jack’s collar the way a new-born pup, its eyes still closed, finds its mother’s teat. In an instant the two were off and running across Route 209, nearly killed by a screeching delivery truck. Up the laborious climb of Race Street, the Jack recalled feasting on day-old pizza crusts discarded at the rear of a neighborhood pizza parlor.

Meanwhile, back in the park, the tourists debated the fate of the two dogs.

"Isn't that the courthouse over there?" Martha queried. "Surely, the sheriff's office is inside."

Clyde checked his watch. "There should still be someone in there at this time of the day," he said. "C'mon."

Racing down a set of cement steps from Race Street, high above its perch over the town, back down to Broadway Street, the Jack led his sightless friend to the rear of Antonio's. There, the Jack sniffed out discarded pizza, no more than a day old, concealed in a thin, flimsy trash bag.

Buddy, whose sense of smell bested the Jack's, needed no help to find the delicious Italian food.

Before long, both dogs were headfirst into the trash, dining on fettucine alfredo, lasagna, antipasta, and even meatballs.

Buddy could not remember such a flavorful experience. Each bite was a symphony. He reveled in the spices and smells that swirled around him and enveloped him in a fragrant world, the like of which he had never known.

The Jack had had his fill and was washing it all down with some water that had collected in a rain gutter. He looked happily at his friend who, for the first time since the Jack had met him, wagged his tail in complete, unabashed joy.

It doesn't take much to please a dog, and even less to please a stray. Both dogs' spirits were full with the warm satisfaction only a hearty meal can evoke.

Soon, the Jack felt that tiredness so common after overindulging himself. He fancied a nap. He pulled up alongside the mongrel, allowing him to catch onto his collar, and then he was off at once to find a nice, cool spot in the shade where he and his friend could sleep off their meals in comfort.

The Jack knew just such a place.

VII. On the Trail of the Vagabonds

"It is easy to see," replied Don Quixote, "that thou art not used to this business of adventures; those are giants; and if thou art afraid, away with thee out of this and betake thyself to prayer while I engage them in fierce and unequal combat."

– Miguel de Cervantes, *Don Quixote*

"They were right there," Elsie Pendleton told Brady as she pointed to where she'd first witnessed the quarreling ferals earlier that day.

Brady and Mrs. Pendleton stood on her back porch, looking out over her garden.

"Right there is where the big blind one and the little white scruffy thing were trying to kill the black one… and I'm not so sure I'm glad they didn't, if you know what I mean. 'Cause that big black one damn near killed me, he did."

Brady nodded and scribbled some notes in his pad. "How many dogs did you see, total?"

"Oh, I only saw three: the blind one; the white scruffy one; and of course, the black one. Did I mention he damn near killed me?"

Brady cleared his throat. "Which way did they go?"

"Which ones? The blind one and the scruffy one? Or the one that damn near killed me?"

"Both, I guess."

Mrs. Pendleton raised her hand and pointed over her tall picket fence towards the woods and beyond, where the remains of the abandoned coal breaker lay like the skeleton of some long-extinct animal. "The little one led the blind one out that way."

"What do you mean 'led'?"

"The big one bit down on the scruff of the little one's neck like this." She demonstrated by shaping her hand into a claw and grasped Brady's forearm tightly. "Then the little one just led him away like he was his very own seeing-eye dog."

Brady shook free of the woman's grip. "Interesting," he responded, and once more scribbled into his notebook. Mrs. Pendleton's fingerprints remained pressed in his skin. "How about the other one?"

"The one that damn near killed me?" she replied.

Brady winced.

"Well, after he nearly got me, he ran down the pathway, leaped the fence there, and ran off toward the woods. But the other way, I think. I don't believe he ran after the other two fellas."

While Brady was adding some details to his notes, Mrs. Pendleton asked, "Is it true about you and Mindy McGovern?"

Embarrassed, Brady stammered. "Wh-what do you mean?"

Mrs. Pendleton winked at him. "Pitch woo on your own time, Mr. Brady. Not on the taxpayer's money."

"Yes, ma'am," he replied.

Brady finished writing his notes, thanked Mrs. Pendleton for all her help, and then hopped into his county-issued Chevrolet Blazer.

Driving at a snail's pace along the narrow dirt road, Brady hung his head out the window and scanned the loose dirt and soft mud for any signs of fresh animal tracks.

It didn't take him long to pick up on the trail of Buddy and the Jack.

Thanks to the rain, their paw prints were imprinted in the damp soil. They ran together in an unusual way, suggesting Mrs. Pendleton was telling the truth when she had alleged one dog had led the other away.

He followed the animal tracks for some time until they turned off onto a narrow bike path. Unable to negotiate the trail in his sport utility vehicle, Brady removed himself from the truck, but not without first fetching his tranquilizer gun and flashlight.

Cautiously, he made his way along the trail, tracking the animal prints like some big-game hunter in darkest Africa. The dogs' paw prints eventually led him to a weathered, rickety shack Brady recognized as a magazine, which the miners once used to store their explosives.

The door had long since seen the final time it was swung open and now lay carelessly discarded behind the small building. Brady switched on the flashlight and shone it inside. The paw prints followed one another to the center of the building where they then divided, made two independent ovals in the dirt, and disappeared into two larger depressions in the centers of both circles. Here, Brady reasoned, is where the dogs had slept for a while.

He shone his light around the interior of the building. Wherever the animals were, they weren't in the building now. Two piles of excrement sat next to the exterior of the shed like forgotten pyramids. Brady knew dogs don't mess where they sleep. Satisfied the dogs weren't present, he made his way back to the vehicle.

Felix Mortimer's voice alerted him over the radio as he climbed into the truck. "We got another feral sighting," he announced, as if it were as rare as seeing Sasquatch or the Loch Ness Monster. "Two of 'em attacked some tourists in the square, they did."

"When?"

"Not more than twenty minutes ago, Boss. The tourists jus' reported the attack to the sheriff. He was none too happy either, he was." Wonderful, Brady thought. "He wanted to know why you weren't at the commissioners' meeting, too," Mortimer added. "He's saying you should be removed. He don't think it should be too hard to catch a blind dog."

"What?"

"The dogs that attacked the tourists. They said one of the buggers had no eyes."

Brady shook his head in disgust. "I'm coming in."

He keyed the ignition and stomped the gas pedal to the floor, sending a hailstorm of rocks and dirt behind him as he raced toward town.

VIII. A Princess

I'm Nobody! Who are you?
Are you-Nobody-too?
Then there's a pair of us!
Don't tell! they'd banish us – you know!
– Emily Dickinson, from *I'm Nobody*

Josephine had worked the entire day at her arts and craft shop perched high on Race Street, situated in a cluster of sixteen 3-story old stone row homes unimaginatively named "Old Stone Row." They were built in 1848 by Abraham Stack, founder of the Anthracite Railroad Company, and served as home for foremen and engineers who worked for the railroad baron. When Mount Canaan experienced a revival in the 1970's, the run-down and neglected structures were turned into art galleries, craft stores, and cafes and frequented by the aspiring writers and budding artists who lived in the apartments above them. Josie's shop, *For All Seasons*, was located on the first floor of the only stone house to have a porch on the second level.

Inside her shop, Josie sat mostly remembering Barney while she mindlessly assembled miniature scarecrows and autumn floral arrangements and listened reluctantly to the inane prattle of the local gossips.

"Did you hear about Byron Brady and Mindy McGovern?"

"No."

"Well, I heard from a reliable source they were caught hugging and kissing in his own office! And here's the kicker: they were both covered in chocolate chip cookies!"

"How kinky! But it doesn't surprise me one bit. He's always giving Rita, his secretary, the eyes."

"Really? Can you believe how these bureaucrats behave? He's an elected official! We, the taxpayers pay his salary so he can have his own personal love shack down there in the courthouse!"

"And while he's fooling around with loose women, these ferals are having their way with us all! Why, just the other day, Elsie Pendleton was in her yard, minding her own business, tending to what's left of her perennials–"

"She keeps a lovely garden."

"Yes, she does… As I was saying, she was assaulted by one of 'em bush dogs. Leaped right o'er her tall picket fence it did, and had her by the throat. Damn near shook her to death, he did. If she didn't have one of 'em out of body experiences, and found herself inside her house, she wouldn't have escaped."

"Really? Well, I heard two tourists from California were down in the town square, admiring our oak trees, when they were attacked by a big 'un and little 'un, working as a team!"

"You don't say? I heard they were from Scandinavia."

"Nope, California. These dogs just appeared out of nowhere an' attacked them 'cause she was eating sunflower seeds. Stole 'em right out of her hand, the little 'un did."

Gasps all around.

"They're the hounds of hell, they are! They're as old as time itself. Been around a long time, they have. Our mom always said, 'when the hounds appear, trouble's on its way,' and I believe it. Our mom heard a dog howl back when our pop was in the hospital and sure enough, he died that very same day."

"No?"

"Certainly! And our neighbor, you know her, Sylvia Bonner? She'd been up nearly half the night waiting for her son, you know, the one with the lazy eye? What the hell was his name? He went to school with our Annette…"

"Nicholai?"

"Right! Young Nicky. Poor Sylvia smoked nearly a whole pack of cigarettes waiting for that boy to come home… he'd been out with the car, you see."

"Teenagers…"

"Sure… sure. Just before dawn, she heard the most bloodcurdling howl, right outside her door. Well, poor Sylvia knew right there and then that her boy wasn't never coming home again."

"I remember…"

"She picked up the phone and called County Hospital. Sure enough, Young Nicky was there. Wrapped their Corvair around a telephone pole."

"DOA?"

"They scooped him up off the road with a snow shovel, I heard."

Josephine frowned.

"The hounds of hell, that's what they are. My mother-in-law's Welsh, and they got a different name for them, those Welsh: Clean and Win, or something like that."

Cwn Annwn, thought Josephine. Her grandmother was Welsh, too. She continued to say nothing.

"The *Clean and Win* are taking over the town."

"Comin' to the point where ya' ain't gonna be able to walk down the street with a sandwich in yer hand without one of these bush dogs tryin' to kill you."

"The funny thing about these bush dogs that attacked the tourists was, the big 'un had no eyes an' the little 'un had to lead him."

"No, Really? That was what Elsie Pendleton said, too, she did. She said she blasted 'em with her hose and chased 'em away, she did. Made the one that attacked her all the more ornery, I think."

"It's the curse of Ledra Hogstooth, it is! She's behind it! She sent those damned dogs here from hell, I'll bet. Just like she'd sent the rats ages ago. She screamed when they put that noose around her neck, she did, 'I place a pox on this town!' And she sure as hell did."

All the gossips agreed: it was Ledra Hogstooth's fault.

Josephine rolled her eyes and laughed. Over the years, everything from acid rain to the hole in the ozone layer had been blamed on Ledra Hogstooth, the town's one and only accused witch. Heck, she even recalled hearing one of the old timers blame the JFK assassination on the Hogstooth curse, claiming she was the shooter on the grassy knoll.

Eventually the gossips moved on to different stores and virgin ears, and the rumors of the blind feral and his smaller cohort spread through the town much like the considerably doubted, but still highly believed, Hogstooth pox.

Josephine fell back into the rhythms of her work: weaving and manipulating dried cornstalks into the shapes of whimsical scarecrows, adorning them with colorful clothes, and mounting them on wooden dowels with the aid of a hot glue gun. Only twice did she actually stop working to cry a spot of tears. Luckily, she composed herself before any customers returned to her store.

At 3:38 P.M., the yellow blur of a Mt. Canaan school bus flashed past her window, followed abruptly by the sounds of the bus' brakes grinding and squealing, protesting the intent of the driver, and yearning for the lure of gravity and the rather steep hill that awaited them.

Soon, narrow and winding Race Street was filled with the chatter of children as they spilled from the bus, onto the dusty cobblestone street, and past the storefronts and galleries embellished with burnt orange, ruby red, and bright yellow. Sinister pumpkins grimacing from within the windows reminded the children that Halloween would soon be here, pouncing on them like a black cat.

They discussed what costumes they'd be wearing and debated how much candy they'd plunder as they anxiously anticipated moving through the darkened streets, begging for treats, but not opposed to playing a trick should they receive something in their booty not to their liking.

"What are you going to be for Halloween, Sara?" a little boy asked an equally little girl. Her clothes were not as fashionable as the other children's and her white sneakers were dirty and scuffed.

Josephine paused from her work and listened intently from inside her store.

"Noodlenose?"

"She should go as a bum," another little girl exclaimed. "She's already got the wardrobe." All the children laughed.

"I'm going to be a princess," Sara replied, as if she didn't hear the remark.

Josephine knew she was used to such carping, and was quite practiced at pretending she didn't hear the criticisms at all. But she also knew Sara was a very tender, sensitive thing, who loved animals with all the enchantment in her heart and preferred the company of a puppy or kitten to that of children her own age. For she often found herself on the receiving end of cruelties and torment directed at her by callous children.

The only child of a single mother who rented the one-bedroom apartment above Josephine's shop, Sara spent evenings with Josephine until her mother returned home from her waitressing job at the Mt. Canaan Inn.

Josephine didn't mind. She enjoyed Sara's company and took tremendous pleasure in the way Sara's eyes would scan over her latest creations with the innocence and wonder that only children possess. They would often pass the evenings telling each other stories and listening to the local oldies station while Sara would sit in the big comfortable chair beside the window and hold the sleeping Barney in her arms.

Barney – how was she going to break the news to the child?

"You're such a noodlenose, VanMeter!"

"Sa-ra is po-or," the children sang out, in a song that seemed well rehearsed. "She lives in the sew-er… she gets her clothes from lost-and-founds… she wears hand-me-downs…"

At the last verse, Josephine angrily threw down the hot glue gun and stormed to the door. Enough was enough! She'd give these wicked children a good piece of her mind.

But as her hand hovered over the door knob, she heard Sara reply, "They're not hand-me-downs, they're vintage clothes. They have history and character. Great people before me have worn these clothes and have gone on to great things."

Josephine smiled.

"Like who, Noodlenose?" a girl asked sarcastically.

"Like for instance…" Sara thought for a moment. "Jane Goodall."

"Who's Jane Good?"

"Jane *Goodall.* She studies chimpanzees by living with them in the jungle." At this information, some of the boys seemed impressed. Living in the jungle with chimps was very appealing to them. The girls, however, looked at it as merely another thing to tease Sara about.

"You're a liar," one girl accused.

"You're so weird, Sara," another girl said. Then she sang, " Sa-ra smells fun-ky… she wants to live with mon-keys!" All the children laughed. But Sara raised her head defiantly and smiled. She did want to live with the monkeys. At least they didn't make up stupid songs that weren't funny at all. She brushed past them and clutched the door handle to the store.

Josephine rushed back behind her counter and work area. So as not to appear she'd heard the teasing, she picked up the hot glue gun and resumed working on her scarecrows.

"Sa-ra's a monkey…" the children's voices cried out, as the singing followed Sara into the store like an unwelcome guest.

"Hello, sweetie," Josephine greeted her. "How was school?"

Sara closed the door, silencing the remainder of the malicious song, dropped her book-bag onto the floor, and plopped into her usual seat by the window. The last of the children sauntered past Josephine's window, sticking out their tongues and making silly faces. "Good," she replied flatly.

Josephine watched as the smile Sara bore gradually diminished and was replaced by a look of relief and exhaustion, as Sara's tiny frame slowly slumped under the burden of the children's ridicule. She pulled her knees up to her chin and hugged them to her chest. Her usually bright emerald eyes turned gray and her pink cheeks glistened with fresh tears.

"Sweetheart!" exclaimed Josephine, dropping the glue gun. In an instant, she was at Sara's side. She draped her arms around the weeping child, and squeezed her tightly against her generous build.

"Oh, Josie!" Sara cried.

"I know," she told Sara, "I know."

Sara looked around the room. "Where's Barney?"

Josephine squeezed Sara even tighter.

It helped Josephine to share her grief with Sara, who had loved Barney as much as she did. They cried together for a time, until Sara reminded her Barney was a jovial spirit and he wouldn't want them to be carrying on like they were.

"He liked parties," Sara told Josephine. So they had one to celebrate his life.

At 7:00 PM, Sara's mother, Linda, returned home and found her daughter singing and laughing and dancing with Josephine to Chubby Checker's "The Twist." Linda stood for a moment in the doorway, admiring the Reubenesque, middle-aged Josephine strutting about the shop with her diminutive pixie of a daughter. When the song had finished, Linda applauded, prompting Josephine's cheeks to turn bright crimson with embarrassment.

"Mom!" Sara exclaimed, and hurtled herself into her mother's arms.

"Have you been a good girl for Mrs. McGillis?"

"She's been an angel," Josephine assured her.

"Josie's made scarecrows," Sara said.

Josephine smiled as she watched Sara lovingly cradled in her mother's arms. She'd wanted so much to have a child with Jim, but God had other plans and left Josephine barren.

"Let's go order us some dinner," Linda said to her daughter as she opened the door.

"Antonio's Pizza!" Sara cheered and ran out into the darkened Race Street.

"Thank you again, Mrs. McGillis," Linda told Josephine. "For everything." Josephine and Jim charged Linda very little to rent the apartment upstairs.

Josephine dismissed Linda's graciousness with a wave of her hand. "It's my pleasure, really."

She watched out the window as Linda and Sara walked hand-in-hand. Slowly, the echo of Sara's laughter faded away and her eyes were inevitably drawn to the empty chair beside the window. *I didn't realize how much company he really was*, she thought.

She remained by the window and waited for Jim, hoping every set of headlights that approached belonged to the old Cherokee.

IX. A Pleasant Discovery

"Don't be alarmed," said a voice.

"None of your ventriloquising me," said Mr. Thomas Marvel, rising sharply to his feet. "Where are yer? Alarmed, indeed!"

– H.G. Wells, *The Invisible Man*

"The hinges we need for the gate are out of stock at the hardware store," Jim told her. "I guess I'll have to make a trip to Hazleton tomorrow and see if I can find them there."

The headlights of the old Cherokee washed over their brownstone, which was sandwiched between a bed-and-breakfast and a small candle shop. The wooden sign hanging from the front of the house read "The McGillis Family – Established 1969."

Josephine sighed. "The McGillis family minus one," she thought. That dog was like a child to her. He was always there to greet them. Now nothing inside awaited them – except maybe the ghost.

It was an old house, one of the oldest on Broadway Street. It predated the revolution and served as an inn during the war.

Fresh out of Penn State, just back from Woodstock, this was the house they wanted. They didn't choose this house so much as it chose them. Stepped right up, pushed the realtor aside and said, "How do you do?"

Stained glass windows, hardwood floors and a ghost; it was everything they were looking for.

Josephine imagined all sorts of intrigues about the place. Maybe Washington slept there, or maybe a respected patriot named "Arnold" shared a pint – and secrets – with the British there.

There'd been talk over the years that the place was haunted, that a lonely redcoat still walked about. Josephine had never seen a thing, but after the loss of Barney, she almost wished the house *were* haunted.

Oh, Jim was good company, and she wouldn't trade him for any ghost – even one as interesting as Washington, but they had slipped into that comfortable rut, that rut that long-married couples often find themselves in.

He liked to keep himself busy, to work with his hands, whether it be a piece of oak or a frosty mug down at Molly MacGuire's Pub. And when not at her shop, she liked to curl up on the sofa with a nice paperback and a cup of tea to help her relax. And so usually, they were off doing their own thing.

But he loved her – he loved her when she was one-twenty and had every boy in town chasing her; and he loved her now at one-sixty– ah, let's just say, "not one-twenty anymore."

He was gentle and kind and decent with the strength of a bear and the temperament of a church mouse. He farted in his sleep.

She loved him, too.

The gate to Josephine's secret garden rested off to the side of the walkway, illuminated by the flickering gas lamp streetlights on Broadway. Jim went inside the brownstone, while Josephine lingered in the garden, tidying up after her careless husband, who'd left his tools lying about where someone could easily fall over them.

Swearing under her breath, she picked up his drill, screwdrivers, screws, and tool belt, and nearly slipped on his forgotten hammer that lay along the walkway. As she bent forward to retrieve the hammer, something struck her as odd. A pair of eyes stared out from beneath her rose bushes. The amber glow of the gas lamps was captured by the strange eyes and reflected out into the darkness like two lighthouse beacons pouring out over an ocean.

Josephine froze. The tools slipped out of her hands and fell with a thud in the grass. All the gossip and rumors she'd heard returned to her like a string of echoes. Could this be one of the very ferals that gripped the borough in fear? Right here in her own yard? She thought of the predicament Elsie Pendleton had found herself in her brush with the ferals. She'd nearly had her precious throat ripped out.

"Jim…" Josephine called out, or at least tried to, but terror stole away her voice. Slowly, she backed away, her own eyes locked on those of the mysterious beast. As she moved, her foot kicked something made of metal. It rolled off to the side of the walkway. Jim's flashlight! God bless his irresponsibility!

Cautiously, she knelt beside the large, flat stones and pawed the ground next to her for the lost flashlight. Her hand passed over the smooth stones and the grass damp with condensation until finally her fingers fell upon the cool metal.

Slowly, Josephine stood. It took her a moment to once again locate the eyes, but there they were, still staring at her. She raised the flashlight and passed her thumb over the plastic button. The beam spread across the entire expanse of her garden as if liquid light had been spilt from the cylinder.

She directed it toward the space beneath her rose bushes. She expected to find a savage and snarling wolf-like creature. Josephine was pleasantly surprised.

Instead of finding such a beast, she found not one, but two. The eyes belonged to a small, cute white dog. Lying snugly against him was a large dog who appeared to be missing hair in places.

Josephine's fear quickly subsided. She wondered why she'd only detected the small dog's eyes glowing out from the darkness. She shone her flashlight on the large dog's face. Two empty sockets looked back at her. The dog had no eyes.

"My God," Josephine gasped. These were the two ferals who'd attacked the tourists.

Curiously though, the dogs seemed neither vicious nor threatening. The white dog simply lay still and watched her, while the blind dog rested his head contentedly on the smaller dog's body. What should she do? Should she go inside and call Byron Brady? Surely he'd be glad to have these two ferals off the street. He'd... Josephine thought. He'd euthanize these two, that's what he'd do.

She thought of Barney. He was old and sick and not much else could be done for him. But these two, they seemed healthy enough, even the blind one, and neither seemed to be foaming at the mouth as if they had rabies. Anyway, how could she be sure these two were even ferals?

They didn't look like bush dogs. Why, the little one even had a collar on, so he could be someone's pet. Besides, the gossips had said these two had attacked the tourists alone, not in a pack like the other ferals. If they were ferals, what were they doing alone? Shouldn't they be with the other dogs?

Josephine made up her mind. She'd go inside and fetch the poor animals the cold cuts she'd bought for Jim's lunch. And if Jim didn't like it, he could go and eat crow. He was already in her doghouse for leaving his tools on the walk.

"Don't you go anywhere," she ordered the dogs. The white dog responded with a flicker of his ears while the blind dog raised his head and emitted a hesitant bark.

"Hush," she commanded the big dog. Josephine turned and entered her house.

In the kitchen, Jim had made himself two bologna sandwiches, one of which he was just about to eat. Josephine rescued the sandwich from Jim's gaping jaws. "Thank you," she said. She stole the second sandwich waiting patiently on his plate, as well as the pack of bologna still on the table.

"Uh... I was going to eat that," said Jim.

"Pick up your tools," Josephine scolded, and raced out the door.

She placed the sandwiches and cold cuts on the grass approximately ten feet from the dogs.

"Here's some goodies for you two," she said aloud. "And no fighting."

The dogs, however, did not move, though the white dog eyed the food intently.

"I get it. You don't want to eat with me around. I'll give you some privacy."

She turned and went back inside the house, where Jim was standing at the kitchen window looking out at the dogs.

"Who are they?" he asked.

"They're the ferocious dogs attacking everyone in town," she replied.

"Oh," he said.

"Now go out and pick up your tools."

X. The Legend of the Hogstooth Pox

His was an impenetrable darkness. I looked at him as you peer down at a man who is lying at the bottom of a precipice where the sun never shines.

– Joseph Conrad, *Heart of Darkness*

Ledra Hogstooth was a witch.

At least that's what the good people of Mt. Canaan had believed in 1739. Afflicted by what is today known as schizophrenia, the old woman would pass her time muttering to herself, a prisoner of her own dementia and hallucinatory visions, wandering up and down the river's edge, calling out to her children.

Her "children" were large, aggressive rats who crawled freely about her one-room shack feeding on the exposed remains of the old woman's grains and gatherings. Some say they weren't really rats at all, but the result of some midnight conjurings. Although the townspeople believed she was a witch, or at least infected with some unclean spirit, the Mt. Canaanites left Ledra alone.

But as the rats multiplied, they found their way across the river into the borough of Mt. Canaan which consisted then of simple brick houses lining quiet, cobblestone streets. Soon, children began dying in unusually high numbers, their tiny bodies laid in neat rows of ten in the town square, waiting to be burned.

Unknowingly, the rats, which may very well have been descendants of rodents who stowed away in goods aboard a ship from Great Britain, found their way to the Pocono Mountains and into Mt. Canaan, carrying with them a form of the dreaded plague. It was one of the rare outbreaks ever reported in the New World, and it curiously sought out the very susceptible lymph glands of the town's children.

When the horrid plague ended as suddenly as it had begun, nearly three-quarters of the children of Mt. Canaan were dead.

On All Hallows' Eve, 1739, Ledra Hogstooth's writhing, contorted body, her face concealed by a burlap sack, was hanged from a massive oak tree which still stood in the town square, a symbol of Mt. Canaan's dark past. From that time on, even as the streets of Mt. Canaan once more sang out with the joyful voices of burgeoning, healthy children, the mere mention of the name Hogstooth brought about a deafening silence as if the entire town had been swallowed whole.

Generations later, mothers still warned their children when they misbehaved, saying, "Ledra Hogstooth is going to get you."

As long as the story has stayed with the Mt. Canaanites, so too, has the stigma of the Hogstooth legacy. All descendants of the Hogstooth witch were treated as though the very plague still flowed through their veins, waiting again to be unleashed on the unsuspecting children of Mt. Canaan. Therefore, each and every member of Ledra Hogstooth's family were driven from the town and forced to lead a nomadic existence in the wilds surrounding the borough.

Arlen Hogstooth, the very last descendant of them, a bitter, hunchbacked old man and not a warlock at all, was determined to punish the ignorant townspeople for the centuries of torment he and his clan had endured.

It was his voice the Alpha heard this night.

In their den nestled in the desolate coal fields west of Mt. Canaan, the Alpha and the other ferals huddled close together to conserve their warmth. Among the sleeping beasts, his female at his side, the Alpha lay awake staring out into the moonlight glistening off the fragments of scattered coal and slate. He could not sleep this night because, on the transcendental edge of slumber, that most illusory place between worlds, when voices long silent speak once more, he'd heard something call to him.

The voice, neither angry nor amiable, only indifferent, was a familiar one, the only voice to ever speak his name.

"Lazarus," it called. "Lazarus…"

The Alpha's ears pricked, and his lucid eyes scanned the darkness for the shrouded, twisted figure to whom he knew the voice belonged. But no man nor beast separated itself from the shadows and appeared to him. Mildly dejected, he lowered his head back to the ground.

Long before he became the alpha dog of the feral pack, the dog once named Lazarus, now simply known as The Alpha, was a mixed-breed pup born to an AKC-registered Bull Mastiff female in the nearby town of Nesquehoning.

After Mike Riley's Bull Mastiff, Shasta, had become impregnated by a roaming Rottweiller who, like some marauding invader, had forced itself into the Riley yard, Riley was enraged. He'd never allowed his beloved Shasta outside his fenced property without her first being securely fastened to a leash. And now she'd been raped in his own yard no less.

Riley knew the kind of animals the litter would produce. An uneasy feeling gripped his body. He knew he must do the unthinkable: a pup with a bloodline of Rottweiller and Bull Mastiff would prove to be too much of a bad combination.

For the safety of the local children, as well as for the pups themselves, whose aggressiveness would more than likely lead to a short, unpleasant life, Riley devised a plan.

Weeks after the pups were born, he gathered all seven, their eyes yet to see the light of day, and placed them into a pillow case, ensuring their captivity with a knot. The darkness of a winter's night lay upon the land like an old blanket, and the moon peeked out through holes in the clouds. He drove his black Range Rover to the Anthracite River, the pups protesting their confinement with anguished yelps, and tossed the sack containing the helpless newborns into the icy water. The bundle hardly made a splash.

In the cold February water, their faint, drowning cries fell upon deaf ears.

Almost.

For in the darkness that night, something stirred. Something ancient and forgotten. Spouting out a stale, wicked breath, it freed itself from its limbo, rushed into the waters, and retrieved the sack. Once on the shore, the dark, shivering form loosened the knot and dumped the contents onto the ground.

All were dead save one, and the figure's clawing, malformed hands pulled the lone survivor from the lifeless bodies of its less fortunate siblings. It scooped up the tiny pup and pressed it against its breast in an effort to banish the cold night air and restore warmth to its chilled bones.

The wet and shivering pup snuggled against this being clad in all black, whom most men and beasts would certainly fear should they encounter him. But curiously, the pup did not. He felt safe, cradled in his arms as the being carried him to a warm, dry shack not far from the river where a fire raged inside.

The warmth of the leaping flames drove off the last of the pup's chill, and the warm rabbit stew cooking above the fire in a hot kettle restored the pup's vigor.

Over the months that followed, the pup grew steadily on a diet of rats, snakes, bats, and lizards, and any other vile creature that crawled or flew. The strange prey fed an increasing rage within the dog, whom the being had named Lazarus.

Though he loved the dog in the best way he knew how, he showed him no compassion other than to feed him and allow him to sleep against himself at night because he didn't desire love nor needed it, and this philosophy he passed on to the dog.

This being lived in exile outside Mt. Canaan, for no one dared have relations with him, and for that reason he hated the very inhabitants of the town. He placed a curse on them.

This curse manifested itself deep within the young dog's heart, a living, breathing, all-consuming darkness; a seed. A mere suggestion of evil, a reflection of its own master, the pup embraced it, suckled it, like it was its own mother's teat.

Soon, the dog, who was growing larger and stronger each day, learned to hunt and to kill for his own food. Sometimes he'd kill merely for sport, playing with the ravaged carcass for a time before leaving it to rot in the sun. This pleased his master, whose bitterness and contempt for the people of Mt. Canaan was as real as the oak tree from which they hanged the Hogstooth witch.

The man was Arlen Hogstooth of course, the last surviving descendant of Ledra Hogstooth, and the unfortunate heir to a legacy of superstition and tragedy. He continued to groom his canine protégé, fashion him in his own image, as if the dog was his own son. As it is often said of dogs and their masters, Lazarus grew to resemble Hogstooth more and more each day, much to the sinister delight of the old man. Oh, if only Arlen could have lived to see the fruits of his labor. But fate sometimes has a wicked sense of humor.

On a brisk autumn morning, many months after Arlen Hogstooth had plucked the drowning pup from the icy waters of the Anthracite River, some vacationing turkey hunters from New York, who knew nothing of the Hogstooth legend, stumbled across the old man's body floating face down in the very same waters. He had drowned while attempting to catch some dinner for himself and his canine companion.

Reluctantly, the county medical examiner removed the body from the river and hurriedly buried it in an unmarked grave at the very back of the municipal cemetery, much in the same way his ancestors and other relatives had been buried, too.

Lazarus, who was never called that name again, disappeared into the mountains, where he soon joined up with a roving pack of bush dogs.

Their leader was an aging wolfhound, and Lazarus easily murdered him in his sleep. With his victim's blood fresh on his tongue, he cried out a piercing howl for any of the remaining dogs to challenge him. Not a single one did. The pack was his to lead, and every female for his pleasure. Hogstooth would have been proud.

The Alpha pushed the old man from his mind. They were just shadows, memories of a long forgotten animal named Lazarus. That animal, like Hogstooth, didn't exist anymore. There was only the pack now.

But that hatred Arlen Hogstooth carried with him for so long, which he then instilled in the Alpha, *that* still lived on. And soon that hatred would spread throughout the ferals like the Hogstooth pox reborn, and Buddy and the Jack would bear the full extent of its wrath.

XI. A Most Repugnant Ultimatum

"So now," he thought, "somebody else will have to do something, and I hope they will do it soon, because if they don't I shall have to swim, which I can't, so I hope they do it soon." And then he gave a very long sigh and said, "I wish Pooh were here. It's so much more friendly with two."

– A.A. Milne, *Winnie-the-Pooh*

A pair of rather curious brown eyes watched Byron Brady as he pulled up to his apartment on Poplar Street in the less fashionable "new side" of Mt. Canaan.

Dusk lay upon the town like the beginning of a tale which, once begun, could only end unpleasantly. For the tired Brady had endured a thorough browbeating from both the county commissioners and sheriff over what they perceived was his ineffectiveness in managing the wild dog population in Anthracite County. Furious over the "attacks" on tourists – whom, the commissioners reminded him, were the life blood of the community – the commissioners demanded immediate action be taken to remedy the problem.

"Ever heard of the Cwn Annwn?" one of the commissioners asked. Brady shook his head. "You will, you will. It's an old name, Brady. And it's been getting thrown around quite a bit lately."

Brady was puzzled.

"Mind you, I'm not the superstitious kind, Brady. But many people in this town are. A lot of people here still have strong ties to the Old Country..."

"Not to mention the whole Hogstooth legend," another commissioner chimed in.

"My grandfather was from Greece," still yet another commissioner added. "When I was a boy, he told me a tale about the goddess Artemis releasing the fifty hounds of hell..."

The sheriff scowled. "Let's stick to the realm of reality here, boys." He was a burly, middle-aged cowboy who'd seen one too many John Wayne movies. Brady didn't like him. His father had once beaten the sheriff for the seat of "grand poobah" or something at the local lodge, and the sheriff had never forgotten it. He had a feeling the sheriff was enjoying this inquisition.

"Cwn Annwn?" Brady repeated. He assured them he and his people were investigating the attacks and even told them he'd discovered a location on the outskirts of town where some of the ferals had been holed up. Why, he'd even gone so far as to put Felix Mortimer on 24-hour surveillance of the stronghold in an effort to catch the culprits and incarcerate them.

The commissioners looked at each other and cleared their throats. "Perhaps…" they started.

But the sheriff, who was less diplomatic than the elder statesmen commissioners, helped express their intentions in more understandable terms.

"Shoot them, Brady. Shoot them dead." He grinned a crooked grin beneath that pencil thin "True Grit" mustache of his. "No cages, no pounds, no meals. These 'dogs,'" he continued, "aren't the cute little puppies at the mall. These 'dogs' aren't ever going to fetch anyone's slippers. Don't let them fool you. They're wild animals, Brady. And they should be treated like wild animals: shot and killed. Pronto."

Brady noted the sheriff's hand pass over his sidearm several times while a distant look, like the way fog veils a mountaintop, glazed over his eyes.

He was already shooting them, pursuing them through the dark wood of his mind, taking pleasure in every whimper, every cry as each shot rang out and each slug found its mark in the fleeing dogs' hides.

"That's what's gotta be done, Brady," he said, almost a whisper – a hoarse, unpolished whisper.

Brady, an animal lover, also loved his job and while admittedly he had euthanized hundreds of animals, both wild and domesticated, he prided himself on putting down the animals in the most humane manner possible. As an animal control officer, Brady was obligated to respect the strict guidelines handed down by the American Veterinary Medical Association concerning the practice of animal euthanasia. To be ordered to shoot these animals in cold blood, damn it, he didn't know if he could do it.

Sensing Brady's apprehension, the sheriff said, "You're not a tree-hugger are you, Brady? I mean, you're going to be a man about this, right? 'Cause we don't need a sprout and tofu eating sissy on this, understand?"

Brady nodded, reluctantly.

The lines near the sheriff's eyes relaxed. He patted his own stomach and a guffaw leaped from his bowels. "Good, 'cause you had us kind of worried. We got the integrity of the Fall Foliage Festival to protect, son. We don't need no wild dogs mussin' things up, you hear? I mean, for as long as I can remember, there's almost always been a Brady holding your position in Anthracite County."

The sheriff was right. Since the position became an official county office in 1892, all but one generation of Bradys had held the office of chief animal control officer. The one exception was Byron's grandfather, Morris Brady, whose plans to run for office were nullified when he was accidentally shot and killed by his own troops on Omaha Beach.

The tragic plight of Morris Brady not withstanding, the position of chief animal control officer had been a proud and long-standing tradition for Brady men, who've approached the job with all the zeal and tenacity of Hoover's G-men.

True, his great-grandfather and even his father had to put down an animal with a firearm, but that was back in the day before the use of the morally acceptable lethal injection so commonly administered now.

To turn a firearm on a defenseless animal now would be a serious breach in Brady's code of ethics. Still, he'd never wanted to be anything else than an animal control officer, nor was he qualified to be, and the feral problem unfortunately would not go away by itself.

So Brady faced a monumental decision as he drove home across the viaduct spanning the Anthracite River, crossing over from the proud history of Mt. Canaan's past to the less certain, economically challenged future of the town.

"We're counting on you on this one, Brady," the sheriff told him, the county commissioners nodding their white heads in agreement. "It'd be a shame to have to remove a Brady from a post the family practically invented themselves."

The sheriff's words rattled in Brady's mind like an iron kettle full of nails. It took three attempts to unlock the door as he fumbled the set of keys.

"Byron!" a voice called out from the darkened street.

Brady turned to see a figure shrouded in mystery approach him from the shadows.

"Byron? Hello?" It was Mindy McGovern.

She was wearing a black raincoat and her mother of pearl necklace, and the heels of her shoes made a clicking sound on the otherwise silent street. Beneath the overcoat, Mindy wore her second favorite dress: a silk number with a floral print that showed just the right amount of her dancer's legs.

"Hello," she repeated, upon reaching the steps to Brady's apartment.

Brady groaned. He wasn't in the mood for company, unless it was a deep glass of aged scotch.

"I hope I'm not bugging you. It's just that I was passing through your neighborhood and I saw you. I thought maybe you'd like some company..."

She was lying, of course. She did often pass through his neighborhood, nightly, at 9:00 PM and 10:00 PM, in the mere hopes of catching even the slightest glimpse of Brady passing by his illuminated window. Sometimes she'd pull to the side of the street like some seedy private eye and stake out his building. She'd stare up at the warm glow emanating from the second story windows and she'd imagine herself in there with him, laughing, or sharing a sophisticated cocktail while some smooth jazz flowed melodiously in the background.

In that simple fantasy, Byron Brady would realize how special she was and how fortunate he was to have the love of just such a woman. For she'd loved him most of her life, since the sixth grade when, as the new girl, she sat behind Brady in Ms. Higgin's class.

Everyone else shunned her, for she was strange and new, and her Alabama drawl was so different from the Pennsylvanian coal region dialect the other children spoke. But she didn't seem so strange to Brady.

He'd helped her with her locker combination, showed her to the cafeteria, and was genuinely interested in her and her life in Alabama. From that day on, her southern drawl gradually ceased, though her admiration for Byron Brady, whose sensitivity and maturation far exceeded the expectations of any sixth grader, continued to grow only stronger.

"Hi, Mindy," he said tiredly. "Now's not a good..."

"I mean I was just passing by..." Subconsciously, she drew her hands to her face and found her old pair of thick, burdensome glasses resting on her nose screaming, "Look at us, Byron! Look at us! Look how thick we are! You can see the rings of Saturn with us!"

Mindy splayed her fingers to silence them, and wrestled briefly with them before removing them from her face. Mindful of the fate of her other pair, she carefully placed them into a case which she held inside her raincoat. "It's just... how have you been?"

She squinted and strained her eyes in an effort to see Brady, who'd once again become a beautiful pink mass of light and color.

"Uh, not so good, really."

"Oh? Is it something you'd like to talk about?" She reached out and touched what she hoped was his forearm.

"Actually, I think I'd really just like to go to sleep. I'm sorry, Mindy. I just wouldn't be very good company tonight."

Dejected, she said, "I understand, I guess." She turned, took two steps, misjudged the curb, and fell headfirst into the gutter.

When Mindy came to, she found the beautiful, pink mass she recognized to be Byron Brady hovering over her, the ceiling light crowning his head just like in a 16th century religious painting.

"Are you all right?" he asked, his large hand stroking her head tenderly. At that moment, Mindy believed she had died, for an angel was looking after her.

"Wh-where am I?" she struggled to say.

"You're in my apartment," he told her. "You took a nasty spill off the sidewalk."

"H-how did I get here?"

"I carried you," he replied.

Mindy's heart leaped. After all these years, she'd finally found herself inside his home. "M-my glasses…"

Brady frowned, though Mindy couldn't see it. "I'm afraid you've broken them in the fall."

Mindy began to cry. All those nights of stalking Byron Brady, she'd finally gotten inside his apartment and now she wouldn't even be able to see it. She'd never be able to imagine his apartment in her fantasies in which he'd cook them both dinner or they'd sip champagne by the window. The notion made her cry even harder.

"It's okay, sweetheart," he reassured her, pulling her head close to his chest. But his gentleness made her cry all the more loudly.

"H-how am I going to drive home?" she thought aloud.

"I'll drive you," he offered.

"Okay," she responded coyly.

Sitting on the passenger's side of Brady's Chevrolet Blazer was just like a wonderful dream. Brady, the beautiful pink mass who'd taken on a greenish tint from the light of the illuminated dashboard, had rescued her once again.

"Will your mother be worried?" he asked her, as the Blazer came to a stop just outside the McGovern home on quiet, tree-lined Chestnut Street.

"No," she replied, sheepishly.

Brady looked at her for a moment. Without her glasses, she no longer looked like the Mindy McGovern he'd remembered from sixth grade. Why, Mindy McGovern had grown up and become a woman, and a quite lovely woman at that. "You should really think about getting contact lenses," he commented.

"I've tried them already. Unfortunately I can't put anything in my eyes."

"Oh," he replied.

"Do you think I look better without my glasses?" she queried.

Brady looked into Mindy's eyes and for the first time felt something completely different for this girl he'd been friend to all his life. There was a queer stirring inside himself, mixed with anticipation and, oddly, hope.

"Different," he remarked.

Mindy McGovern smiled. He'd noticed. He'd finally noticed.

Long after they'd said their good nights, and Byron's taillights faded into the night, Mindy lingered on her front porch, rocking on the swing, staring up at the twinkling stars above her that she swore she could see.

XII. Assault on the Lair of the Jack

Allowed to roam the neighborhood, the JRT (Jack Russell Terrier) feels compelled to range far afield and may not return for days, or at all…

– D. Caroline Coile, Ph.D., from *Jack Russell Terriers: A Complete Pet Owner's Manual*

The morning sun felt nice on Buddy's fur as the Jack led him through the woods to the old magazine shack. The hearty meal of Josephine's cold cuts still sat comfortably in his belly and the effects of a good night's sleep beneath her rose bushes proved remarkably well for the weary mongrel's spirits.

The dogs had lingered in Josephine's garden until the early morning hours in the hopes of breakfast, which if Josephine had been awake she surely would have served. But when no breakfast was forthcoming, they used the remaining cloak of darkness to flee the town and return to the Jack's sanctuary near the abandoned coal breaker.

The Jack was glad he had led his new friend to that garden. He'd been there once before and had met an old dog who did little more than sleep in the sun. That dog had a bowl of food he cared not to protect, so the Jack helped himself to it. The poor old dog did not even seem to notice.

Trotting alongside the Jack, Buddy felt invigorated. They'd finally found another kind human, one who wouldn't chase them away with harsh words or stones, or even worse, pluck their eyes from their heads. Buddy's trust in humanity was restored, if only momentarily.

As the Jack turned down the familiar bike trail leading past the magazine shack, he pulled up abruptly, causing Buddy to nearly topple over him. Something wasn't quite right. A strange smell was on the air.

Buddy, in his euphoric state, failed to seize upon the queer scent – but not the Jack.

The scent reached his keen nostrils and poured over him like a wave of icy water. A stranger was about.

The hair on his back bristled, his limbs tensed, and a low, forceful growl emerged from within. He shook free of Buddy, who understood almost immediately the Jack's intent.

Although Buddy's sense of smell was sharp, he was still blind, and not much use when it came to defending the Jack and himself from an enemy.

Instinctively, he sought the thick bushes off to the side of the road, which he hoped would protect him against any searching eyes.

Meanwhile, the Jack cautiously pressed on along the trail, scanning the bushes and trees for any signs of the intruder, as well as sniffing the ground before him in an effort to uncover any additional clues. He'd show this stranger, whoever he was, this was his home, and he'd defend it to his last breath.

As he moved closer to the magazine shack, his nose skimmed over Byron Brady's shoe prints in the soft earth. A man had been here, but the tracks, as well as the scent, had faded. The scent was different from the one that gripped him moments before. Whoever had left that footprint was gone, but the scent of the present intruder still lingered strongly on the air. Someone or something was waiting for him; waiting with the deadly patience of a spider. The thought made him tremble.

He cursed himself. He had had a good home once, which seemed so long ago. He had had a family who cared for him, who loved him, and had a comfortable bed, too. But a public utility worker had carelessly left the backyard gate open while he read the electricity meter, and the temptation to roam for a Jack Russell terrier is strong.

He had never meant to leave his home or travel so far, but the strange and exciting scents he encountered were so intoxicating, they kept luring him along like an invisible leash. Before he even realized it, the Jack had traveled miles from his home in Lansford, and his sense of direction soon failed him. The night crowded in all around him. Suddenly he'd found himself alone. He cried out into the darkness for the family he loved, and far away in the town of Lansford, the family who loved him just as much cried out, too.

However, the children who adored the spunky young Jack – so young the poor Jack never even learned his own name – never saw him again. All the posters seeking the lost dog, held by thumbtacks to so many telephone poles, failed to return him safely to their keep.

The Jack shook his head, his ears flapping from side to side. The memory faded. Their present predicament struck him like a rolled newspaper across his muzzle. There was no mistake about it. Something was waiting for him – waiting just inside the ramshackle structure – ready to pounce.

Fear of the unknown should have driven the Jack away, but a Jack Russell Terrier's curiosity is nearly as robust as his will to roam, and he needed to know what was waiting for him, even if it should prove to be his end.

Showing no signs of the fear that held his pounding heart – held it rigidly with a merciless grip – the Jack drew nearer. At the darkened entrance, he paused, mindful of the danger which awaited him just within. He growled a warning to the stranger. He wanted no trouble, and a confrontation even less.

Inside, the stranger stirred. He sucked in air from between his teeth and the Jack's supersensitive hearing easily detected it.

He remembered the raccoon – the dead raccoon, lying twisted and broken on the roadside. Doom washed over him. The world seemed such a dangerous place.

So be it, thought the Jack. He lowered his head and rushed blindly into the shack. Growling and snarling, and carrying on quite raucously as if some form of madness had seized his brain, he stabbed the darkness like a knife.

The shape of a large man fell upon him. For an instant, the Jack was captured in a pair of thick, gloved hands. But the gloves proved cumbersome, and he managed to slip the man's uncertain grip. A bare forearm – pale and thin like a sick chicken – flashed beneath the Jack's nose. He attacked – gave the arm a tug with his teeth.

Felix Mortimer cried out in pain. The Jack's fangs had torn into his leathery flesh and found blood.

Cursing, Mortimer fell to the ground and clutched his injured arm.

The Jack escaped. He did not look back. He found Buddy still hiding in the brush and quickly led him away.

Their sanctuary had been discovered.

They were homeless again.

XIII. Sara's Troubles

Thus let me live, unseen, unknown;
Thus unlamented let me die;
Steal from the world, and not a stone
Tell where I lie
– Alexander Pope, from *Ode on Solitude*

The bus ride home from school was tiresome, and Sara waited eagerly to reach Race Street and Josephine's warm shop, where she could take her familiar seat by the window and delight in Josie's entertaining conversation. For she hated school, particularly the other children, though she did love her teacher, Ms. McGovern, whom the children also took great joy in ridiculing.

But this morning her teacher seemed changed in some way, and it wasn't the fact she'd worn a different pair of glasses for the third straight day. It was something deeper than that.

Sara had always considered Ms. McGovern a beautiful woman, despite her thick glasses and social awkwardness, but today she had seemed absolutely gorgeous.

She wore a floral print sleeveless dress, which was her usual custom, but instead of hiding it beneath a cardigan sweater, Ms. McGovern elected to allow her porcelain, freckled shoulders to be exposed for all to see. Instead of having her light hair tied back so tightly in a French braid which sometimes seemed as though it was ready to explode, she'd chosen to wear it down so that it rested just shy of her shoulders. And when she taught today's lesson on the Louisiana Purchase, Ms. McGovern bounced on her toes as if the very ground she walked on was made of rubber.

Never had Sara witnessed Ms. McGovern so carefree. She wished maybe some day she could be as happy as Ms. McGovern was today.

As the bus rambled and backfired along Broadway, they slowly passed the thrift store advertising "like new" clothing, displayed haphazardly in the cluttered store window. Sara slumped slowly in her seat. She knew what was coming next.

"Hey, Sara," one girl called out from the rear of the bus. "Should we stop so you can buy some new clothes?"

The school bus erupted in laughter. Sara could feel their stares upon her.

She slid down, so far she hoped they could not see her, and she felt her pigtails catch on the high seat back.

Sara did her best to ignore them and stared out the window. Just a few more stops and the bus would be on Race Street. Then it would be only a matter of minutes before they reached Josephine's shop, where she could finally be off the bus and away from these miserable children for the remainder of the evening. But the bus was not moving fast enough.

She looked to the drawing in her hands for comfort. It was of herself holding Barney while sitting in Josie's comfy chair. She'd made it for Josie and Sara was sure she'd hang it in her store.

Aaron, who was in the other sixth grade class across the hall from Sara's, walked right up to her seat and cursed at her.

Sara looked back at him for a brief moment, in which she scanned his eyes for any redeeming quality and regrettably found none.

The boy countered with the timeless rhetorical question, "Duh?!"

She turned her head away from him and redirected her gaze out the window. But the little boy, the monstrous product of a union between a school board member and a hairdresser, wasn't quite satisfied with her lack of a reaction. He maliciously yanked her hair.

"I'm talking to you, Noodlenose," he said.

The assault hurt her feelings more than it did her head, but a steady flow of tears soon made their way down her cheeks nonetheless.

"What's this?" he said, snatching the drawing from Sara's hands.

"Give it back," Sara responded, starting to rise. But the boy pushed her back onto her seat with one hand.

"Look at the stupid picture Noodlenose drew," he said, holding it up so everyone could see.

"Please, Aaron," Sara pleaded. "Give it back."

"You want it back?"

Sara nodded.

"Okay," he said. "Here." He started to hand the picture to her. Devilishness sparked in his eyes. He withdrew his hand. "Wait a sec…"

A half-smile turning up one corner of his mouth, he shredded the drawing. His malevolent eyes never blinked. He sprinkled the pieces onto her lap.

Sara began to cry harder.

"Look, everybody," he announced. "The baby's crying! Cry, little baby, cry!"

All the children were soon chanting, "Cry baby! Cry baby," at the top of their lungs, despite the protests of the tired bus driver.

Sara couldn't take any more. She refused to give these horrible children the satisfaction of watching her cry. She collected her things beside her, sprang to her feet, and fled the bus at the very next stop.

As the bus pulled away, the unrelenting chants of "cry baby" echoed in her mind long after the bus had traveled from view. She stood on Broadway among the tourists and wondered where to go.

In order to get to Josie's shop, she'd have to climb the steps behind Antonio's Pizza, but by the time she reached the shop, the school bus would have arrived, and the same wicked children would be there waiting.

Sara cried all the louder. She tucked her books under her arm and ran as fast as she could toward the river.

The Anthracite River was surging. Its pace was hurried and deliberate; it was a very busy river and it kept a tight schedule. It had other rivers to meet.

It was a mild autumn evening, and a light easterly breeze coaxed many blazing leaves to descend from the trees jutting out over the river's edge and gently freefall to the rushing water below.

Sara sat on the old stone wall erected many years before to prevent the mighty waters of the river from overflowing the gorge. She hummed softly to herself as she listened to the strong current over the rocks beneath her. The rhythmic flow of the relentless water eased her mind and made her forget the callousness of her classmates.

She could stay here forever, she could, just like Ledra Hogstooth. Sara fancied the thought of raising some rats of her own and unleashing them on the hateful children who tormented her each and every day.

She stomped at the wall. Poverty wasn't something she brought on herself, she was born into it. That wasn't something she could help, nor could she be responsible for it, either. And she couldn't blame her mother, for Sara knew her mother worked very hard at the Mt. Canaan Inn so that they could afford the tiny apartment above Josie's shop.

Besides, what should it matter what kind of clothes a person wears? It's what's inside that counts, at least that's what Josie said.

Sara wept. She wanted her daddy. *A blaring horn...* It'd been nine years since he'd died in the automobile accident, back when they still lived in New Jersey. Sara remembered very little about her father or their home in New Jersey, though her mother had told her plenty about both. *Screeching tires...*

She knew her dad had been a claims supervisor with an insurance company, that he was tall, and that he loved animals just like her. *Glass shattering...* And she thought she remembered lying on the floor with him on Sunday afternoons, watching football. He'd hold her on his chest and cradle her until she fell asleep to the blissful voices of the play-by-play announcers.

Did she really remember that? Or was that something her mother had told her? Sara couldn't be certain. *Blood...* All she was sure of was if her father had not died, they would not be poor; at least not as poor as they were now. *A crash.*

Unsettling images often tainted her fractured memories of her father. She shuddered. Why did she remember him this way? If they *were* memories, even.

Sara stretched out atop the wall and stared up at the sky. Somewhere up in the clouds he was looking down at her, constantly watching her, because he loved her. And when you truly love someone, you never leave them, even if you die.

True, something was watching Sara, though it wasn't her father. For in the nearby woods a pair of sanguine eyes pierced the darkness and stared hungrily at the child on the wall.

XIV. A Confrontation on the River

He had never seen dogs fight as these wolfish creatures fought, and his first experience taught him an unforgettable lesson.
– Jack London, *The Call of The Wild*

Silently, as if an apparition, the Alpha emerged from the twisted trees around him and glided effortlessly toward the floodwall and the child perched atop it.

Sara continued to hum to herself, unaware of the danger racing toward her. Within seconds, the Alpha was near the wall. His eyes were focused intently on the child's unprotected, dangling foot. Targeting Sara's exposed leg, the Alpha lunged toward her.

Perhaps sensing a disturbance in the air, Sara withdrew her foot just as the savage feral reached her. He impacted with a harmless thud against the wall.

Sara screamed. Behind her, the rapids of the Anthracite River licked and lapped hungrily at the base of the wall, some 100 feet below. In front of her, the Alpha stood upright, his front paws scratching against the century-old brick levee. She edged toward the water.

The dog clawed at Sara. "Oh God!" she cried inside her head. "Someone help me!" She felt her balance slip away. The Alpha clutched her pants leg as she teetered backward. If not for the strength of the dog, she would have fallen headfirst into the river. Sara's mouth gaped open and a muted cry emerged. The dog tugged swiftly at her leg and pulled her off her feet. She fell sharply onto the top of the wall and nearly rolled off. The impact compressed the air in her lungs and Sara struggled to breathe. Her foot touched something sitting on the wall. Her books! In a desperate ploy, she kicked with her free leg and sent them hurtling to the ground near the feral.

Forgetting Sara, the Alpha threw himself atop the books with crazed tenacity, and turned the texts into a mess of confetti on the ground. Sara took advantage of the dog's distraction to jump from the wall.

She ran as fast as she could for the town square, praying the dog wouldn't notice. Leaving the remains of the books behind him, the Alpha tore after her. Soon he was at her heels.

She could feel the dog snapping at her feet as she ran, and she could sense his demoniac gaze upon her. Oh, God she hated those children! If they wouldn't have been teasing her, she'd be safe in Josie's shop right now, sitting in her big, comfortable chair by the window and listening to Josie's fanciful stories.

But wishful thinking was no defense against a feral. The dog, who weighed more than Sara, was nearly upon her, biting at her, much in the same fashion he had done away with her school books. Ahead of her lay the old train station and Hazard Square. She could see people strolling about, unaware of her plight.

"Hey…" she strained, but her voice abandoned her. To her right along a narrow path parallel to the floodwall, two more ferals were fast approaching.

Oh God, she thought, *more of them.*

The Alpha lunged for Sara. He tackled her in a way a linebacker might bring down a ball carrier in the open field. At last, she found her lost voice and screamed a dire scream as the feral grinned.

"Oh God, please God," Sara pleaded.

But the Alpha, who served no God, paid no heed to the girl's prayers. He lashed out at her in a dizzying rain of razor claws.

Sara pulled her hands to her face and shielded herself against the attack. She fended him off briefly with a flurry of futile kicks. But the Alpha, despite all his darkness and wrath, had a gracefulness about him, and he effortlessly bounded over Sara's extended legs. In one fluid movement, he landed on her chest.

Lying beneath him, his stale breath in her face, Sara's entire body quivered. His dark, fathomless eyes scanned over her and widened as they fixed upon her throat. They weren't the eyes of a dog; they were hypnotic, like a cobra's. They swirled, changed shapes, danced – the Danse Macabre – the dance of death. They thirsted, thirsted for blood – innocent blood. They promised death, a swift, painless death if she gave herself freely to him. She sensed it was an offer he'd extended to other unfortunate creatures before her. She also knew she was powerless. He was deadly silent.

He had the patience of a cobra, too.

But as quickly and suddenly as the direction of a summer breeze can change, so, too, did Sara's fortunes.

Buddy and the Jack, who had been roaming about the river valley since the attempted assault at the magazine shack, had picked up on the Alpha's frequent markings and had followed them to the floodwall. The Jack spotted the Alpha attacking the girl.

He reached Sara first, with Buddy trailing not far behind, following the Jack's persistent bark. The Jack lowered his head and blind-sided the Alpha, knocking him off of the girl. The Alpha scrambled for his footing, but before he'd regained his balance, the fearless Jack was atop him. First attacking his friend, Buddy, and now this defenseless girl… why, he'd show the Alpha a thing or two.

But with the advantage of surprise gone, he was no match for the Alpha. He threw the pesky Jack from his back, grasped him by the loose skin of his neck, and shook him like a toy. Then he flung the Jack toward the floodwall as if he was nothing more than mere rubbish.

The Jack tumbled end over end – head over tail – and struck his head against the base of the wall.

Sara shrieked. It seemed as though the little dog was dead. His small, pink tongue had pushed out the corner of his mouth and his eyes were shut.

While the Alpha admired his own handiwork, Buddy's sniffer zeroed in on the Alpha's scent. He leaped upon the Alpha's back and pulled him to the ground. The two giant dogs rolled upon one another like angry lovers; a primordial song of growls and gnashing teeth arose from their coupling. The smell of blood stung the air.

Sara knew she should run away. The Alpha was no longer interested in her. But the little dog looked so sad lying there all alone… Anyway, he had saved her life, whether he intended to or not, and Sara felt compelled to be at his side.

She rushed past the warring canines and dropped to her knees beside the fallen Jack. Showing no sign of fear or hesitation, Sara placed her hand on the lifeless dog's chest and felt for a heartbeat. A faint, infrequent thumping signaled the dog was still alive, if barely. She gently raised his battered head and rested it on her lap. The dog emitted a slight moan and his ears flickered. Sara passed her hand through the disheveled fur on his head.

She said to him calmingly, "It's okay… everything will be okay." But she was not sure the little guy was going to make it.

While Sara looked over the Jack, Buddy and the Alpha continued their struggle. In the lightless labyrinth of Buddy's mind, he saw the Alpha, all rage and flashing teeth and blood red eyes, taut muscles flexing beneath a black velvet coat, razor-like claws honed on the bones of its hapless victims. Buddy saw himself, too. A giant, hairy, pitiful wretch, so despised by his own master, he sent him away to have his eyes plucked out. Both dogs were bound by darkness.

Their battle raged all around Sara. She knew if it were allowed to continue, the fight most surely would end in the death of one of them. Sara feared for the mongrel. In his blindness he fought a courageous battle against what she knew was a superior foe.

But the Alpha appeared to be slowly gaining the upper hand. Buddy was scrambling for footing, losing ground, and the Alpha was driving him backward. But he kept his head down, protecting his throat from the feral. Without the aid of the Jack, Buddy's chances of besting the Alpha were washing away like teardrops in the rain.

Sara screamed at the Alpha. His hideous muzzle contorted like a laughing jack o'lantern.

There must have been something in the urgency of Sara's voice. The little dog in her lap suddenly stirred. He lifted his heavy head and looked up at Sara through unfocused eyes.

"Hello," she said to him.

The Jack lowered his snout, sought out Sara's hand and gently licked it. He had found his way back home with his family in Lansford, or so he thought. This girl reminded him of their youngest daughter, Ginny. But even in his foggy state, he knew that couldn't be true. The sound of the Alpha methodically destroying his friend sliced through the fog in his brain like the cold steel of a sword. Buddy needed him.

The girl's lap was warm and comforting. Under the right circumstances, he would have liked to stay there longer. But his friend was running out of time.

Buddy fell.

The Jack pulled himself upright. His legs were wobbly. His vision somewhat blurred, the Jack could barely discern the shape of the Alpha towering triumphantly over the shape of a fallen Buddy.

He managed a growl and bristled his fur. He searched for the courage that had, just moments earlier, propelled him onto the Alpha's back. But this Alpha was too strong. Surely he could not triumph over him.

But the Alpha was killing Buddy, and if something wasn't done soon, he was about to lose his best friend. He couldn't let Buddy die. Ahead of him, the Alpha readied for the kill.

Seeing three Alphas, the Jack threw himself at the middle dog. The Alpha was all muscle. It felt like hitting the wall again. He succeeded in once again knocking the Alpha off balance – more importantly though, he turned the Alpha's attention away from his hurting friend.

The Alpha quickly recovered. The Jack swayed. The Alpha seethed. There was a sense of unfinished business in the Alpha's manner, and the Jack knew it. The Alpha had taken the Jack's assault in their first meeting as a personal affront. He had held a grudge. This dark creature was no normal dog.

He could ill afford to be caught in the Alpha's jaws again, he was fortunate to have been trapped once and still breathing. Slowly, he felt his strength and vision return. The Alpha lunged for him, but the Jack sidestepped the attack. He'd have to be quick to stay alive. The Alpha lashed out once more, trying to end the Jack's life in one fatal snap of his jaws. The Alpha's teeth glanced his chest, but the Jack managed to roll away from him.

Sara rushed to Buddy's side. But Buddy wanted no comfort from her. He struggled to his feet, his fur wet with blood and saliva. He barked a defiant, hoarse bark at the Alpha, his throat dry from fatigue.

"You're going to have to face the two of us," he seemed to say.

Sara, bolstered by the courage of Buddy and the Jack, advanced on the Alpha while Buddy approached the sinister hound from behind. "We're not afraid of you, you stupid feral!" Sara exclaimed.

Weary, the Alpha paused and looked around. He was surrounded on all sides. Buddy, the Jack, and Sara, all once his intended victims, stared audaciously back at him. He swore at them a dog's profane curse. The insidious growl echoed off the wall. He considered continuing the battle, for the coppery taste of the mongrel's blood was still fresh on his tongue. He could kill all three of them, he was certain of it. But he had not become the alpha male of his pack by making brash decisions. He'd have his chance at these dogs again.

His gaze fell on Sara. He'd have another chance at her, too.

The Alpha hissed and, in one leap, bounded into the clearing. With a vengeful howl, he melded into the shadows of the wood and was gone.

Sara collapsed onto the ground beside the two exhausted dogs.

"Thank you," she said.

The Jack, still reeling from his head wound, managed to wag his tail. He sauntered over to where she sat and allowed Sara to stroke his unkempt, matted fur.

Buddy, however, wanted no part of her or any person. His mistrust of people was still strong. He kept his distance from Sara and resisted her attempts to beckon him to her.

In their exuberance at turning away the Alpha's aggression, neither Sara nor the Jack saw the county-issued vehicle fast approaching, just beyond the square.

XV. The Uninvited

Oh, I am a Texas cowboy, right off the Texas plains.
My trade is cinchin' saddles & pullin' of bridle reins,
And I can throw a lasso with the greatest of ease;
I can rope and ride a bronco any damn way I please.
– Cowboy Song, from *A treasury of Western Folklore*

Darkness was rapidly descending on Mt. Canaan, as Felix Mortimer returned home from the emergency room of County Hospital. He'd spent most of the day being treated for dog bites. God, he hated animals – every last stinking one of them.

As he struggled to steer his car with the large bandage on his hand, he imagined capturing the miserable little Jack Russell terrier and locking him away in the pound's stainless steel cages. He could almost hear the clang of the cage door, he could almost see the dog cowering in the shadows of the bars. The dog's imaginary fear filled his nostrils. A warm feeling enveloped him, like blackberry brandy on a winter evening. Like Leroux brand, not that cheap stuff they had down at the liquor store. Never again would the contemptible little creature roam free.

Mortimer was beside himself. He knew dogs with ornery dispositions were euthanized, and he'd arrange to administer the lethal dose himself. The fantasy delighted him so much, he almost didn't recognize the very same small, white dog frolicking with a little girl near the floodwall.

A little girl! His cigarette nearly dropped in his lap. Mortimer stomped the brake pedal all the way to the floor, commanding his vehicle to a grinding halt along Route 54. A little girl was playing with the white dog. The same dog responsible for the nine stitches in his forearm! And the small dog's blind pal was not far away, either.

He removed his control stick from the rear of the car. The control stick was a six-foot long pole with a steel noose coated in plastic, attached to the end. It was a common tool used by most animal control officers to subdue an animal. Mortimer hurried toward the child.

Sara giggled as the Jack, crouched in his play bow pose and wagging his tail, nipped pleasantly at her extended hand. Sitting here playing with the Jack on the grass lawn, in the shadow of the floodwall, Sara had forgotten all about the frightening attack by the Alpha, as well as the taunting she'd suffered at the hands of her classmates earlier in the day. She was having as much fun with this outcast dog as she had ever had.

The Jack, too, was enjoying the good-natured exchange between the girl and himself. It was like being with Ginny again.

But Buddy's mistrust of humans was very strong and he denied himself the opportunity for such affection. Instead, he waited quietly at a distance. In fact, the idle Buddy was the first to detect the scent of a strange man approaching. He ran in a circle and barked out a frantic warning.

The Jack sprung to his feet. Instinctively, he backed toward Buddy and raised the hair on his back. *Keep away... stay back.*

Sara also stood and placed herself between the dogs and the approaching stranger whom she instantly recognized as a dogcatcher.

"Now step aside, Missy," Mortimer ordered.

"Why? What are you going to do?"

"You're playing with fire, Missy. These two buggers are dangerous."

Sara laughed. "These two dogs?" She motioned to Buddy and the Jack behind her. "They saved my life," she replied. "I don't believe they'd intentionally hurt someone. Unless that someone was asking for it, of course."

Mortimer raised his bandaged arm. "They done this to me, they did."

"I wouldn't blame them," Sara scoffed. "I'd probably do the same thing to you, if I were them."

Mortimer sneered. "So that's the way it's going to be," he said.

Sara nodded. "Yup."

"So be it," he replied, and attempted to brush past her. Sara stepped defiantly in front of him and was knocked to the ground.

Angered, the Jack leaped toward Mortimer. He stopped just short of the dogcatcher and growled. This raised the ire of Buddy, who also growled at the unseen foe.

"Uh-oh. You shouldn't have done that, I'm afraid," scolded Sara. "They protect me and now they think you've hurt me." She sat up and brushed the grass from her pants. "You're in big trouble now."

"We'll see about that," Mortimer countered.

He raised the control stick and attempted to loop it over the Jack's head.

But Jack Russell terriers are exceptionally agile dogs. The Jack easily avoided Mortimer's laughable attempt at capturing him.

"Bugger!" Mortimer nearly fell on his ass. He waved his bandaged hand at the Jack. "Lousy bugger! If I can't get you, I'll get your blind pal, I will."

Buddy was a much easier target for the dogcatcher's noose. Mortimer seized the blind mongrel in his first attempt.

"Leave him alone!" Sara cried out, as Mortimer tugged Buddy toward him.

"Stand back, young Missy. Or you'll get my size 11 boot in your arse."

Buddy was frightened by the sudden restraint around his throat. He pulled away from Mortimer's snare; however, the more poor Buddy attempted to free his throat from the dreadful loop, the tighter it constricted about his neck. Buddy struggled to breathe. An even darker, colder kind of darkness consumed him. He realized any further resistance would be futile and reluctantly followed the dogcatcher's lead.

The Jack paced a wide circle around Buddy and Mortimer. What could he do? The man had Buddy… and his head hurt… and he was oh, so tired. Bark? Maybe he could scare him away.

He snarled and yapped, and created quite a ruckus. But the man paid no mind. He continued to pull Buddy toward his car.

Sara kicked the ground. First there were rotten kids, then a killer dog, and now a dogcatcher? She'd had just about enough for one day. These two dogs had saved her life and she wasn't about to just let them be carted away to some dog pound.

As fast as she possibly could, Sara ran toward Mortimer.

"Now young Missy –" Mortimer started.

Sara kicked him in the kneecap.

"You – !" he cursed her.

Instantly he surrendered his grip of the long choker. He fell to the ground and clutched his knee in agony.

Buddy shook free of the noose.

"Run!" screamed Sara.

The Jack ran alongside Buddy and allowed him to grasp his collar.

"Go on, now!" Sara commanded, and clapped her hands.

Frightened, the dogs raced for the wood.

Meanwhile, Mortimer writhed on the ground, wincing with pain. Soon, both dogs vanished from sight.

"You're in a heap of trouble, Missy," Mortimer grumbled, clasping his knee firmly in his hands.

Sara looked down at the ground where the remains of her schoolbooks lay scattered on the grass like freshly fallen snow. "Take a number," she said.

XVI. Several Days in Mt. Canaan

Suppose time is not a quantity but a quality, like the luminescence of the night above the trees just when a rising moon has touched the treeline.

– Alan Lightman, *Einstein's Dreams*

When Sara didn't come home from school at her usual time, Josephine became worried. It was not like Sara to be late, or for her not to at least call Josephine and let her know she'd be late. Every laugh of a passing child prompted Josephine to her shop's door in the hopes it was Sara. *Where could that child be?*

Josephine's hand hovered over the telephone for remainder of the afternoon; however, she resisted her urge to contact the police. She didn't even call Sara's mother at work, for she knew Linda could ill afford to miss any time.

Instead, she simply waited inside her shop, busying herself with inane work and whittling at her fingernails until they throbbed with pain. At least there were no howling dogs.

At 6:10 P.M., Sara arrived in Felix Mortimer's car, to the relief of the much worried Josephine. She found Mortimer was in a foul mood, grumbling about how Sara had bungled his attempt to capture some ferals, and he littered his description of the incident with various four-letter words.

As he sped off, Josephine turned her attentions on the tardy Sara and began to scold the child for being late; however, Sara excitedly apologized and then went on and on about how a little white dog and a big blind dog had saved her life from the jaws of a really vicious feral.

"You don't say," Josephine commented, instantly forgetting her anger.

Without another word, she pulled the small child close to her and held her tightly for some time.

Over the next few days, Josephine noticed a considerable change in Sara. Though the other children continued to taunt and tease her, Sara seemed indifferent to their tormenting, and continued to fill Josephine's ears with stories of her new "friends," the dogs.

She recounted time and again of the dark moment when the Alpha had pinned her to the ground, intending to rip out her throat, when the two angels had descended upon the feral and saved her from a most certain and painful death.

When Josephine had told Sara that the same two dogs had spent a night in her garden a few days before, it prompted the most insistent Sara to accompany Josie home every night in an effort to see her new friends once more. But Buddy and the Jack had found an ideal home west of the borough along the river.

It was a magnificent cave, its opening long since grown over by bushes and vines. The Jack had stumbled across it quite accidentally while chasing a wily hare. The rabbit got away, but not before revealing the cozy confines of this small cavern which suited two homeless dogs like Buddy and the Jack just fine.

A bed of dried leaves, which had been chased into the cave by the wind, blanketed the cavern's floor and provided a comfortable place to sleep for the two weary dogs. For after their bouts with the Alpha and Felix Mortimer, the dogs were battered and exhausted and needed the regenerating powers that only good rest and sleep can bring.

So for the next few days, the dogs avoided the town, opting to stay close to their new home and the good hunting it provided.

That was a good decision on the their part, whether they realized it or not, for the coming of autumn was a big event in Mt. Canaan and the townspeople celebrated it with a Fall Foliage Festival held every October in Hazard Square.

Celebrating the brilliant colors of the season, which made this borough such a special place to live during the fall, food and arts and crafts stands, games of chance, and a large stage were erected in the town square, attracting tourists and locals alike.

Also, with Halloween fast approaching and its strange connection with the Hogstooth witch, the town also became a mecca for real witches, Wiccans, spiritualists and other new age types who held their own gatherings in observation of the execution of Ledra Hogstooth and other occult holidays which coincided with the season.

This was a very busy time indeed for the borough of Mt. Canaan, and the town stood to reap a good amount of wealth from the free-spending tourists.

No one knew more about that than Byron Brady. He continued to endure the pressure to eradicate the feral problem placed upon him by the county leaders as well as the arrogant sheriff, and Felix Mortimer's botched attempt to catch two of the most sought-after offenders nearly cost him his job.

"One more chance, Brady," the sheriff warned. All the county commissioners nodded their gray heads in agreement.

"If these two dogs attack another tourist, heads will roll, Brady. Starting with yours, my friend."

Strangely, though Brady felt the loaded guns pointed at him, and the utmost urgency to catch these ferals, it didn't affect him the way he thought it might. For Brady's mind wasn't entirely focused on his work. He couldn't stop thinking about Mindy McGovern.

My God, the way she'd looked that night in his car, he couldn't forget it. Why didn't he ever notice it before?

She was beautiful, and his heart raced whenever he thought about her, which was quite often. Why, they had been friends since the sixth grade. Was it possible he'd loved her all this time? Love? *C'mon, Brady, get a hold of yourself.* But he did feel something for her, something different than he had ever felt before for her, or any girl.

Maybe he was coming down with something. It was that time of year. No, it was Mindy McGovern, he was sure of it. He was falling in love with Mindy McGovern. Or had he loved Mindy McGovern all this time?

Mindy McGovern played the next few days very cool. After years of chasing her white whale, Byron Brady, she had the boy right where she wanted him. For there was no mistaking the look in Brady's eyes that night: he'd finally noticed her for what she really was, a woman. Brady would never look at his little buddy from the sixth grade quite the same way, that's for sure. And just think, all it took was to be knocked unconscious in the gutter in front of Brady's apartment building.

In the days leading up to the Fall Foliage Festival, Mindy was feeling somewhat of a free spirit. She'd finally shed the shackles of unrequited love, and it showed in everything she did.

At school, she dressed whimsically, but still in the bounds of good taste, and she quite suddenly stopped giving homework assignments.

"Go home and play," she commanded them. "And fall in love if you may."

All the children looked confusedly at each other. Was this the same mousy Ms. McGovern, afraid of her own shadow, who ordered them to read a chapter per night? Even when confronted by the ludicrous story that Sara

VanMeter had told her, the one in which a crazed feral had eaten her textbooks, did Mindy remain her new, jovial self.

"There's plenty more textbooks in the closet, dear. Go on and help yourself. In fact, take as many as you like, just in case the hungry feral should come back for more."

Even her fellow teachers noticed a change in her. Why, in fact, several of the single male teachers approached her and asked if she had a date for the Fall Foliage Festival.

"Why, yes, I do... but thank you," she said with a smile, for she was certain the great love of her life, the man whom she planned to marry, would call her and ask her to the square, where the annual autumn dance would be held this weekend.

So positively certain was Mindy that she knew her man so well, she avoided him the rest of the week. No surprise visits to the courthouse with freshly baked cookies, no stake-outs outside his apartment building, and no late night telephone calls to his home just to hear his sleepy voice and then hang up... ahem, she'd never done that, of course not. That was someone else.

So when her telephone rang on Thursday night, she wasn't the least bit surprised to hear Brady's somewhat nervous voice stammer and struggle to ask her to the Fall Foliage Festival.

"Why, Byron Brady, are you asking me out on a date?" she said, her sweet southern Alabama drawl making a reappearance after all these years.

"Uh, yeah... I mean, yes... I guess so."

"Hmm, I don't know. I did have some plans this weekend..."

It was cruel, she knew it. But she also knew if she was going to have a chance of keeping him, she had to seem somewhat indifferent – at least that's what her latest issue of *Cosmopolitan* said.

"Well, I..." Brady started.

"Sure," she interrupted, letting him off the hook. "Why not? It sounds like fun."

"Great," he replied. "I'll pick you up Saturday at 8:00 PM."

Mindy replaced the handset onto the telephone and did a mock tap-dance in her stocking feet, until her mother walked in on her.

"I've got a date Saturday night with Byron Brady!" she announced.

"The dogcatcher?" her mother responded. "Tell him to do something about these damned ferals."

XVII. A Dreadful Revelation

"Just the same, I don't envy you," said the old sheep. "You know why they're fattening you up, don't you?"

"No," said Wilbur.

"Well, I don't like to spread bad news," said the sheep, "but they're fattening you up because they're going to kill you, that's why."

– E.B. White, *Charlotte's Web*

As the remains of October dwindled until only a few days were left, the annual Fall Foliage Festival turned the usually serene Hazard Square into a bustling center of activity and song. The aromas of funnel cake, potato cakes, pierogies, and baked goods swirled about the wind-swept park, transporting the traditional smells of autumn throughout the anxious town.

Locals and tourists alike strolled among the wooden stands which peddled such staples as warm apple cider and pumpkin bread, and games of skill like "Dunk the Mayor."

Truly, it was one of the year's biggest events and no one profited more from its annual appearance than the local merchants themselves, who, thanks to the festival, experienced an increase in business more so than at any other time of the year.

One of those merchants, Josephine McGillis, even set up a stand of her own in the square, in the hopes of boosting her annual profits.

While her good-natured husband Jim ran the shop, Josie and Sara, with her mother's blessing, sold Josephine's autumn-themed crafts to the festival-goers, who were eager to purchase a memento of their visit to Mt. Canaan.

All day long, the square remained filled with browsers satisfying their cravings with the wide variety of ethnic dishes, while a diverse schedule of musical groups entertained the masses from the wooden stage erected in front of the old train station. Never was the old town so alive like during the Fall Foliage Festival.

While Josie sat at a makeshift work-table behind her stand, creating such fall-themed crafts as jack o'lanterns and scarecrows, much to the delight of passersby, Sara waited on the customers and graciously accepted their money in exchange for one of Josie's unique creations. For all her hard work, Sara would receive 15% of the day's take.

She hoped it would be enough to buy herself a princess costume, since Halloween was only days away. Although her mother would be working overtime this night at the Mt. Canaan Inn, where the revelers would eventually seek refreshments a bit stronger than apple cider and tips would probably reward her mother quite well, the money could be better spent on necessities like food and utilities rather than such foolishness as a Halloween costume.

So, like the good little girl her mother raised, Sara kindly accepted Josie's offer of employment at her festival stand and worked on Saturday, instead of marching in the annual Halloween Parade that commenced on West Broadway and ended several blocks later at Hazard Square.

Most, if not all, of Sara's classmates would be in the parade, proudly adorned in their store-bought costumes, and putting their best foot forward in front of the judge's stand in the hopes of garnishing first prize. They would be judged, appropriately enough, in front of the courthouse for creativity, scariness, humor, and originality.

From Sara's position in the park, she could easily see the all-decisive judging of the parade participants, which was only a mere 50 yards away.

As Josephine continued to assemble her crafts, Sara waited on a man she recognized instantly as a dogcatcher, although not the same one she had encountered days before.

"Hello," he greeted her.

His kindly eyes looked beyond Sara to the busy Josephine working behind her.

"Hello, Josie," he called.

Josephine looked up from her crafts at the handsome young man dressed in a well-tailored three-piece brown tweed suit. "Why, hello, Byron. How are you?"

"Just fine, Josie. And you?"

"Very busy, Byron, very busy," she replied. "I see you're all *gussied* up for our little festival here."

Brady looked down at himself. "Oh this," he said, tugging at the lapel of his coat. "I have a date tonight."

"You do? And with whom might that be? Anybody we know?" Josie asked, although she had a pretty good inkling who it was already, thanks to the gossips who visited her shop.

"As a matter of fact, you probably do know her," he said, proudly. "Mindy McGovern."

"Ms. McGovern!" Sara exclaimed, and then quickly covered her mouth with her hand before any other words could escape.

"That's right," Brady replied. He crouched so he could look Sara in the eyes. "Do you know her?"

Sara nodded. "She's my teacher."

So that's why Ms. McGovern was acting so strangely, Sara thought. She was in love... with the dogcatcher. Suddenly, Sara felt dejected. Of all the eligible bachelors in Mt. Canaan, why did she have to pick a dogcatcher, and the chief one at that.

"Do you like her?" Brady asked.

Sara nodded again. "Do you?"

Brady smiled at her warmly. "Very much. Mindy... Ms. McGovern, I mean... she and I have been friends since we were your age."

"Are you going to get married?" Sara asked him.

"Sara VanMeter!" Josephine exclaimed. "Don't you answer that, Byron," she said, to Brady.

Brady laughed heartily. He had a warm face, Sara thought, and despite his job, Sara liked the way the corners of his mouth crinkled when he smiled. She could see why her teacher had fallen for him. But Sara wasn't completely sold yet. If this Brady character was a snake, Sara was determined to find out.

"You're the dogcatcher, aren't you?" she queried.

"I prefer the title 'animal control officer,' because we catch more than just dogs," he replied.

"Like what?"

"Well, let's see," he said. "We patrol all the county roads in an effort to round up and impound stray and runaway animals... we respond to complaints from the public... we investigate–"

"What do you do with the dogs when you catch them?" Sara interrupted.

Brady cleared his throat. "Well... first we check them out for any type of disease, and once we find that they're healthy, we clean them up and put them up for adoption." He smiled at her, hoping the explanation was adequate.

"What if no one adopts them?" she asked, innocently.

"Sara," Josephine interceded. "Perhaps Mr. Brady doesn't have time to talk to you right now. Remember, he does have an important date to keep."

Sara ignored Josie and continued to stare at Brady, awaiting an answer.

Brady shifted, uneasily. "Well, you see..." He cleared his throat once more and recited, "Uh, well, as you know, the unwanted animal population is at an all-time high right now. And even though we try to make every effort we can to find a home for each animal... well, sometimes no one wants a pet. Unfortunately, we don't have enough space at the uh... animal shelter. So when new animals come in, we need to make space for them." Brady felt sweat collect over his brow.

"Byron," Josephine pleaded. "You don't have to explain all this right now..."

But Brady raised his hand and silenced her. Educating the public was part of his job, like it or not, and he honestly felt he did what was best for the animals. "So," he continued, "some of the animals that have already spent some time in the shelter and have yet to be adopted... they need to be put down, so other animals can have their fair chance at being adopted, too."

"Put down?" Sara asked. She understood what the words meant in the context of Brady's explanation, but she wanted him to elaborate anyway, for she needed to examine his eyes when he spoke in an effort to find any redeeming quality in them.

You see, Sara had a habit of looking for the good in most people, even her tormentors at school, and she regarded Brady no differently, despite the fact he was a dogcatcher. Her teacher was in love with him, and Sara greatly admired her teacher. She thought Ms. McGovern deserved a man at least her own equal in kindness.

Brady looked to Josephine who held his gaze for only a moment before directing her eyes downward at her work. He was alone on this one. Apparently, even Josephine had a difficult time justifying Brady's actions.

"Well Sara," he started. "When I say 'put down' I mean euthanasia..."

"Euthanasia?"

"Yeah, euthanasia... that's a, uh... that's a fancy word for..."

"Killing," she offered, more than asked.

"Uh..." Brady laughed, nervously. "Yeah, that's another name for it –"

"How do you do it?"

Brady hesitated. The innocence in the girl's eyes was unwavering. At that moment, he'd have rather faced one hundred county commissioners and sheriffs than this child's bold interrogation. Finally, he repeated, "How do I euthanize..."

"Kill them... how do you kill the animals? Do you shoot them with your gun? Do you poison them by placing something bad in their food or water? Do you beat them with something like a baseball bat?"

While Sara asked him these questions about this morally complex problem, Brady shook his head to each one. "No, Sara," he told her, when she'd finished. "We – I give them an injection that makes them go to sleep, and they never wake up again. Believe me, Sara, they don't feel anything. I would never harm any of them... I love animals."

While Brady explained this to Sara, she thought of the small white dog and his blind friend. The emotions in her young body swirled inside her heart and mind until finally she lost control over them and her eyes inevitably flushed with tears. "If you love them, why do you kill them?"

It was a question Brady could not answer, at least not to a child Sara's age. For how could she understand such complex issues as the overpopulation of animals, the lack of spaying and neutering of pets whose owners allow them to run free, and the mere absence of rights for animals which human citizens of this country all but take for granted. So he did not answer her, at least not that question.

"I care for them very much, Sara… I really do."

Looking down at the sensitive little girl whom he'd made cry on this joyous Saturday evening, Brady felt his hold over his own emotions slip away and his sight blurred, too. He dropped to his knees, not caring what stains might be left on his pants.

"It's not easy, Sara… it really isn't. I don't like doing it… in fact, I hate it."

"Then why do it?" she countered.

Josephine, wrestling with her own emotions, stepped silently behind Sara and draped her arms around her. "Because he cares, Sara."

She looked at Brady, who held his head low. "You're too young to understand now, but there are things in life everyone must do, things that no one likes. There are some very dirty jobs that everyone would prefer someone else do, and Byron does one of them. If he didn't, there would be animals starving in our streets and dying with disease. Be glad there is someone like Byron in our town, someone who does what he does out of love for the animals, because there are certainly men out there who would take *great joy* in the very same task."

Brady felt a tiny hand find its way inside his clenched fist. Looking up, he discovered Sara was holding his hand.

"It's okay," she told him. She thought once more of the stray dogs by the river and hoped in her heart that neither would ever find themselves inside Brady's animal shelter. If that ever happened, she'd be forced to hate this likable man who, for the good of the town, bore the blood of the innocents on his hands.

XVIII. The Fall Foliage Festival

Well it's a marvelous night for a moondance
With the stars up above in your eyes
A fantabulous night to make Romance
'Neath the cover of October skies...
– Van Morrison, *Moondance*

Brady pulled the chair out for Mindy. "Thank you, Mr. Brady," she shouted, over the conversation of a hundred other guests, the chatter of silverware on china, and the clunk of heavy glass beer mugs on the hand-carved bar.

"My pleasure, Ms. McGovern," he replied, and seated himself.

They were inside the very crowded Mt. Canaan Inn where, for this special night, Brady had secured a reservation days in advance. He stared across the table at Mindy who was wearing a most elegant flower dress, each color of the season represented, as well as a subtle autumn corsage Brady had purchased from Josephine and Sara.

Mindy, sans her glasses which were banished away in her purse, stared dreamily back at him, imagining what he looked like in his tweed suit.

A fire was raging in the giant stone hearth next to their table, and Brady admired the reflection of dancing flame in Mindy's eyes.

Despite the large crowd gathered at the inn this night, service remained prompt, and a waitress was soon at their table.

"Good evening, my name is Linda and I'll be your..." the waitress stopped and looked at Mindy. "Why, hello, Ms. McGovern. I didn't recognize you without your glasses."

Mindy squinted at the stranger through crossed eyelashes. "Hello..." she replied, curiously.

"It's me," the waitress told her, "Linda VanMeter... you have my daughter, Sara, in your class."

Brady perked up at the mention of Sara's name.

"Oh, hello Mrs. VanMeter," responded Mindy. "working late tonight, I see."

Linda exhaled. "Yeah, it's a busy weekend, that's for sure." She turned to Brady. "Hello," she said to him.

"Hello," Brady returned, pleasantly.

It was interesting that he'd meet both Sara and her mother on the very same day. He mentioned this to Mindy after Linda had taken their orders and moved on to the next table.

"She's a very sweet, sensitive thing," Mindy explained, referring to Sara. "Somewhat of a loner. The children pick on her unmercifully."

She looked both ways to see if anyone was listening, although it was all for show, inasmuch as Mindy couldn't really see, anyway. "She and her mother don't have much money. Her father was killed when Sara was quite young... he was some type of relative to Josephine McGillis, a cousin or something. Anyway, after his death, her mother moved them here from New Jersey and they took an apartment above Josephine's shop on Race Street."

Brady's heart sunk. In a matter of moments, he'd fallen in love with the little girl. Now he was saddened to learn of her poverty.

"It's a shame, it really is. She's the nicest child in my class, but isn't that always the case?" She shook her head, and frowned. "My heart goes out to her, it really does. Every time I hear the other children tease her about her out-dated clothing... I could just... just... grab them and shake them." While talking, Mindy unconsciously picked up a butter knife from the table setting, and wrapped both her hands around it. Realizing she'd been strangling the silverware, Mindy let it slip from her hands.

Brady caught the knife before it hit the table and quietly positioned it back on the folded napkin. He could see this really troubled her. But there was something else, some other connection between Mindy and Sara. He hadn't noticed it before, but now it was all too clear. Sara was Mindy, or at least she was Mindy when Mindy first moved to Mt. Canaan from Alabama so many years before. The comparison was uncanny.

Brady poured Mindy and himself some water from a carafe Linda had left on the table. He raised the glass to his lips, regarded Mindy over the rim, and smiled at the sound of Mindy crunching her ice.

They ate dinner mostly in silence.

After they had finished, they each enjoyed a glass of the house wine and reflected thoughtfully on the time they'd known each other.

Gently, Brady reached his hand across the table and attempted to place it atop Mindy's; however, the sudden contact startled the nearly blind Mindy and caused her to instantly draw back her own hand. As a result, she knocked over her glass of wine and spilled it on her dress. "Oh damn it!" she exclaimed. "These damned eyes! I can't see a damned thing!"

Brady sprung from his seat and quickly placed himself behind the frantic Mindy.

"It's ruined... it's all ruined. I've ruined yet another dress!"

"Easy now, Mindy... easy. I'm just going to take off my coat and place it around your shoulders. Okay?"

Mindy nodded.

"I'm taking the coat off now, okay? Now I'm putting the coat around you nice and slow..."

"Uh, Byron?" she squinted at him and raised her brows.

"Sorry. Here you go."

"Thank you," she replied and allowed Brady to slip his much larger suit coat around her. The coat, tailored especially for Brady, easily dwarfed the diminutive teacher and made her look like a small child playing dress-up in her father's clothes. "Does it look bad, Byron? Be honest."

Byron looked at her and laughed. "It covers up the wine stain, that's for sure."

If she could actually see what she looked like, she definitely would not want to go to the Fall Dance after dinner. Thankfully, her glasses were still tucked away in her purse.

"You look absolutely breathtaking," he told her, and he meant it.

There was a slight chill in the air that night, though neither Brady nor Mindy felt it.

The band, perched high above the revelers on the make-shift wooden stage, played songs which reminded them of their youth spent in this village, often described in tourism literature as the "very essence of Victorian elegance."

They laughed and danced, and sang along to the songs they remembered, and hummed over the lyrics they'd forgotten.

Brady, dressed in his cream-colored shirt, bronze tie, and tweed vest, led Mindy, still hiding in his much larger coat, onto the dance floor where they quickly fell in step with the rhythms of the other dancers. They danced several fast tempo songs before the band decided to slow down the pace.

Then, without a word, Mindy raised her arms and draped them around Brady's strong shoulders, while Brady's arms found their way around Mindy's narrow waist.

Soon, lost in the music of a song she listened to a lifetime ago, when every song reminded her of this boy, now a man, Mindy rested her head against Brady's chest, closed her eyes and dreamed no more. All she wanted, *needed*, was here in this moment.

Brady also found he was taken by a strange, inner calm and a feeling that all was set right within the world. Thoughts of work and feral dogs, and the civic leaders bent on destroying them, seemed to drift away and dissolve in the moonlight pouring over the town. At that moment, he thought neither of the future nor the past, and simply concentrated on the synchronicity of their bodies moving so slowly in unison to the familiar melody.

After the song had ended, Brady and Mindy continued dancing as if they had not realized the music had stopped, like they were listening to a secret song that only they could hear.

Moonlight dripped from her long eyelashes. Mindy's fingers unclasped and worked their way up to the back of his head where he felt them softly stroke his hair. He felt the tingle and he knew she knew it. She had him. She looked up at him and smiled, a dream-like, distant smile.

She was sunlight across a page of poetry; a stray raindrop on the tongue; a shooting star in an otherwise starless sky. The same far away look held Brady's face also, but Brady knew Mindy couldn't see it. But she needed to see it, too.

"Put your glasses on, please?" he asked her.

"Why?" she protested.

"For me… please?"

"I hate –" she started, but he silenced her with a forefinger to her lips. Reluctantly, she complied.

She removed the glasses from her purse and slipped them on over her freckled nose. The kaleidoscope world of colors she'd been moving blindly through the entire evening, suddenly became acutely clear. She looked up at his eyes and noted they were glistening with a queer wetness about them.

"Byron?" she said.

But Brady opted not to use words and answered Mindy with a kiss. A long, drawn out, though gentle kiss, not too wet, lasting just the right amount of time, or so Mindy thought. When their lips finally parted, she felt as though her glasses had melted, for she saw the world once more through a swirl of colors.

Across the park, Sara watched them eagerly and held her tiny hand to her chest. It was one of the most precious moments she had ever witnessed and she marveled in wonder at the emotion emanating from her teacher and the dogcatcher her teacher loved.

Even at her young age, Sara knew true love was rare, for she was witness to her widowed mother's hapless love life, and she wished and hoped that

Brady and Mindy could somehow hold forever onto the feelings they shared this evening.

But the moment of serenity passed. Just beyond the square, a raging darkness loomed.

XIX. The Night of the Ferals

He had come like a thief in the night. And one by one dropped the revellers in the blood bedewed halls of their revel, and died each in the despairing posture of his fall.

– Edgar Allen Poe, *The Masque of the Red Death*

Out of the shadows surrounding the festival, the ferals descended on the fairgrounds.

The square, which moments before was a place of laughter and song, was now filled with the screams of horrified women and children, and also of the growling beasts which had made it that way. It seemed as though the very gates of the Netherworld had burst open, releasing its long captive inhabitants.

"Cwn Annwn… the hounds of Annwn," Josephine gasped. She grabbed hold of Sara and pulled her beneath her worktable. Evil spread through the night air like the smell of something rotting and long dead. Sara wept into Josephine's bosom while Josephine did her best to comfort her.

"It's him," Sara cried. "It's the dog who tried to kill me. He's come for me, Josie! He's come for me!"

Josephine said nothing, for she knew which dog Sara meant. The beast's gaze had fallen briefly on her before finally resting upon the small child standing beside her. An unmistakable look of recognition flared in the dog's eyes. Whether or not he'd come looking for Sara, Josephine could not determine, but now his stare was locked upon her.

In an instant, the feral was charging straight toward her.

Elsie Pendleton was also at the festival. She'd had more than a few beverages at the beer stand, but she recognized the Alpha with the sober clarity of a hundred saints.

"That's him!" she bellowed. "That's the one that damn near killed me!"

She spied Brady lifting Mindy up onto the stage.

"There he is, Brady!" she exclaimed, clutching his arm. "There's the one that damn near killed me!"

Brady, satisfied for the moment that Mindy was out of harm's way, pointed his nose in the direction of Elsie's crooked finger. A black dog raced toward Josephine's stand.

It was a hauntingly sleek and muscular animal, and it moved with the grace and beauty of a thoroughbred. But why was it speeding so urgently toward Josie's stand? And where were Josie and Sara?

Sara peeked out from behind the wooden stand.

My God! Brady thought. *He wants Sara!*

With no regard for his own safety, Brady rushed for Josephine's stand and the beast speeding toward it.

Without a break in his stride, he picked up a partially empty garbage can and dumped its contents on the ground.

The Alpha vaulted the wooden counter and disappeared behind it, where Josephine and Sara were hidden. The onslaught elicited a scream from Sara and a wail from Josephine. Their anguished cries made Brady quicken his pace.

Just as he reached the stand, Sara flew over the wooden counter as if she'd been launched from a catapult. She fell sharply to the ground.

The Alpha leaped from behind the stand, his fangs bared to the gums and his muzzle fresh with blood. The feral lunged at Sara for the kill. Brady slammed the trashcan down on the animal's head.

The blow stunned the Alpha, long enough for Brady to pick up Sara and run with her toward the stage.

"Josie!" Sara cried out. "He's killed Josie!" And then she fainted.

On the stage, Mindy had watched the horrific scene. She helped Elsie Pendleton up when an enraged German shepherd nearly knocked her to the ground, and she briefly comforted one of her frightened students who had been attacked by a hound.

It just didn't seem real. Moments before she'd been kissing Brady and singing joyfully to the music. Now she was on this stage alone while Brady dashed off to God knows where.

Across the square, a shot rang out. The sheriff dropped a collie mix in its tracks.

A second dog, a large black and tan mongrel, went down with another of the sheriff's bullets in his side.

"That's how you do it, Brady!" the sheriff cried. "That's how –" he started once more, but a third beast attacked him from behind.

It took several of the band members brandishing their instruments to beat the dog from the fallen sheriff.

"Brady!" he yelled madly. "Damn you, Byron Brady!"

Brady didn't hear him. He only heard Sara's words reverberating in his head: *He's killed Josie!*

Mindy was waiting for him at the stage. She took off Brady's warm suit coat and laid it upon the floor, and Brady gently rested Sara atop it.

"Look after her," he told Mindy.

A mighty thud shook the stage. Brady turned to find the Alpha staring at him.

The crowd that had gathered on the stage quickly left. Only the Alpha, Brady, Mindy, and the motionless Sara remained. Brady placed himself between the Alpha and the women, prompting the Alpha to snarl at him, contemptuously.

Brady had encountered many animals, but never before had he witnessed a beast with the ferocity and intelligence of this creature. It both captivated Brady and terrified him. Its deadly eyes gave away no secrets, and its hatred for men felt as real as the dew forming on the grass.

Brady scanned the stage for anything that could be used as a weapon against the feral. There – blazing tiki torches.

The flames should be enough to scare the dogs away. But in order to get to them, he'd have to leave Mindy and Sara unguarded.

"Brady!" the sheriff called out from the grounds below. He'd shot and killed a third feral and now had his gun aimed at the Alpha.

"This is how you deal with wild animals, Brady!" He squeezed the trigger but missed. Apparently, his aim was not as accurate from a greater distance away. The shot buried itself in the stage floor, mere inches from where Brady was standing.

Angered by the shot, the Alpha leaped toward the sheriff.

The sheriff remained calm. He raised his gun and leveled it at the hard charging feral.

He squeezed the trigger. *Click. Click. Click.* The revolver was out of bullets.

He threw his useless gun at the dog and fled.

Brady grabbed a blazing torch, jumped from the stage, and chased after the Alpha.

The portly sheriff, not nearly as agile as his feral pursuer, slipped in the wet grass and fell. The Alpha landed on top of him and buried his fangs in the sheriff's meaty shoulder.

The sheriff cried out in agony.

"Get!" Brady ordered the Alpha.

The Alpha hissed. He winced in the brightness of the flame and turned away.

"Get!" Brady repeated. The Alpha looked toward the lumpy shape of the sheriff in the grass as a string of drool escaped his jowls. Brady waved the torch over the dog's head. "Go on, now!"

The Alpha gnashed his teeth.

Defeated, he barked out a command to his minions, and ordered them to retreat. The Alpha and the remainder of the feral pack receded from the square and dissolved back into the shadows from where they had come.

"Nice work, Brady," the sheriff sneered.

But Brady ignored him. The sheriff looked no better than the animals he'd killed, Brady thought. He headed for Josephine, unsure of what he would find.

"Josie!" he called out as he reached the crafts stand.

Josephine, slumped in the corner, her head bleeding from a laceration above her brow, stirred at the announcement of her name. Her sweater and blouse were stained with her own blood, and her bare arms were filled with more bites and scrapes.

"Didn't your mother ever tell you not to play with strange dogs?" she responded.

Through her pain, she forced a smile at Brady and even managed a wink.

Elated, Brady leaped over the wooden stand and threw his arms around Josephine.

"My God!" he exclaimed. "I thought we lost you!"

Hugging him back, Josephine retorted, "It'll take a bigger dog than that to get rid of me." Then, turning deathly serious, she asked, "Sara?"

Brady sprang to his feet. He cast a glance at the stage. The resilient Sara was sitting up and talking with Mindy.

Relieved, he dropped to his knees, smiling, and kissed the battered Josephine lightly on her forehead.

XX. The Cwn Annwn

Am I thus conquered? have I lost the powers
That to withstand, which joys to ruin me?
Must I be still while it my strength devours
And captive leads me prisoner, bound, unfree?
– Lady Mary Wroth, *Am I Thus Conquered?*
From Pamphilia to Amphilanthus

The remainder of the weekend inevitably passed, though the memory of the feral attack lingered long into the week like a bitter taste on the tongue, reminding the bewildered town at every bark of a fenced dog and every cry of a frightened child.

The coming Friday brought Halloween, and by late Thursday afternoon, Sara had yet to find a costume she could afford. The last of the princess costumes she'd sought at Hillman's Pharmacy were gone, and all that remained in her price range were the usual assortment of monsters, witches, and, ironically, hoboes.

But Sara fancied none of them, for she wanted the children to see her in a different light. An appearance at the school's Halloween party hiding behind a grotesque persona would only further fuel the children's already distorted image of her.

Considering the scarce variety of the costumes left, Sara chose not to go to the party at all, nor would she go trick-or-treating afterward. She'd concede victory to her poverty once more, and settle for a few vicarious thrills as she'd watch Josephine bestow treats to her more fortunate classmates.

Her mother would be working again, as it seemed she did on most of the important events in Sara's life, and she wondered whether her mom even realized tomorrow was Halloween and her daughter had yet to find a costume.

Lately it seemed as though she was spending more and more time working, and less time being Sara's mother. Sometimes Sara felt she'd lost both her mother and father in that car accident, for ever since they moved to Mt. Canaan, her mother had been slowly fading away.

But Sara guessed working long hours did that to you, and her mother had the responsibility of raising a young daughter, too. But as she'd grown older, it seemed to Sara as if her mother wanted to work more, and actually preferred it to spending time with her. It was almost as if she couldn't even look at Sara anymore, like the very existence of Sara brought a pain to her heart.

For as perceptive as Sara was, she could not possibly realize she was growing to look more and more like her father each day.

Sara was right. Her mother couldn't bear to look at her, for Sara reminded her too much of her deceased husband. But it did not mean she didn't love Sara, only that the loss of Sara's father was deep, far deeper than Sara or anyone else knew. And this emptiness her mother carried in her heart and, whenever possible, quelled its demands with work and the avoidance of idle time. But in her efforts to vanquish her own sorrow, she neglected to see the effects it had on her daughter.

Sara frowned. *What doesn't kill you, only makes you stronger*. That's what Josie told her, anyway. She'd said it again that night, after the feral had attacked her and Sara had believed she was dead.

Damn those ferals, Sara thought. Their attack brought an early end to the festival and any hopes of Sara earning enough money for a decent costume. As she walked along Broadway, Sara felt her sadness gradually overcome her like the evening shadows creeping across the tops of the buildings.

A blaring horn... Screeching tires... Glass shattering... Blood... A crash.

The image jolted Sara. She turned suddenly cold. She held herself until the moment passed. What –

The driver leaned on his horn once more.

"Get the hell off the street, kid!"

Sara found herself standing in the middle of Broadway, staring at a gray sedan. Its front bumper was just inches from where she stood.

"Are you gonna move or what?" the driver howled.

She opened her mouth to speak, but no words came out.

"Go on, now. Beat it!"

Her legs finally getting the message, Sara bolted for the sidewalk, allowing traffic to resume along Broadway.

What had just happened to her? Whatever it was, it was gone now. Was it another memory about her dad again? Why was she such a weirdo?

Sara wished she could be like Josie. Nothing ever got the best of her, she was indomitable. Why, after she'd spent half the night at the emergency ward with a score of other people, being tended to her cuts and bites, and even receiving the first of a series of rabies shots, she still managed to have the shop open by noon the next day.

With a big bandage over her eye, and an equally big bandage around her left forearm, Josie sat at her workplace and continued to assemble her crafts as if the horrible events had never even taken place. Why, she even made jokes about the alpha male, and quipped she'd throw a saddle over the beast the next time she'd see him, and ride him across the square like a horse.

Sara looked overhead. The sunlight was quickly fading behind the courthouse clock tower. Even though Josie made light of the feral attack, she still had a respectful fear of their might, and wanted Sara back safely in her shop before dusk.

Empty-handed, Sara reluctantly climbed the cement steps behind Antonio's Pizza.

Josephine was in her shop, looking out through her window at the very same diminishing light. Though she did not show it, the alpha male of the feral pack worried her immensely.

The Alpha disturbed Josephine in the way it had selected Sara out of the crowd, and the manner in which his eyes beheld the child like a coveted prize. And when she and Sara had hidden beneath the counter of the stand, it had not deterred him from seeking them out in the least.

He leaped over the counter in one fluid, effortless motion, and his mouth peeled back to the corners of his snout, revealing a white, thorny grin. The damned dog smiled at her!

Sara had been weeping at that point, and Josephine covered the distraught child's head, burying her face in her chest. Josephine watched as the beast's eyes fixed on the bundle of trembling, pink flesh Josephine held tightly in her arms. The dog didn't want Josephine… he wanted Sara. The creature wanted Sara!

Josephine turned away from the dog, shielding Sara from his gaze. She prayed that someone, anyone, would come and chase the animal away.

With her back facing the Alpha, her plentiful frame concealing Sara, she comforted the child.

"Hush… hush, Sara," she told her. "Everything will be all right."

But the ominous growling, steadily growing louder in her ear nearest the feral, told her otherwise.

The Alpha, with one blow of his mighty paw, came around to the front of Josephine's face, caught the flesh above her eye, and pulled her onto her back. She could feel the fresh, warm blood trickle down around her eye socket and continue on along the side of her face.

With Sara exposed, the Alpha seized the opportunity and lashed out at the child's head with the tremendous speed and strength of his jaws. Josephine barely had enough time to raise her arm and deflect the Alpha's advance, but not before his teeth found the soft skin of Josie's forearm. Blood from the wound stained Josephine's clothing, making the injuries appear worse than they actually were, and prompted Sara to believe she was dead.

At that moment, Sara struggled free of Josephine's arms and threw herself over the wooden counter. The angered dog then climbed over Josephine and chased after the fleeing child.

Josephine shivered. "The hounds of Annwn," she said, repeating the words she spoke that night. Just like her grandmother had told her so many years ago.

Her grandmother, born and raised in Wales, would often gather the children on dark, autumn evenings and recount tales of her Welsh homeland. That's where Josephine first heard the name of the Cwn Annwn. They'd appear routinely in her grandmother's stories, a sign to the children the tale would have an unpleasant end. For the Cwn Annwn were the harbingers of death, quite literally; ghost dogs whose very appearance signaled the death of someone in the village. It was just silly superstition from the Old Country, Josephine told herself, and she didn't believe in such things. Still…

Josephine remembered the day her grandmother died. She'd been playing hopscotch on some carelessly drawn squares etched in chalk on the front sidewalk. Her schoolbooks lay on the cool pavement. The sun had just set behind the houses across the street and twilight hung in the air like a hint of night. The children's laughter echoed. The smell of some fifty neighborhood dinners swirled about. The soles of her shoes scraped the sidewalk as she bounded unsteadily on one foot.

The screen door pushed open, its rusty spring protesting.

"Josie, come inside," her father's voice cracked.

She did as she was told. The living room was full of her aunts and uncles and cousins and brothers and sisters, and of sorrow and remorse, and the scent of lilac. Black was the color of choice, and a dry handkerchief was a rare commodity. Her mother sought her out from a group gathered in the kitchen and without a word, she grasped her hand and led Josephine upstairs.

The hallway was crowded with even more people clad in black: friends, neighbors, strangers. Her grandmother's orange tabby, Mona, slinked through the legs of several people and fled down the steps. Josephine and her mother pushed past the people and Josephine felt strange hands stroke her head. At the doorway to her grandmother's bedroom, two men in dark suits, whom she'd never seen before, smiled at her before parting.

"Grandmum's gone," her mother told her. *Grandmum's gone? Where?* Josie wanted to ask. Her mother tugged her into the room before she could.

Her grandmother lay motionless on the bed, her eyes closed, her hands resting on her chest. Why, her grandmother had not gone anywhere, she was right here. Several neighbors were standing at her grandmother's bedside, remarking on how peaceful she looked. Well, of course she looked peaceful! She was sleeping! She looked up at her mother, puzzled. Her mother was crying.

"Grandmum's dead, sweetie," she whispered. She let go of Josephine's hand and dabbed her eyes with a handkerchief.

Josephine walked along the perimeter of the bed, her eyes locked on this familiar face always so full of love and comforting words. There were no words to comfort her grandmother. Josephine had never seen a dead person before. Her grandmother seemed empty, like a package with its contents removed. Her mother was right; her grandmother *was* gone.

More people entered the room and commented on her grandmother's appearance. One person said it was for the best.

Josephine didn't understand. She went to the window and looked out. She wanted to be back out there playing, to be around the living again. She scanned the street for the children, but Broadway was silent. Her eyes passed over the hopscotch squares where she'd played only moments before. A sleek, black dog, as if carved from ebony, was standing there, staring back at her. Death made its presence felt. The Cwn Annwn had come.

Its eyes glowed yellow in the twilight and its coat gave off a luminescent quality not seen before by the young Josephine. It lifted its hind leg and urinated on the chalk drawings. Josephine looked away in horror.

"Mum?"

Her mother, speaking with one of the neighbors, replied, "Yes, sweetie?"

Josephine pointed out the window without looking. "Cwn Annwn."

Her mother looked out, past her. Her eyebrows raised, "They're here to take Grandmum away," she said, matter-of-factly.

They? Josephine swallowed hard and tried to muster enough courage to look. She closed her eyes, turned, and faced the window. They? Had more arrived?

She opened her eyes.

A black Packard hearse was parked along the street. Several men in dark suits were removing a casket. The dog was gone. Josephine exhaled and looked at the chalk drawings. They were partially washed away.

Josie swatted the memories away like gnats from her face. Silly superstitions, that's all.

She smiled to herself as Sara wandered in off the street.

"Hello, precious," she greeted Sara.

Sara contorted her mouth into a smile. "Hello," she replied through clenched teeth, and climbed into her usual chair by the window.

"Where's your Halloween costume?" Josephine queried.

Sara sighed. "I've decided not to go," she said.

"What?" Josephine responded. "To the party? What about trick-or-treating?"

"I've decided all that sugar is bad for my teeth. Anyway, I'm sure you'll need help handing out candy to all the other children."

Josephine chewed on her lip. She knew Sara enjoyed Halloween, and she recalled how excited the child had been earlier in the day when she set off to buy her costume.

Josephine walked over to the chair and knelt down beside it. "What's wrong, honey?"

"Nuthin," Sara returned.

"Why didn't you buy a costume?"

"I already told you, I'm not going."

Josephine didn't press her. She knew what was wrong. Sara didn't have enough money to buy a costume.

The rest of the evening, Josephine avoided the topic of Halloween. Sara remained in a somewhat depressed state and showed no signs of improvement, even when her mother arrived to pick her up.

The next morning, after Jim had his breakfast and had gone to work, Josephine traveled to Hillman's Pharmacy and inquired about a princess costume.

"They're all gone," old man Hillman told her. "On Halloween morning, don't expect to find much of any of the good costumes left."

Hillman was right, for Josephine failed to find any cute costumes that would even remotely fit the tiny Sara. Undeterred, she ventured next door to the Thrift Store.

Inside, she found a long, white dress, a roll of lace fabric, a simple, white mask one could hold up to his or her face, and even a sparkling tiara, crowned with shimmering blue jewels.

If she couldn't buy Sara a princess costume, then damn it, she'd make her one. The supplies were cheaper than if she'd actually purchased a costume, and she had enough money left over to buy Sara a plastic jack o'lantern to hold her candy while trick-or-treating.

Pleased with herself, she struggled with the bags back up Broadway, pausing once to look at the new hardcovers in the window of Pendragon's Bookshop.

Upon arriving home, the tired Josephine, who in her exhaustion stumbled over the yet to be replaced garden gate, nearly failed to notice the inhuman creatures lurking in the shadows of her withering rose bushes.

XXI. The Law of Stray Life

And in that town a dog was found,
As many dogs there be,
Both mongrel, puppy, whelp and hound,
And curs of low degree.
– Oliver Goldsmith, *Elegy on the Death of a Mad Dog*

The Jack, lying next to Buddy beneath the rose bushes, stared back at the portly woman. She had a kind voice and smiling eyes, and he didn't mind at all that she came stumbling into the garden in the middle of their afternoon nap.

"Why, hello again," she said.

The Jack wagged his tail in reply while his friend voiced a hesitant growl.

"Now that's no way to greet a friend," she admonished the mongrel. "Your partner's a bit cranky, isn't he?" she said to the Jack.

The Jack wagged his tail even faster. He didn't know what she was saying, but her voice sounded so warm. He liked her voice – he liked the woman, too – and the way she smiled at him when she spoke. That's why he'd led Buddy back here.

"I'll bet this isn't a social call, is it?"

Buddy barked at her, a hoarse, though timid retort.

"I knew it," she said, and abruptly entered her house. Watching the woman walk into the house evoked a Pavlovian response in the Jack. He felt his mouth fill with drool in anticipation. The last time she'd entered the house, she'd returned with an array of treats. This time was no different.

She exited, bearing an assortment of food she'd raided from her own refrigerator.

At the reappearance of the woman and the variety of goodies she held against her bosom, the Jack jumped to his feet and broke into an excited dance.

"Are you doing a dance for me?" she asked him.

"*Woof!*" the Jack replied.

"Are you doing a dance for me?" she repeated, louder.

"*Woo-oof!*" the Jack asserted.

The woman opened a package, freeing a wonderful smell that rushed straight for the Jack's nose. It was obviously cold cuts – sweet Lebanon bologna – he'd found the slightly spoiled kind in some trash, not long ago. He watched as she rolled a slice into a mock-ball.

"Here," she called to him.

The Jack barked again and then fell into his play-bow pose with his head lowered and his rear-end raised behind him. All the while, he kept right on wagging his tail.

"Do you want this?" she asked the Jack.

The Jack barked an affirmative.

"Then come here, and take it."

He edged closer to the woman. The unwritten law of stray life taught the Jack to exercise apprehension when dealing with humans, though his instincts told him this woman intended no animosity. So he struck a compromise between his heart and head – and let his stomach break the tie. He inched his way closer to the woman and barked out a proclamation to stay back.

"I'm not afraid of you," she assured the Jack. "I've already been bitten once this week by a beast four times the size of you, so I'm not going to be frightened by a piss-ant like you."

"*Woof!*"

"I wholeheartedly agree," she told him. "Now come here and eat this bologna before I feed it to your blind buddy."

At the chance mentioning of his name, Buddy perked his ears and tilted his head to the side. The connection did not go unnoticed by the woman.

"Did I strike a chord with you, buddy?"

Again, Buddy flicked his ears and leaned his head to the left. Someone knew his name! Why, he thought he might never hear it again. And how beautiful it sounded!

Buddy! Here, Buddy! Daddy loves his Buddy! Does Daddy love his Buddy? A resounding "*woof!*" *Daddy loves his Buddy! Right, Ol' Buddy-boy?* Buddy missed his old master. Why, maybe this woman knew him.

"Come here, Buddy," she called to him. Buddy leaned forward, wanting to get up, but still, he did not move from his place beneath the roses. Caution and mistrust still ruled him.

Meanwhile, the Jack barked at the cold cut still held in the woman's hand, now only inches from the Jack's probing, wet nose.

"That's yours, Jack," she said.

In one swift motion, the Jack stole the meat from her hand without even touching her fingers. It was delicious! He swallowed the ball of meat in one voracious gulp and was campaigning for seconds before it even reached his stomach.

"My, you *are* a hungry lad, aren't you?" she commented, and fed the Jack a second helping. "You best get over your shyness," she warned Buddy. "Or else the Jack here is going to eat all this food."

The Jack was not sure what the woman was saying, but he hadn't forgotten about his friend. Instead of hungrily gobbling down the second roll of cold cuts as he did the first, he carried it over to Buddy, held it under his nose, and allowed him to take it from his muzzle.

The woman fell quiet. The Jack noticed she was holding her heart, and a strange wetness leaked from her eyes. Silently, she spread the rest of the food onto the ground in front of her and then moved away from it.

The Jack nudged Buddy under the chin, signaling him to grasp onto his scruff.

Buddy complied, and followed the Jack. Calmly, both dogs shared the food, neither even so much as snarling at the other.

When they had finished, the Jack approached the woman and licked her hand. For her kindness, the Jack figured she'd earned that much.

The woman wiped her eyes. "You're welcome, Jack."

He wagged his tail, hitched Buddy to his scruff, and led him to the street.

"Be careful," she told them. "And do come back again."

The Jack wagged his tail one last time. He didn't have to understand what she was saying, to know what she'd meant.

It was a rather warm, sunny day on this Halloween, and Buddy and the Jack took advantage of the unseasonable weather to explore Mt. Canaan. They roamed about South Avenue, North Avenue, Cedar Street, Cherry Street, and even Center Avenue.

It was along Center Avenue that Buddy began acting strangely, as the Jack led him past an enormous, freshly painted Victorian home. The Jack wanted to continue on, for it was getting late, and his tired paws yearned for the soft blanket of leaves in their cave overlooking the river. But Buddy was immovable, like a large stone gargoyle.

While his perplexed friend watched him curiously, Buddy's mind's eye, the only vision left to him, wandered back to a time not so long ago, when he and Angus shared a blanket in the kitchen of this very same house. Although the appearance and smells of the home had changed, enough of his and Angus' scent remained to let Buddy know he had returned *home*.

XXII. Home

Now he could see the Castle above him, clearly defined in the glittering air, its outline made still more definite by the thin layer of snow covering everything.

– Franz Kafka, *The Castle*

A high wrought-iron fence, armed with spear-tipped spires stabbing at the sky, surrounded the home as it did when Buddy had lived there. He pressed his nose to the cold iron of the fence and recalled how he'd often gazed out through these same spires, curious about the peculiar scents and sounds that drifted to him on warm, gentle breezes. He would've done anything now to be back on the other side of that fence with Angus, once again watching the world go by in the comfort of his master's care.

His master? He wondered if he was in there now. If he was, Buddy was certain he'd invite him and this friendly terrier inside, because his master was a kind and gentle soul. He couldn't still be angry at him – angry for the unknown crime Buddy had committed which prompted his master to summon the stranger – the stranger who'd taken him away.

Buddy barked in the direction of the house. He hoped his master and Angus were inside and would hear his call. He remembered Angus had exceptional hearing and could often detect the minute pitter-patter of a chipmunk upon dried leaves, clear across the yard.

But the truth was Buddy's master did not fall angry with Buddy. He simply surrendered to old age and the persistence of his children to sell his home and move in with them.

He was reaching an age where he'd often forget to turn off the stove or stub out his cigar or unplug the iron. And he'd taken the unfortunate habit of falling down quite a bit, and one time had fallen down the steps and lain for a considerable amount of time, unable to get up until his son checked in on him, hours later. And the old man himself would probably admit that although he loved Angus and Buddy very much, and enjoyed their company, the two dogs were quite a chore in the end.

So he agreed, reluctantly, to give up his house and his pets – and in essence, his independence – and moved in with his son and his son's family outside Philadelphia.

The man's son placed an ad in the classified section of the local newspaper seeking a good home for Buddy and Angus. Buddy, the more fortunate of the two, was quickly adopted by a lonely man who'd lost his wife and daughter in an automobile accident.

Angus, however, was much older than Buddy and suffered from rheumatism in his legs. He did not find a home and was given up to the animal shelter.

Angus spent the mandatory two weeks in the shelter allotted every dog, and not a day more. Everyone wanted a cute puppy, not an old, decrepit dog like Angus. He was kept in the back room, in the intentionally darkened cages where the old dogs were housed, waiting for the end to come in the form of an unassuming prick of a hypodermic.

Angus fell victim to the needle. A cold, unscrupulous needle – its acute, steel point bore through his soft fur and found a vein in the old dog's hind leg. A numbing cold crept inside him like a thief and stole the light from his eyes. So like his old friend, Buddy, he was plunged into a world of darkness, falling – falling – falling into a bottomless chasm, until he was Angus no more.

The man who adopted Buddy, a once kind though now emotionally scarred man, hoped the mongrel could fill the void left in his life by the passing of his wife and daughter, and help restore a bit of the man's sanity, which seemed to deteriorate with each passing year.

The man lived alone in a large, four-bedroom house on the east side of Mt. Canaan. Originally bought for himself, his wife, and young daughter, the home was a desolate and sacred place, filled with rooms such as his daughter's bedroom and wife's sitting room, where all time had stopped that fateful day their mini-van had stalled on the railroad tracks.

These rooms were off limits to Buddy, but how could he have known? Buddy was as distraught and saddened as the man who had adopted him. He'd also lost the only family he'd known or cared about.

But the man, who alternated between kindness and cruelty toward Buddy in the hours after he'd brought the dog home, could not see Buddy's melancholy through his own despair, which lay before his eyes, thick like fog.

Buddy was frightened by his new surroundings and the sense of suffering and anguish exuding from the walls. He sought out a place in the house, away from the strange man who seemed to like him and hate him at the same time.

To his great misfortune, he chose the room of the man's daughter, and curled up contentedly among her dolls and stuffed animals atop the bed.

How was he to know the man intended to preserve the girl's room exactly the way it had been prior to the accident, when he and his wife and daughter were a family, and darkness had yet to replace the love in his heart?

It was not long before the man found Buddy, who in his broken-heartedness, had fallen asleep. The man's leather belt cut deep into his hide and ripped him from his peaceful slumber.

Buddy catapulted from the bed and fell to the floor. But the man continued to beat the defenseless mongrel with his belt. No words were spoken – the man's rage spoke for him.

Buddy had never been the recipient of such a beating, and it confused him. His master never raised a hand to him. A strange feeling came over him. He struggled to his feet, bristled the hair on his back, and bared his fangs.

The mongrel's normally friendly brown eyes narrowed into two dark mirrors – mirrors that seemed to reflect the man's own ugliness back at him.

Horrified and repulsed at once by the insights into his own soul revealed to him through Buddy, the man leaped upon the mongrel and wrestled him to the ground. He was a physically strong man, stronger than most, and he easily carried Buddy out of the bedroom and returned him downstairs.

He couldn't allow this dog to spend another second in his house, for the beast had sullied the sanctity he had striven so hard to preserve. The animal had to go.

He looped Buddy's collar around his neck, and Buddy allowed him to do so, all too glad to be soon departing from this place which smelled of death and decay. Buddy hoped he might be going back to his master and Angus, now that he had suffered his punishment. Whatever he'd done wrong to deserve this, surely this beating had made up for it.

Without protest, Buddy exited the house and did not look back. Eagerly he complied when the man opened the door of the sport utility vehicle. He hopped inside, climbed into the back with the spare tire, and looked out the rear window as the man drove off. Poor Buddy did not even notice the man's .22 caliber rifle beside the spare tire, almost touching his front paws.

The man drove out Route 903, several miles north of the town, to a secluded area he knew well. In happier times, he'd taken his wife to shoot target practice there while he was still courting her. Now the business at hand was much, much dirtier.

Buddy cringed at the strange surroundings, but he still felt relieved to be away from that place where hate and sorrow set as thick upon the house as the dust accumulated on the furniture.

The man brought the vehicle to a stop along a dirt road, which seemed halfway around the world from the man's house. He pulled Buddy out of the truck by his leash and tied him to a giant, ancient oak tree. Buddy pressed his back against the trunk of the tree and felt some of the bark come loose in his fur. The earth, sky, and everything felt like it was crumbling around him. The man turned his back toward Buddy, and Buddy could not see what he was doing at the open tailgate of the truck. He feared what the stranger had planned for him.

The man turned and faced the mongrel with his rifle. Freshly cleaned and oiled, and loaded with the appropriate ammunition, he pointed the gun at the dog and centered the sight on a point just above the animal's eyes. His eyes – the man recalled the reflection of himself this beast had revealed to him.

He had become a monster, a detestable, wretched thing undeserving of this life that was spared to him. He had been the one driving the mini-van that night, the one who had made that fatal error in judgment and chose to cross the tracks with the train so near. He had also been the one who had instinctively jumped from the van when it stalled on the tracks.

His wife had also exited the van safely, but not their daughter. Frightened by the blinding light and the train's whistle shrieking – shrieking like a wild beast racing toward her – she fumbled with her seatbelt and was unable to free herself.

A mother's instinct propelled the man's wife back to the van for her child. She lost time struggling with a door that would not open – it was like she'd lost all basic motor skills. *Hurry, Karen – damn it!* The man remembered standing there watching, like a spectator at some morbid, new sporting event. In the final seconds of her life, his wife succeeded in freeing their daughter from the seatbelt – free, as the mini-van crumbled around them. The man couldn't watch. He closed his eyes and shrieked like the train whistle.

The nightmarish sound of twisted metal, like the cries of an animal caught in a trap, filled his ears and his head until it seemed the very night had crashed down upon him. He opened his eyes to where the mini-van had been moments before – but it was gone. Broken glass and maligned metal were strewn among the tracks.

He had done this. He had killed his family. All he had loved was erased – erased in one inordinately violent mishap that could easily have been avoided by a simple display of patience.

Those damned eyes! He let his rifle fall to the ground. Brandishing the penknife he'd always carried with his car keys, he threw himself on top of Buddy. He could feel the dog resisting, fighting him, but he was so much stronger. He easily pinned the dog to the ground. "Damn those eyes!" the man howled. And then he went about the fiendish business of carving them from Buddy's face.

The piercing, cold metal of the man's blade probed deep into Buddy's head. It was the worst feeling he had ever felt.

The pain radiated from his face, down his jaw and into his limbs. No part of his body escaped it. He gnashed his teeth in protest. A crimson shadow, warm like a summer rain but smelling coppery, streaked across Buddy's sight like an angry storm. Everything around him faded away as if the world had just suddenly ended. The man, the trees, and the sky diminished to a fine pinpoint of light. He cried out for that pinpoint, that last hint of light – that last hope of ever seeing anything again. But it disappeared. Someone had turned the sun off. Buddy whimpered. It hurt to breathe – to think even – and for the first time in his life, he wanted to die. He wailed and pleaded for the man to put an end to him, to finish the job. It was his wailing that eventually prompted the man to stop.

The man peeled himself from the now sightless Buddy.

"My Lord, my Lord… what have I done?" he cried out. "Oh, my God, what have I become? What have I become?"

He looked accusingly at the knife in his hands, as if the blade alone had committed the atrocity against the dog. Then he let it slip from his fingers onto the ground. A sobbing overtook him, shook him like a tremor beneath his feet, and he fell next to the pitiful creature he had blinded. "Forgive me, Buddy. Forgive me… I'm sick… so very, very sick."

But Buddy didn't hear his apologies. He heard nothing. A switch had been turned off somewhere inside himself – some kind of self-defense mechanism to guard against his suffering.

Gradually the pain diminished, and feelings of confusion and fear took its place. He had never been in total darkness before, not so dark that he couldn't at least see something. Nighttime, or even a darkened room, has a certain quality that allows the eye to still observe something, even in the absence of almost all light. But this darkness was a final, complete darkness – a world without sun. It panicked Buddy. He was just a dog – but a dog so bad, it warranted the sun to be shut off.

After some time, the man gathered his wits, or at least as much of his wits as he had remaining, and picked up his rifle from the ground. He'd brought this curse upon himself and now upon this innocent animal as well, and it was time to set things right. He couldn't restore the dog's sight – it was irreversible like the train crashing into the mini-van. He'd done a good job up until now of suppressing *that* memory, of forgetting – forgetting the role he'd played that fateful night. *This was just a minor slip-up*, he assured himself. He could tidy this little mess up, too, and file it away deep inside his muddled brain.

He raised up the rifle, trained it on the dog, and prepared to squeeze the trigger.

Buddy was unaware of the man's intent, or even his presence at that moment. He sat awkwardly on the ground, whimpering, as he attempted to shake the nonexistent veil from his face. He blinked his eyelids again and again in a desperate bid to regain his sight. A trail of bloody tears streaked down his face.

"God…" the man gasped. It was barely audible above the dog's anguished cries. Staring at the creature he'd blinded, he was unable to pull the trigger and at least put the poor, miserable animal out of its misery.

A complete and utter failure at everything in life, the man cut the collar from the dog's neck, entered his truck and drove off, leaving a newly blind dog to fend for himself in the wilds.

The rattle of the engine, the gravel crunching beneath the truck's tires as the man drove away, the smell of exhaust fumes, and darkness; Buddy remembered it all. He shivered as the past inevitably caught up with the present. He was still standing outside the gates to the house that some other dog named Buddy had lived. That dog, an immense, friendly dog, was always ready for a game of catch or a scratch behind the ears.

But that dog died that day – that day the sun was shut off.

The door opened. It squeaked, as it had when Buddy lived there, and that one-note song always signaled the master wanted him.

Buddy barked a reply. An unfamiliar voice cursed at them. "Go away, you damned ferals!" the voice cried. "Go away, before I get my gun!"

Buddy sensed the Jack was frightened – he felt him prod his side with his muzzle. The Jack wanted to go.

But Buddy still lingered. He thought it might be his master, everything else seemed the same, and he stayed frozen – listening.

"I said, 'get going!'" the voice cried out, even louder.

The voice belonged to a round, balding, middle-aged man with a smoldering pipe clenched in his teeth. The Jack growled as the man moved quickly along the porch. He picked up a piece of firewood and flung it at them.

The Jack shut his eyes and winced. But the wood fell short of the dogs and clanged harmlessly against the fence. It was enough to scare Buddy though, and the Jack felt him grab onto his collar. With Buddy firmly in tow, the Jack made a hasty retreat.

He wasn't certain what Buddy's connection was to that house, but he swore he could smell him there – in the grass, in the earth – buried, asleep in the soil, like a memory waiting to be remembered.

He did not like to think about his friend that way, dead in the ground – dead and forgotten. It made him feel alone and very small.

The cave was not that far now.

A peculiar scent weaved its way through the air like the tentacles of some horrific beast. It reached the Jack's nose just as the cave moved into his line of sight.

It was a unique odor – the smell of unwashed fur – and the persistent markings of aggressive dogs stretched across their path, impeding their progress like the wall of an impregnable fortress.

A cloud passed over the setting sun. The first of the ferals emerged from the woods. In a matter of seconds, the remaining dogs appeared and circled, forging a ring of evil around Buddy and the Jack.

The Jack backed close to Buddy.

The sun, burning through the cloud's attempt at hiding it, cast a red hue over everything. The Jack looked at Buddy and shivered.

It seemed as though his friend's brown fur was covered in blood.

XXIII. Brady Investigates

"Quite so," he answered, lighting a cigarette, and throwing himself down into an armchair. "You see, but you do not observe. The distinction is clear...

– Sir Arthur Conan Doyle, *A Scandal in Bohemia*
from *The Adventures of Sherlock Holmes*

Brady had been to the cave.

The paw prints of both Buddy and the Jack were quite numerous along the river where the Jack had hunted for several days, and were as easy to follow as road signs if you knew how to read them.

Brady did. His father had been quite a skilled tracker in his day, and he passed on his considerable knowledge of the subject to his eager son. Brady knew the ferals, like all animals, needed water to survive and therefore, he reasoned the dogs would most likely secure a den in the area of the river.

Brady called on his experiences as a boy growing up in Mt. Canaan, and his explorations of the nearby woods, where he'd spent a good deal of his youth. He recalled summer days spent crawling about a small cave – small for a rambunctious 12 year-old – but large enough to comfortably house a pack of dogs. It overlooked the river, not far from the town.

It took Brady a good hour until he quite accidentally stumbled across the entrance, much in the same way the Jack had, days earlier.

Inside, it was very similar to the way he had remembered it, though obviously, the roof of the cave seemed taller as a boy.

Brady shone his flashlight throughout the cavern until the light fell upon a curious formation in the rock wall. The initials "BB" were scratched into the wall and looked as fresh as the day they were inscribed there. Below it, in much smaller lettering, was "MM."

Brady remembered that day with a smile. They'd spent the whole morning skipping rocks on the white tops of the raging river. But the morning inevitably gave way to afternoon and the summer sun soon grew too warm for such strenuous activities. Brady knew a place where they could escape the relentless sun. He held young Mindy's hand in case she would stumble, and embarked on a perilous climb.

Mindy had never been in a cave before, and wouldn't enter unless he promised there were no bats. Mindy quickly overcame her fear of bats, and any other thing that might choose a cave as a home, and was soon searching for fossils hidden within the rocks. They did find some fossils that day, coniferous ferns entombed in a sheet of slate, and Brady still had them – kept safe in a shoebox beneath his bed.

He remembered they later sat sharing a large flat stone, their backs resting against one another. They talked about all sorts of things that would spark the imaginations of twelve-year-olds: their favorite scary movies, what they wanted to be when they grew-up, their schoolmates.

And then Mindy kissed him. Right in the middle of a tale involving his dog, Skippy, she just kissed him! There was no warning or indication, she just found his mouth in the darkness and kissed him. Her lips were delicate and smooth, and sweet like a Jolly Rancher (she had a watermelon candy inside her cheek), and her mouth hovered next to his like a persistent hummingbird sampling the nectar of a buttercup. Brady could not feel his legs. The lightless expanse of the cave was suddenly filled with Technicolor wonder.

Brady directed his flashlight to the stone. It was still there. Feeling that same weak-in-the-knees condition, 16 years later, he walked over to the old rock and sat numbly atop it.

When Mindy finally pulled her lips away, he felt her breath trail up the side of his face until it stopped by his ear. She whispered, "I'm going to marry you, Byron Brady." He put his arm around her, felt the goosepimples raised on her arms. The darkness and the silence filled the space all around them, insulated them, and preserved the moment forever – like a fossil.

Mindy McGovern was his first kiss? No – certainly there had to be someone before that… playing post office or spin-the-bottle? But there wasn't. *Mindy McGovern* was his first kiss. How could he not have remembered that until now? It was Mindy from the beginning. It had always been Mindy. The darkness suddenly became stifling. He wanted to leave the cave – run from it – run all the way to the school, throw open the door to her class, and kiss –

Where the hell did that come from? *Get a hold of yourself, Brady. You've got a job to do, and time's running out.* He ran his hand through his hair, took a deep breath and forced himself to concentrate on the ferals.

Telltale signs of the cave's inhabitants were everywhere. Discarded animal bones, once belonging to assorted rodents and small game, lay upon the pliant bed of leaves like secrets, anxiously awaiting to be told. Cast-off fur, a short, wiry white and a longer, softer brown variety also mingled amongst the leaves where the dogs had most likely slept. But perhaps the most telling clue of the dogs' presence inside the cave was not found inside the cavern at all.

Brady had noticed several deposits of dog mess in a clearing not far from the mouth of the cave. There was a strong presence of urine near the cavern entrance which could just as well been a "No Trespassing" sign, since it served in the same capacity to the animals who lived there.

It's widely known a dog marks his territory with urine so other dogs will know into whose land they have wandered. The more frequent the markings, the more dominant and territorial the dog is. Though it's not unusual for another dog to come along and leave his marking over that of the already existent dog, in effect evicting him from his territory. When this happens, a confrontation of the two rival dogs, or packs, is inevitable.

Content for the moment that he had found what he believed was the home of the elusive ferals, Brady descended the mountains and returned to his sport utility vehicle, parked on the road below.

Perhaps this whole sordid affair could be resolved in the next few days, bringing an end to this conflict with the sheriff and the commissioners. And then he could get back to more reasonable work, namely finding homes for the animals already overpopulating the shelter.

Brady sighed. His father had never experienced a problem such as wild dogs attacking townspeople, nor did he have a malevolent sheriff riding his back.

Why, he had thought for sure the sheriff was going to call for his dismissal after the fiasco at the Fall Foliage Festival. If it wasn't for Brady saving the sheriff's life from the alpha male, he was sure he'd be in the unemployment line right now. The festival was one of the big money makers for the town, and the commissioners reminded Brady again.

"All the county workers may have to take a cut in pay, son," one of the commissioners warned him.

All except for the commissioners, Brady thought. No doubt, many of the vendors at the festival stood to take a loss after the ferals attacked and scared off their customers, though the vendors had already paid their entrance fee for the festival, and to the best of Brady's knowledge, they were not refunded by the county.

Brady especially felt bad for Josephine. A good amount of her crafts were destroyed by the marauding ferals and the ensuing effort to drive them off. He marveled at her resilience. Even after she'd been attacked by the Alpha, she still managed a smile.

As Brady hopped into the driver side of his truck, slipped the transmission into reverse, and peered over his shoulder at the road behind him, a curious pair emerged on the path: a small, white dog seemingly leading a larger, brown dog by its scruff. It was the blind dog and his partner!

Brady earnestly jammed the transmission back into park, snatched his tranquilizer gun and binoculars, and dashed into the cover of some nearby trees.

For a moment, he thought the dogs may have detected him, for they both froze in their tracks along the path; however, soon the situation became even more peculiar.

Members of the feral pack descended upon the two dogs from the woods flanking both sides of the road.

Brady's heart pounding, he wrestled with the binoculars to keep them steadied on the two dogs who suddenly found themselves surrounded.

"I'll be damned," he said to himself.

As quickly and as quietly as he possibly could, Brady hurried back to his vehicle and the CB radio inside.

"Felix," he said into the receiver. "Felix... you copy?"

"Yeah?" Mortimer responded, as if he'd just stuffed an entire half of a bologna sandwich into his mouth. Brady figured he probably did.

"I'm on the old dirt road that runs along the river beneath the viaduct on the east side of town. I need you to get here as fast and as quietly as you possibly can. Leave your truck beneath the bridge and follow the road out on foot."

"Why?"

"We have a situation here..." Brady replied.

"Ferals?" Mortimer asked.

"Ferals," Brady repeated, and then shut off the radio.

XXIV. Sara's Costume

Her shirt was o' the grass-green silk,
Her mantle o' the velvet fyne;
At ilka tett of her horse's mane
Hung fifty siller bells and nine.

– Anonymous, *Thomas the Rhymer*, from *The Oxford Book of the Supernatural* by D.J. Enright

When Sara arrived from school at Josephine's shop late that afternoon, the first thing she noticed was Josie's peculiar behavior.

An almost complete turnaround from the previous day, Josie encouraged Sara not to go to the Halloween party, and in fact, insisted she stay in her shop and help Josie pass out candy to the anticipated trick-or-treaters who were fortunate enough to have a costume on Halloween.

Sara sighed. That's the way this world is, she thought. Some people get everything, some people get nothing: the "haves" and "have nots." Sara was resigned to the fact that she was a "have not." And why not? She was at least good at it. The best, at least in this small town.

So you could just imagine Sara's delight when Josephine dropped the façade seconds later and revealed to Sara the results of Josie's most-productive afternoon: A long, flowing white gown, complete with sparkles that glistened when the light fell upon them in just the right way, and a scintillating silver tiara, which Josie had burnished with some silver polish and an old toothbrush she had once used to brush Barney's teeth.

"What's that?" Sara asked Josephine, her eyes surveying every inch of the garment as it hung proudly from Josie's talented hands.

"What do you think it is, Sara?" Josephine returned.

"I dunno," Sara replied, breaking into a smile. "Is it a princess costume?"

"Just your size, precious," Josephine told her, unable to hold back her self-satisfaction any longer.

"Oh Josie!" Sara exclaimed and leaped into Josie's unsuspecting arms. Josephine had barely enough time to set the costume down before the child bolted toward her.

Crying, Sara told her through an assault of kisses on her cheek and mouth,

"I love you, Josie... I love you so much."

Crying herself over the little joy she'd brought into Sara's world, Josephine replied in a whisper, "I love you, too... Now stop your crying this instant, you hear? Your eyes will be all red and puffy for the party... and you'll make mine all red and puffy for the trick-or-treaters."

"Okay, Josie," Sara sniffled. She planted one last kiss on Josie's already moist cheek. "Josie?" Sara asked.

"Yes, sweetie?" Josephine replied, composing herself as she chased the last tear from her eye.

"Can I try it on?"

"Well," Josie said, "you better if you want to be the 'belle of the ball.' It's only an hour away, you know, and I might have to make some alterations." She crossed her fingers behind her back and hoped the dress would fit, for God knows how long it might take to alter the darn thing.

Sara anxiously gathered up the costume and rushed into the back room of the store.

Luckily for Josephine, her measurements were precise and no further modifications were needed, for the gown fit Sara just like Josephine had intended it to, transforming the already angelic child into a chimerical vision of sheer beauty.

Josephine placed the "closed" sign in the front window, lowered the lights, and led Sara into the shop's tiny bathroom, where she proceeded to "clean up" Sara for the party.

Josephine brushed the knots from Sara's hair and then curled it with an electric curling iron. "Try not to move around," she instructed Sara, "I don't want to burn you."

Then, with what seemed like a hundred hair pins clenched in her teeth, Josephine gently pulled back Sara's hair from her face, and fastened her now-spiral hair in place with the pins. But she left two long curls coil down from either side of Sara's head so the hair would frame her pretty face.

"There," she said, handing Sara a mirror.

Sara's eyes enlarged as she admired her hair, but only for a moment, for Josie quickly retracted it from her hands. "I've still got to do your make-up," Josephine insisted, "and we're running way short on time."

Sara silently complied, for she was excited. Never before was she allowed to wear make-up, and she thrilled at the cool feeling of the lipstick gliding across her lips.

"Now, don't lick your lips," Josie warned her. "And close your eyes."

Sara did as she was told, and Josephine applied a light coating of silver eye shadow and mascara to Sara's restless eyes, restless because Sara stole a peek every now and then.

But the party was only fifteen minutes away, and Sara had to get dressed. "You can see the complete and finished project when I'm through, hun," Josephine said.

"Okay," Sara conceded.

Josephine helped Sara into the dress, complete with puffy shoulders just like in Elizabethan times, and zipped her up from the back. Then she slipped onto Sara's hands, a pair of long, silver gloves that extended all the way back to her elbows. Josephine had worried the gloves might be too large for Sara's hands, inasmuch as Josephine had worn them to her own senior prom, many years ago. But like everything else thus far, they fit perfectly.

Sara watched as Josie removed a large, velvet-covered jewelry case from a drawer inside Josephine's worktable.

Inside was a pearl necklace and a matching pair of pearl earrings. The set had been an anniversary gift from Jim several years ago, who'd given it to her during an intimate dinner at a little bed and breakfast in the Poconos.

It was one of the most expensive and precious things that Josephine owned, yet she had no apprehensions at all about loaning it to this little girl whom she cherished as much as life itself.

Luckily for Sara, she'd had her ears pierced just the summer before, though the earrings still hurt when they pushed through the tiny holes in her ear lobes.

Josephine draped the necklace of fine pearls around Sara's awaiting neck and then, just like in a coronation, placed the shimmering tiara upon Sara's head like a glowing halo.

"There," Josephine commented, admiring her own work. "Now, what are we missing?"

Sara held up a foot from beneath the gown and wiggled her toes at Josie.

Shoes! Good Lord, how could she have forgotten shoes! Josephine looked at the clock. They had five minutes until the party. What was she going to do about shoes? Josephine knew the wrong kind of shoes would ruin the entire ensemble. She had to think…

"Do you have a silver pair of shoes?" she asked Sara.

Sara shook her head.

"Do you have a pair of dressy shoes?"

"Yes, but they're black."

Josephine shook her head, vehemently. "No, no, no… black shoes just will not do –" But then, just as suddenly, Josie had an idea. "Run upstairs and bring your black shoes down," she ordered Sara.

Sara returned in seconds with a pair of black shoes sporting a quarter-inch heel on them.

"Place them on my table there, dear," Josie said, while she rummaged through a storage cabinet. "Ah-hah!" she exclaimed, removing a can of spray paint. "Silver," she told Sara. "Be a dear and open the door up, just a crack."

Josephine shook the can vigorously for several seconds while the tiny ball inside clacked against the cylinder. Then she placed her hand inside one of the shoes, turned it up side down, and proceeded to cover the black with a glimmering coat of silver paint.

"Forgive me, Linda," she said to herself. "I'll buy the child a new pair, I promise." She then repeated the process with its matching partner.

When she had finished, she said, "Let them dry a minute or two." She winked at the anxious Sara who stood in anticipation next to the door like a tiny, barefoot pixie.

After several minutes had passed, Josephine cast a glance up at the clock. It was nearly six o'clock.

"You had better be dry," she warned the shoes, "'cause we can't wait a minute longer." She picked them up, squatted near Sara, and slipped both shoes onto her diminutive feet. "You must be Cinderella!" she remarked.

"Oh Josie!" Sara exclaimed once more, and fell into Josephine's arms.

"None of that again, sweetie… none of that again. We've got to get you to the party." She smiled, and kissed Sara on the forehead. "C'mon."

They rushed out onto Race Street, and into Josephine's awaiting Jeep Cherokee. But once inside, both were nearly overcome by the sickening odor of the painted shoes.

"Good Lord, what else?" Josephine asked, aloud. She leaned on the power window switch for the passenger side window and depressed it until the window was completely down. "Stick your feet out the window, Sara." she told the child.

Sara placed both of her feet out the window and leaned her head back toward Josie, so the air would not muss up her hair.

"Off we go," Josephine said, and slipped the automatic transmission into drive.

And off they went, Josephine and the little princess, as the children in their store-bought costumes were already making their way inside the Mt. Canaan Elementary School gymnasium for a night of Halloween festivities.

XXV. The Strays Attacked

Let them be confounded and put to shame
that seek after my soul: let them be turned back
and brought to confusion that devise my hurt.
– Psalm 35:4

The ferals surrounded the Jack and Buddy on all sides. Curiously, the Alpha was not with them.

The Jack backed in close to Buddy. He bared his teeth and raised the hair on his neck. His eyes scanned over the ferals, the whole snarling lot of them. They had been sent here by the Alpha – sent here to do his bidding. His chief concern was to defend his blind companion. But there were so many of them, and he was tired.

He heard Buddy growl his familiar mantra, *keep away, stay back*, and it bolstered his courage. His friend was prepared to do his part. The Jack would have to be his eyes.

The ferals, moving as one ominous, hateful beast, lacking both compassion and remorse, tightened the circle of growling, sharp teeth around the two dogs. The Jack could feel the ferals' hot breath upon his own muzzle as if the jaws of some giant dog were closing down on them.

Because of his fear, or in spite of it, Buddy lashed out at the invisible growling. He seized one unexpected feral and clutched it by the throat.

The feral was a rather emaciated short-haired terrier mix, who had been with the pack only a short time but had already won the respect of its members for his cunning and fearlessness.

The dog struggled a bit in Buddy's powerful jaws, but he had a firm hold on the feral's windpipe. The feral's lungs craved precious, life-giving air, but Buddy denied him. He felt the feral manage one final kick of his hind leg and then the animal fell limp in his jaws. Buddy dropped the dead dog at his feet and raised his head, defiantly.

A wave of silence washed over the pack. All contemplated the matter at hand in the best way a dog can. But in a canine world, brutality begets brutality – and the dogs could reach only one conclusion. The remaining ferals fell upon Buddy and the Jack like a swift and merciless plague, swallowing them up in a cloud of gnashing teeth and bared claws.

The copper-like smell of blood, both feral as well as Buddy's and the Jack's, mingled with the scent of unkempt animal fur that was falling to the ground in clumps.

The Jack battled back. The ferals were attacking from all sides. Razor-like claws raked his back and pointed fangs buried in his shoulder. The Jack howled, and rolled away from his attackers. He scrambled back to his feet. A hound was assailing Buddy from behind. The Jack slipped under the frothing jaws of a seemingly rabid cur and charged the hound. He caught him in the side with a glance of his claws and felt them cut into the thin layer of skin covering the ribs. The hound wailed and fell away from Buddy.

Two more dogs quickly replaced the hound and continued the assault on Buddy. The Jack could see Buddy was busy enough with a fair-sized mongrel and was in no position to fend off the attack. Bitten and bleeding, the Jack threw himself at the two ferals, snapping his jaws. He rolled beneath the legs of the nearest dog, pushing him into the other feral. He grasped one of the feral's front paws in his mouth and bit down until the dog shook free of him. The feral whimpered. He held his paw above the ground and limped away.

Tirelessly, the Jack continued on, waging war on their enemy, and turning back countless encroachments by the pack.

Buddy downed his second and third opponents much slower than the first. He felt the ferals gaining the upper hand. His thick, pink tongue spilled over his black gums to keep from overheating.

While Buddy was occupied by a fairly large collie-mix, two smaller dogs succeeded in opening a large wound on his hind leg. Exhausted, Buddy allowed himself to be pulled to the ground by the relentless ferals. The dogs swooped down upon him and bathed their muzzles in Buddy's blood.

The Jack used his agility to keep the remaining dogs on the move. He could feel two of the ferals nipping at his tail. He veered into a tight circle. The faster of the two ferals was right behind him. The feral was fast – but the Jack was so much more agile. He pulled up abruptly, and the faster feral ran past him. The Jack changed direction and ran right at the second feral, causing the two pursuing ferals to collide with one another. The colliding dogs fell into a brief battle amongst themselves, before remembering their fiendish intent and resuming their onslaught.

But while the Jack succeeded in escaping serious injury at the jaws of the ferals, his friend was slowly slipping away under their unrelenting attacks.

Buddy was overtaken by several ferals atop him, savaging him brutally. His paws kicked and clawed in a vain effort to shield his underbelly from the enemy. Buddy cried out for his companion.

The Jack charged the dogs assaulting his friend, knocking two of the four off balance. Then, in a blur of white fur, the Jack darted for the safety of the trees, leaving only two ferals for his comrade to face.

The befuddled ferals regained their balance and scampered off in pursuit of the Jack. The Jack had to lead them away – far away from Buddy. He hoped Buddy could protect himself against the remaining ferals. He'd have to.

Buddy struggled to his feet. The odds were more evenly matched now. He leaped into combat with the two lingering ferals, a beagle-terrier mix and a medium-sized mongrel. He knew his disability and weakened condition favored a brief and deadly fight.

Buddy bared his teeth and lunged forward. He caught the beagle-terrier's throat firmly in his jaws. With all his weight, he forced the smaller dog to the ground and ended the dog's life with one violent tug. The dog's body protested for a moment, quivering in Buddy's mouth. Its limbs clawed in a futile defense – then its life leaked from him – a crimson puddle in the dirt.

His victim's blood dripped from Buddy's whiskers. He sensed the second dog's fear and sniffed the air urgently for his throat, too; however, this feral refused to meet the same fate as the last, and ran away.

Exhausted, Buddy collapsed to the ground, bleeding profusely from his rear leg. Too tired to even clean the wound, the blind dog was unable to sense the last feral some one hundred yards away, being loaded into Byron Brady's Chevrolet Blazer.

XXVI. The Halloween Party

Then old Fezziwig stood out to dance with Mrs. Fezziwig. Top couple, too; with a good stiff piece of work cut out for them; three or four and twenty pair of partners; people who were not to be trifled with; people who would dance, and had no notion of walking.

– Charles Dickens, *A Christmas Carol*

Sara arrived at the party late.

In her haste to get the child to the gymnasium on time, Josephine stalled her Jeep Cherokee several times, and as a result, flooded the engine at an intersection several blocks from the school. After waiting fifteen minutes, the engine still refused to start, so Josephine walked Sara to the school.

"You have a good time, honey, you hear?" Josephine told her when they arrived outside the gymnasium.

Sara nodded. She was afraid of how the children would react to her, and Josephine knew it.

"Remember," Josephine said, "the best thing about Halloween is you don't have to be yourself. You can put on a mask and pretend to be anybody you want, and it's okay." She smiled at Sara. "Not that there's anything wrong with who *you* are."

Sara grinned. "I know," she replied.

"Look how pretty you are, Sara VanMeter," Josephine gushed. "This is your night. Enjoy it. After the party, Jim and I will take you trick-or-treating, okay?"

"How will you get home?" Sara asked.

Josephine dismissed her with a casual wave of her hand. "The car should start by now… it's had enough time to rest."

"But what if it doesn't start?"

"I've got a thumb, Sara," Josephine said with a wink, "and I know how to use it. Now you get your butt inside that gym this instant, you hear?"

Sara nodded, turned, and walked slowly to the two, large double doors that marked the entrance to the school. As she approached the doors, the sounds of music and merriment reached her ears and made her pause. She looked back over her shoulder at Josephine.

"They're never going to like you if they don't get to know you first,"

Josephine said.

Sara nodded once more, rather reluctantly, leaned her petite frame against the metal door, and pushed it open. Instantly, the amplified sounds of the party within rushed by her and escaped into the night-time air, where they became echoes and joined the memories of Halloweens long past.

Darkness greeted Sara inside the school. A long, unlit hallway stretched before her, lockers lining the walls like ancient tombs. *Whispers.* Someone else was in the hall – hiding.

Sara was well aware there were more than just lockers in this hallway. There were classrooms, too. At the opposite end, there was a faint, dim light pulsing like the fading heartbeat of something dying. Sara reached out for this light, this glimmer of hope, a tiny ship struggling against a stormy sea. A beacon – it was the gymnasium.

Damn it, she'd forgotten all about the hallway – the haunted hallway. It was an annual occurrence, just like the Halloween party. Upperclassmen – seventh and eighth graders, hid in the classrooms of the haunted hallway, waiting to pounce on the hapless partygoers as they made their way to the gymnasium. That in itself wasn't all that bad – it was all meant in fun. But often, the upperclassmen would enlist the aid of fifth and sixth graders – at least the cool ones, to participate as well, when some of the eighth graders stole away to the auditorium to make out. The cool ones translated to Sara as the terrible clique – the kids from the school bus.

Her hand tightened around her mask. She could feel the cool, autumn air seeping in from the doors behind her and she knew it would be so easy to just turn around and walk back out those doors. But Josie put *so* much hard work into her costume and she would be *so* disappointed in Sara if she didn't make it into that gymnasium. But it was *so* far to go.

Sara stepped forward, reluctantly. Her shoes *clacked* against the polished tile floor, each step a signal to the lurkers she was coming nearer. She thought about taking them off – taking them off and running as fast as she could down the hall, to the light. But they already knew she was here. They'd known since the moment she walked through those doors.

The absence of light was unsettling. She thought of the blind mongrel she'd met by the floodwall. This was his world, every waking minute of his life. For a moment, she drew strength from this notion – strength in knowing she was not alone after all.

There was a stirring. It was brief – a rustling of fabric – the impatient shifting of weight from one leg to another. But Sara heard it. Someone was waiting in the doorway of a classroom just ahead. What would the mongrel do? He'd peel back his jowls and show those great big teeth of his –

Sara... a phantom voice whispered. *Sara... Sara VanMeter? It's Sara VanMeter!* Stifled giggles. *Sara VanMeter! Can you believe she came?*

Sara's hands trembled. *Sara...* The whispers seemed to originate from all around her. *Sara...Sara VanMeter...* She felt the tears coming. Oh, God, no. Please, no. Not here, not now. Please don't let me cry. *Sara... Sara VanMeter... Sara!* Think of something – anything. *We're going to get you, Sara...* Think – the mongrel. What would he do? But then she realized it – she could never be that mongrel – he had a friend. *Sara... Sara VanMeter...* the whispers were relentless.

The doors to the hallway opened momentarily behind her and for a millisecond, the hall was filled with light. The lurkers ducked back into their hiding places, scurrying like rats – but not before Sara saw them. The darkness returned, but at least Sara knew now what lay before her.

For the first time since she entered the school, she was aware of music and the smells of baked apple and popcorn. Someone else was coming up behind her, another partygoer, and she'd have to push forward now.

Sara... Sara VanMeter... the whispers started once more. But they're only whispers, she told herself, and whispers can't hurt you. At the halfway point, she thought of her father. When he died, did he pass through a tunnel like this? Was it worth it to reach heaven? To achieve some peace? She convinced herself it was. *Sara... Sara VanMeter...*

She relaxed her hearing and the whispers became just words – words with no meanings – words strung together in nonsensical sentences. *Jabber*, Josie called it. Ahead, the light intensified. It was heaven, and she was nearly there. Inside, her father waited, dressed in his pinstriped suit – the one he wore in the photo she kept on her nightstand. Not much farther to go–

Sara VanMeter... Sara! Strong, clumsy hands wringed her shoulders. She screamed. Laughing... Hot breath on her ear, the smell of sour milk on his breath – *Sara... we've got you...* Being pulled, twisted, turned – stomach cramping – *Sara VanMeter... Noodlenose!* Oh, God, please! Red eyes burning off the darkness – the Alpha! *That's my dress... She's wearing my dress...* Strange hands, pinching, clutching – *My mother gave that dress to the thrift store...* Darkness, spinning darkness – *Cry baby, cry!* Help – Daddy, please... don't die... please Daddy, don't die – *Sara is poor...* I'm sorry, Daddy, I'm sorry... A blaring horn – headlights – a crash – blood. Daddy? Daddy? *Sara is a monkey...* Don't leave me, Daddy – Daddy, please! *Sara...* I dropped my dolly, Daddy – *Sara...* Please don't turn around – *Sara VanMeter...* Don't turn around to pick it up – *Sara...* Don't, Daddy, please – *Sara...* Don't take your eyes off the road – *Sara...* Daddy, No! *Sara...*

A crash.

"Sara?" A soft cheek against hers, warm hands on her shoulders. "It's okay," the voice whispered. "I'm scared, too." One of the hands slid down her arm, leaving a trail of warmth, and firmly grasped her hand. "C'mon," the voice whispered, "we can do this."

Who's that? Do you know? The voices whispered, clearly agitated.

Sara pressed her cheek against the stranger's warmth, clinging to it. "My Jack?" she muttered.

Sara... Sara VanMeter... Sara tensed.

"Don't listen to them," the voice whispered. "They're just jerks." The stranger moved her closer to the light. As it grew brighter, the whispers faded.

Sara... Sara VanMe...

"Almost there," the voice whispered. "Almost–" The illuminated outline of double doors. The light was dim, because it had been leaking from the cracks of the closed doors. A silhouette of a hand reached out.

Light exploded in her eyes; the spell was broken.

"Who–" she turned – squinting – straining against the sudden brightness. But the voice, the whisperer – *her Jack*, was gone.

There was only someone clad in a child's superhero costume melding into the crowd.

The gymnasium was alive with the harmonious rhythms of laughter and music. Pumpkins and black cats and ghosts and witches, symbols of the season, adorned the walls surrounding the chattering children, while orange and black balloons and crepe paper hung from the ceiling above their heads.

The children, whose identities were concealed, often with a grotesque mask, mingled from one group to the next, mindful of their voices and even the very gait of their walk so as not to give away any hints to who they might be. Even the teachers wore costumes and were not easily recognizable.

Ms. McGovern, for instance, arrived at the party dressed as a black cat, complete with painted whiskers, pointy ears and a long tail that waved lazily from side to side when she walked. And she wore a form-fitting black leotard that made more than a few of the male teachers turn their heads for a second look. Of course, she also wore her glasses, so most of the children knew it was her.

Sara stood off to the side, held her mask up to the tense lines near her eyes and mouth, and cautiously scanned the party through the circular eyeholes.

Near the center of the gymnasium, a group of children gathered to dance and sing to the familiar songs playing over the loud speakers usually reserved for the public announcement system. Some of the children, even disguised, Sara recognized as her tormentors from the school bus, and probably from the haunted hallway as well.

They laughed, waved their hands above their heads and pretended to scare one another with their costumes. Sometimes one of the boys would jump into the center of the group and break into an exaggerated dance, his arms flailing about in an effort to make the other children laugh. The boy's clowning elicited an uproarious response from the rest of the group. And despite all their villainy, Sara couldn't help but laugh, too.

"You'll find it's a lot more fun the closer you get," a voice said to her. It was Ms. McGovern in her cat costume.

"Oh, hello, Ms. McGovern," Sara said. "You look pretty tonight."

Ms. McGovern stared at her for a moment, a puzzled look on her face. "Sara? Sara VanMeter?"

Sara nodded and then smiled.

"Why, look at you, Sara. You're absolutely beautiful!"

"Thank you, Ms. McGovern," Sara replied, bashfully.

"Did your mom help make you look so beautiful?"

"No," she said, timidly. "My mom had to work tonight... with it being Halloween and everything. My best friend made me this costume... Josie McGillis."

"Well, you're lucky to have such a friend like Josie."

"I know," Sara agreed.

Ms. McGovern thought for a moment. "And you're lucky to have such a hard working mother, too."

"I know that, too," Sara said.

A comfortable silence then fell over the two as they looked out over the dance floor.

"So are you ready to join the party yet?" Ms. McGovern asked, finally.

Sara bit down on her lower lip. "I don't know..."

"C'mon, Sara. I feel like dancing," Ms. McGovern told her, and grasped her hand.

"But I don't know how..."

"I'll teach you," Ms. McGovern replied, and jerked the rigid Sara onto the dance floor.

Despite her protests, Ms. McGovern led Sara right near the group of children she'd hoped to avoid.

"Now watch me," Ms. McGovern instructed. "And just do as I do, okay?"

Sara nodded and watched as Ms. McGovern swayed her hips to the rhythm of the music.

"Now let's see you do it."

Sara complied and moved her body much in the same manner as her teacher.

"Can you feel the music?" Ms. McGovern asked her.

Sara nodded and concentrated on her motions.

"Can you feel it?" she shouted, raising her hands and hopping up and down.

"Yeah," Sara replied, laughing.

"I said, 'can you feel it?'" her teacher shouted, even louder.

"I can feel it!" Sara shouted back.

Ms. McGovern clutched Sara's hand and made her jump up and down with her. "Can you feel it, sister?"

Laughing, Sara screamed over the music, "I can feel it!"

"Isn't it fun?" Ms. McGovern asked her.

And Sara had to admit it was. It was also funny to see Ms. McGovern, her usually reserved teacher, jumping up and down in a cat costume like a complete idiot, not caring how she looked. But Sara guessed that's what Halloween was all about: stepping out of your skin for one night and just being free.

She had forgotten all about the children she'd been so concerned with and did not even realize they were all doing the same, ridiculous dance right along with Ms. McGovern and herself. Nor did she notice the boys looking at her in a somewhat peculiar way.

Inevitably the principal, dressed as Dracula and acting as the DJ for the night, took a break from the fast tempo songs and played a slow-paced love song.

"Do you know how to slow dance?" Ms. McGovern asked.

Sara shook her head.

"Would you like to learn?"

"Yes," Sara replied. "I think I would."

Ms. McGovern held out her hand. "Here," she said, "take my hand… and place your other hand here." She took Sara's free hand and placed it around her waist. "Now just follow my lead."

Sara did as her teacher said and soon found herself dancing her very first slow dance.

"What do you think?" Ms. McGovern asked her.

"It's nice," she said.

"It's even nicer with a boy," Ms. McGovern suggested with a smile.

"Byron Brady's nice," Sara said, quite unexpectedly.

"Uh, yes, he is," Ms. McGovern returned.

"I saw you dancing at the Fall Foliage Festival," Sara offered.

"Do you know something I don't?" Ms. McGovern queried.

"No..." Sara replied. "Just that I think he likes you a lot."

At that moment, Sara felt a light tap on her shoulder. She turned to face a boy she'd recognized from the other sixth grade class, a quiet light-haired boy who sat at the back of the room and, like Sara, had very few friends. He was dressed as a comic book character, though he did not have his mask on. *It was him.*

"Uh, excuse me..." he said.

"Yes?" Sara replied, expectantly.

"Uh, may I," he stammered. "May I, uh... cut in?"

"Sure," said Sara dejectedly and stepped aside to allow the boy to dance with Ms. McGovern.

He looked up at Ms. McGovern and smiled, uncomfortably. "Uh..." he started.

Sara didn't want to hear any more. She turned and walked away. He liked Ms. McGovern, and not her. *Oh, well,* she thought. *Easy come, easy go.* That's what Josie always said. Why would she expect otherwise.

Feeling sorry for herself, she eyed the punch bowl. She'd just go back to lurking behind it until Josie came for her.

Suddenly, a hand grasped her forearm. She turned to find the superhero.

"Wait!" he pleaded. "You didn't understand me right. Uh, I meant I want to, you know, dance with you..."

She hesitated. *Me? He wants to dance with me? He wants to dance with me!* Eyes wide, she looked beyond him, shooting a glance for approval at Ms. McGovern.

Ms. McGovern nodded. "Say 'yes,'" she mouthed.

Sara's eyes glowed like embers, her cheeks burned. She felt a grin spread across her face. "Okay," Sara replied, finally.

But instead of being relieved, the boy looked troubled. "Uh, except one thing, though."

"Yes?"

He looked down at his shoes. "I don't know how –"

"That's okay," she said. "It's easy... I'll show you. Give me your hand." It was the same warm hand. "I'm Sara."

"I *know* that much."

"What's your name?" she asked.

"Justin." Sara placed his hand around her waist. "But you can call me

Jack if you'd like."

Sara smiled. "No, I like Justin. Justin's nice."

Mindy, flushed from dancing, backed casually away and fetched herself a glass of punch. By the refreshments table, she watched Sara and Justin dance, awkwardly at first, their bodies afraid to touch, neither one speaking.

But one dance led to another, and one word led to a string of sentences, and then quite suddenly, both Sara and Justin were chattering away as if they'd known each other as long as Mindy and Brady had.

They took turns battering away at a swollen pinata, and even shared ice cream and cake. And when Sara bobbed for apples, Justin held her tiara so it wouldn't topple off her head and fall into the water.

By the end of the night, a few other boys and girls who really didn't fit into any of the cliques were attracted to Sara's and Justin's aura, and joined them to form a loose confederation of outcasts. The new group, that Sara likened to the stray dogs she'd befriended, laughed and danced and played games for the remainder of the night until the principal regrettably announced the last song over the din of their resounding jeers.

At 8:00 PM, Sara rushed to Josephine's up and running Jeep Cherokee, where Josephine and Jim sat patiently sipping coffee.

"There's the little princess," Jim declared as Sara excitedly leaned into the window.

"Hullo, Jim," she said.

"How was the party, sweetie?" Josephine asked.

Sara smiled. "Oh, Josie… I had the best time of my entire life tonight!"

"You did? That's wonderful, dear!" Josephine replied. "Are you ready to go trick-or-treating?"

Concern turned down the corner of Sara's mouth. "About that, Josie. I met some friends at the party tonight… and… and they asked me if I could go trick-or-treating with them tonight. Please say it's okay… please?"

Josephine caught her breath. Friends? This was quite unexpected. "Well, of course it's okay, sweetheart," she said, finally. Friends? Sara had made friends.

"You're not mad?" Sara asked.

Josephine shook her head. "Go out and have a glorious time," she told her, and meant it. "But do stay away from the woods and be mindful of the ferals."

"Oh, thank you, Josie! Thank you so very much!" She kissed Josephine on the cheek. "I love you," she whispered in Josephine's ear.

"I love you more," Josephine whispered back.

"Happy Halloween, Jim!" Sara said.

"Same to you, honey," he returned.

"You're going to need this," Josephine said, holding up the plastic jack o'lantern she bought Sara earlier so she'd have something to hold her candy.

"Oh, right," Sara remarked, stealing it from Josephine's hands. She started to run, then stopped. A puzzled look held her face. "Josie?"

"Yes, Sweet pea?"

"Was I with my father when he died?"

Josephine gasped. "I-I don't understand, Sweet pea?"

"Was I with him when he died? Do you know?"

"I suppose both you and your mom were at the hospital." Josephine pursed her lips. "You were so young."

Sara shook her head. "No, Josie. Was I *with* him when he died?"

"You – You mean in the car?"

Sara smiled. "It's okay," she said. "I know."

"I don't – What? You know? How –"

Sara moved to the vehicle. She reached out to Josephine, touched her face. "It's okay, *Sweet pea*," she said to Josephine. "I know, now. I guess I've always known."

"You were so young," Josephine repeated.

"I dropped my doll."

"He loved you so much." She could barely see Sara through her tears.

"I dropped it, Josie. It was my fault," she confessed into the green glow of the dashboard light.

"Is that – is that what you think?"

"He looked away to pick it up –"

Josephine shook her head, adamantly. "The other driver ran a red light." She was sobbing now, so much so, it prompted Jim to grasp her hand. "He was drunk, the other driver. There was nothing your dad could do."

"But the doll –"

Choking, Josephine said, "Sweet pea, that doll was the most wonderful thing."

"He looked away, Josie. He turned to pick it up."

"Sara, the doll was wonderful!"

"How, Josie? How can you say that –"

"You were the last thing he saw!"

"But –" Sara started.

Josephine leaned out the car door and grasped Sara's face in her hands. "You were the last thing he saw, Sara. I know it. He died looking into these eyes." As if in response, they glistened. "I knew your father so well. We were cousins. I knew him since he was knee-high. I know he would have wanted it that way."

"Then I didn't kill –"

"No," she said, kissing Sara. "And don't you ever think it again."

"But –"

"You made him happy, Sara. You're still making him happy."

Sara smiled. "He was good?"

"He was good, Sara. And so are you." She looked past Sara at the small gathering of children waiting patiently in the distance. "All the good candy is going to be gone."

"You're sure you're okay with this?" Sara asked, caution blanketing her words.

"I'll be fine." She patted Sara's head. "It's your time, now."

"Hey, Sara?" one of the children called out. Josephine held Sara's gaze for a moment, not wanting to let go, hoping nothing could ever change between them.

But they both knew something had changed. Sara could go forward now, forge her path. Josephine had no more stories left, no more secrets to share. It was time for Sara to collect her own tales, protect her own secrets. It was time for the world to meet Sara VanMeter.

"Thank you," Sara whispered, her fingertips trailing lightly across Josephine's forearm. She was glowing.

Sara bolted from the vehicle and into the darkness where she joined the other children.

"I can go!" Josephine heard Sara exclaim as she caught up with her friends. She was embraced by a chorus of laughing, cheering voices, any one of which could have been Sara's.

Then their footsteps, which echoed along the cobblestone streets, slowly faded away like the remnants of a pleasant dream.

Josephine sighed, rolled up the window, and rested her head against the seat back. She smiled a faraway smile and her eyes fixed upon nothing in the distance.

"Our little girl's growing up," Jim said.

"Yeah," Josephine replied, still smiling.

"So what do we do now?"

"Go home," she said, contentedly.

"And do what?"

An air of devilishness manifested on Josephine's otherwise tired face. "Trick-or-treat," she responded.

XXVII. The Jack Hunted

Me, I was part of the nastiness now.
–Raymond Chandler, *The Big Sleep*

The Jack led the ferals deep into the woods – deeper than he had ever been before.

Fatigue was setting in, but the Jack dared not stop and rest. If he did, the ferals would be upon him and he would be turned into nothing more than a heap of blood and fur. Fear drove him forward, fear for his own life as well as that of his friend's, who did not seem to be faring as well as he, the last the Jack saw him. The Jack resisted the urge to turn and face his attackers. There were too many, and their barks seemed to be drawing closer. Wearily, he drove forward.

As he made his way up an embankment of loose dirt, the Jack felt the ground fall away beneath his right hind leg. His front paws dug into the soft earth. The ground deteriorated and a small hole opened up. The Jack's rear quarters were quickly consumed by the subsidence and his back paws kicked at the dirt in an effort to anchor himself. The smell of fox wafted up from the darkness. A low, enjoining growl reached his ears, clearly distinguishing itself from the ferals calling in the distance. The Jack struggled to free himself. The source of the growling was coming nearer. He clawed at the ancient roots of a nearby oak and plunged his nails into the crumbling bark. Razor-like talons swiped at his tail. They ripped through his fur like knives. The sharpness of the fox's claws caught the Jack off guard and he cried. Thankfully, the roots of the tree were strong enough to support the Jack's weight. His hind paws found some clay just beneath the lip of the hole, and it held him. He pushed himself up, sprang from the hole, and hurried up the embankment.

He emerged in a clearing with the ferals not far behind. In front of him, the embankment leveled off. It seemed as though the Jack had reached the end of the world – he had run out of land. The setting sun was very large here, and low, too. If the Jack kept running, he was sure he could leap off the world and touch it.

But he hadn't reached the end of the world. He'd reached the edge of a strip-mining pit. Hundreds of feet of deadly, still blue water waited patiently below. The Jack halted abruptly, nearly falling in.

Mere inches from his front paws, the ground ended before him in a two hundred and fifty foot vertical fall. Mesmerized by the height as well as the deep blue water below, the Jack froze. An idea sparked in his brain. He turned and ran back toward the ferals.

Come and get me! he barked defiantly into the woods.

We most certainly will! the ferals bayed.

The Jack caught a glimpse of the lead dog, a hound, and bounded back to the pit. Once again he stopped short of the edge.

We've got you now, the hound barked, pleased with himself.

We certainly do, a lean mongrel snarled.

They leaped toward the Jack, their fangs poised to make a mess of the Jack's soft, pink flesh. They were in mid-flight before the Jack even reacted. Their claws reaching out for him, their sinister eyes glistening with anticipation, the Jack threw himself to the ground and rolled. His hind legs cut through the open air above the pit – the shadow of the first feral passed over him. It was the hound. The mongrel was right behind him.

The Jack scratched the ground in an effort to moor himself. He needn't have worried about the hound. A desperate, futile cry pierced the air, just as the mongrel's claws stabbed the Jack's haunches. The mongrel was hanging from the edge of the pit, saved only by the Jack. The hound had already gone over.

The Jack was unable to find any footing on the rock wall, which had been polished smooth by decades of rain washing over it. The mongrel's weight was pulling the feral into the pit, and taking the Jack along with him. The Jack felt his own grip lessen as his claws raked over the loose rock and gravel. He felt more and more air beneath him. He craned his neck and turned his head. The feral's muzzle was right there, peeled back over his sharp teeth, grimacing. Straining. The Jack bit him. The feral whimpered, his eyes widened, and the Jack felt his grip on him release. The Jack shook free of him, like he'd shake pellets of rain from his coat, and the mongrel slipped away.

The blue sulfur water, like an ancient beast long dormant, parted its icy contents and swallowed the mongrel whole. Just as his friend the hound had discovered, the steep pitch of the rock wall provided the mongrel no respite from the icy waters. With nowhere to escape, the water had its way with the feral.

Numbly, the Jack looked down at him. The unforgiving cold covered over him – a liquid grave. The surface – rippled from the feral's futile attempt at saving himself – became placid once more.

The last two ferals, a German shepherd and a mangy cur, were watching, too, a short distance from the Jack. They stood motionless at the ridge of the pit, staring down at the cold abyss, puzzled by the disappearance of their cohorts.

Fearing the German shepherd too strong for him, the Jack charged the cur. He nipped at the feral's tail and bounded back for the wood. Angrily, the cur all too eagerly followed. The Jack retraced his steps and led the cur to the foxhole. He glanced back at the cur, wagged his tail, and disappeared into the ground.

The feral wasn't about to let him get away that easily. With nowhere to run, he'd make quick work of the little dog, he was sure.

But Jack Russell terriers were bred to be short with strong chest muscles and powerful legs for just this type of work, and the Jack competently negotiated the narrow twists and turns of the foxhole.

The cur, meanwhile, who had no breeding at all, was ill-equipped for spelunking. He burrowed after the scent of the Jack, the hole becoming increasingly smaller. The cur was soon forced to crawl on his belly, and even that was a snug fit. He was having a tough go of it, but he'd gone this far, and there was no turning back now.

The Jack pushed on in the dank, lifeless air of the hole, the smell of the fox becoming prominent, the cur's panting looming behind him. In the darkness ahead, something stirred – the scratching of some dirt. A flash of a half-dozen red, glaring eyes made the Jack stop. A forbidding growl urged him to leave. He'd reached the den's tenants. They were not hospitable hosts.

The cur was almost behind him. The Jack pawed at the darkness in an effort to anger the invisible creatures. It was more than enough.

The foxes charged the Jack, claws reaching, ripping, tearing. The Jack tucked his head in his side, shielding his eyes, and tried to turn around. It was a tight squeeze, but he managed it, his nails digging into the sides of the hole to pull him around.

The cur was right there. The cur's jaws opened and, for a brief second, had the Jack's left front leg in its possession. But the Jack clawed at his head, stepped on it, and was atop him, wedged in the tiny space.

The cur barked in frustration. He was unable to turn around in the tight space. And something else was in the hole with him.

The Jack attempted to push past the cur, but he couldn't get past the dog's rear quarters. Frantically, the Jack began to dig with his front paws in an effort to widen the space above him. He heard a foreign hiss and felt the cur's body tense.

Then the foxes attacked. The darkness, the hole, and everything around it seemed to be breaking apart. The foxes hissing, scratching, the cur yelping, heaving, the smell of fear polluted the air.

The Jack dug all the faster. The cur's fearful panting filled up the hole and consumed the darkness. Then a small beacon of light broke. The Jack pushed his muzzle through it, drinking in the fresh air, putting distance behind the cries of the animal he was still lying upon. First his head, then his front paws, the Jack pulled himself through. His hind paws clawed deep into the cur's back as he pushed off, and he felt the cur's body tremble. With the skill of a mole, the Jack inched and scratched his way to the surface, the cur's anguished cries driving him on. Light exploded in his eyes, ancient earth clinging to his coat. A bloodcurdling howl followed him out of the hole. Then silence.

The cur was never seen again.

The Jack shook the loose dirt from his fur. The sunlight and the air felt nice around him, and the birds chattering in the trees proved a welcome change from the nightmare he'd experienced below. He scanned the forest around him: tall oaks, fallen trees covered in moss, a German shepherd... the other feral! The Jack tensed.

The German shepherd, unable to enter the hole because of his size, had waited patiently just outside. It was obvious what had happened below. Angered by the Jack's trickery, the German shepherd charged him, sending the Jack off and running once more.

The Jack was exhausted, but he had no choice but to continue running.

The German shepherd chased him through rugged terrain, a blur of black mountains, desolate plateaus, and leafless trees. It felt as though they had been running for days. The German shepherd's stamina seemed limitless. Along the way, the Jack seemed to pick up on the scent of the Alpha, and subconsciously followed it as it grew ever stronger.

Upon reaching a summit some two and a half miles from the road outside of town, the Jack had disappeared. Dumbfounded, the German shepherd stood along the summit and strained through the diminishing light for his prey. Even nose to the ground, he could not detect the Jack. Something was dead here. The pungent odor of decaying flesh filled the air and corrupted the German shepherd's senses. The shepherd scanned the black rock for any sign of the Jack. The carcass of a deer lay not far away, an arrow standing defiantly from its neck like a solitary antler. Sniffing the air, where had the terrier gone?

Beneath the carcass something stirred. The shepherd was too far away to notice. On his belly lay the Jack. The smell of death made him shudder. He could very well be the next rotting carcass, dying here alone. An odd shadow crept from behind his eyes and he felt a growling in his chest he could not contain. A peculiar darkness gained control of him, nudged him on, and reminded him of an inner rage, long since tapped.

Suddenly, the smell of death seemed delicious. He had an urge to roll all over the carcass, soak it up in his coat, to commune with it. But the good-natured Jack managed to suppress it, and he pushed the strange feeling away. He leaped from the rotting shell.

The shepherd, startled by the sudden appearance of the Jack, bared his fangs and raised the hair on his neck. A low growl emerged from the dog's throat, not so much a warning, but a promise: a promise to kill the Jack. This was his arena now. Mouth to mouth, claw to claw, fang to fang. Not the game of hide-and-seek they'd been playing.

The Jack clawed at the ground in front of him. He was sure the feral was a more experienced fighter than himself. But the Jack was also certain he was smarter than this animal. The shepherd's rage was obvious. If he could somehow use that against him…

The Jack sat up on his haunches, ears pricked, like he was begging for a treat. *You don't trouble me*, he yapped.

Enraged, the German shepherd instinctively rushed the Jack, baring his teeth, his legs moving beneath him in long, fluid strides.

From his seemingly lackadaisical position, the Jack suddenly leaped toward the feral. They met in a blur of flashing fangs. The two dogs moved in unison, chest to chest, two hateful lovers. They gnashed their teeth, snarled and attempted to gain access to the other's throat. The German shepherd, the much stronger of the two, drove the Jack backward in a bold attempt to knock him to the ground.

Reeling, the Jack threw back his head. It was a weak effort to gain his balance. The German shepherd recognized the deadly opportunity he'd been waiting for. His jaws widened – his strong, brilliantly white teeth glistening – the German shepherd grasped the Jack's exposed throat firmly in his mouth.

The Jack squealed, much like a rabbit caught in the steel cold jaws of a coyote. He had slipped up, he realized too late.

The German shepherd rolled the Jack onto his back, a procedure he'd followed so many times before.

It was too mechanical, and he'd underestimated the Jack, who was stronger than the German shepherd's usual prey of hares and groundhogs. He was more intelligent, too.

But the German shepherd's jaws were doing a masterful job. The Jack could hardly breathe and darkness was gathering along the edges of his sight. He almost gave up. But something stirred inside him, something ancient and wild – a beast. It protested with a growl deep within his bowels. It was not the growl of a dog, it was a beast much older.

Startled, the feral eased up slightly, but it was enough for the Jack. He lashed out across the German shepherd's face with his claws, drawing blood from the dog's nose and right eye. The feral released him and cried out.

The Jack sprang to his feet and shook off the strange wildness. The German shepherd seemed bewildered.

The Jack circled the shepherd and snarled as his enemy turned to keep an eye on him.

There was a good amount of bleeding from the wound the Jack had opened across the shepherd's snout. The shepherd fell back into his mechanical routine once more, but he was blinded by his rage.

The Jack veered to the left and right, dodging each futile attempt by the feral to seize him. The German shepherd grew more frustrated. The Jack's speed proved too much for the sheer brute strength of the German shepherd, who was showing signs of fatigue as evidenced by his labored panting.

But speed alone could not defeat the much stronger feral, and the Jack knew it. He darted past the staggering German shepherd and headed for a towering man-made mountain of loose coal and slate. Reluctantly, the German shepherd followed.

His tired eyes pursued the white apparition moving through the trees and on up the mountain, the loose rocks sliding down behind him. It would take every last bit of energy to stay with the small dog. The shepherd's pride drove him on now. He didn't have much energy left. He reached the base of the mountain and peered up at the Jack ahead. With a ferocious intensity, he climbed after him.

The Jack's hind legs worked like magnificent springs to push him up the mountainside. He continued to pull away. The mountaintop was not more than forty dog-lengths ahead.

Suddenly, a queer sound filled the air around him. It seemed to originate from beneath the very ground the Jack climbed upon. It began as a murmur, a mere allusion to sound. But soon, the murmur gave way to a much more definitive rumble. The Jack had unknowingly created a rockslide.

Frightened, he climbed the mountain with even more urgency. It was breaking apart all around him. Black rocks of all sizes began tumbling beneath him, gaining momentum as they continued down the mountainside. The Jack struggled to keep his footing. The climb was becoming more perilous. The top of the mountain was almost within his reach –

Then the ground disappeared underneath him.

The Jack's back paws caught nothing but air. His front paws stretched in front of him, clawing at the black rock, pulling it beneath him, clinging. The mountaintop started moving away, flying off into the sky. Scratching, digging, every muscle working, the rockslide seemed to pour from him. He had created it, now it was drawing him in, claiming him.

But the Jack had left a job unfinished. He had to see this through to the end. He had to bring the mountaintop back, pull it to him. Stronger, harder, faster, the Jack stretched every muscle, sent signals to every nerve ending. More power, more –

An ominous black shadow materialized in the German shepherd's field of view. What happened to the terrier? The black shadow was chewing up the mountainside, reforming it, spitting it out. It belched rocks and trees and other debris as it moved down the bleak landscape like a fierce, dark storm.

The German shepherd was dwarfed by its enormity. The rockslide surrounded him on all sides. Defeated, the German shepherd opened his mouth to cry out. But his bark and the very air around him were siphoned away.

The black shadow swallowed up everything in one decisive, all-consuming wave of energy. It could have been death itself. It surged over the German shepherd and erased him from the mountainside as if he had never been there at all.

Without pausing, the rockslide rolled on to the base of the mountain where it deposited rock upon rock, as well as everything else in its path.

The mountain had turned upside down. The top was the bottom, the bottom was the top, and the Jack did not know which way was up. *More power*, he commanded his legs. And they complied.

Scrabbling, he gained control again, control of the ground beneath him. The mountaintop drew closer, and he felt the rockslide slip away.

He emerged at the summit, surprised not to see any sign of the persistent feral. As suddenly as the rumbling had begun, it just as suddenly ceased. The quiet was oddly disconcerting. The shepherd was gone, buried away beneath the tons of loose rock. Perhaps he was still alive, clawing, scratching, struggling to free himself. Exhausted, the Jack stared down at the pile below.

Nothing stirred. He had beaten the shepherd, beaten the pack.

But one still remained.

The reality of facing the Alpha slowly crept into the Jack's mind, chasing away any hint of triumph he may have felt. The beast inside his belly clawed to get out.

He stood at the peak of the redefined mountain and unleashed a most dreadful howl.

Not far away, in the den he shared with his female, the Alpha stirred. Something was not right.

None of his pack had returned to him.

XXVIII. Imprisonment

'Why does my action strike them as so horrible?' he said to himself. 'Is it because it was a crime? What is meant by crime? My conscience is at rest. Of course it was a legal crime, of course the letter of law was broken and blood was shed. Well punish me for the letter of the law... and that's enough.

– Fyodor Dostoyevsky, *Crime And Punishment*

The coldness of the steel cage was foreign to Buddy. Fear and lost hope hung heavy on the air, and the anguished cries of the shelter's caged animals invaded his ears like an unwelcome creature clawing at his brain.

He cried out in response to their calls, but his own bark was silenced by a muzzle fastened tightly about his snout. He gnashed his teeth in contempt for the unseen captors who bound him in this steel shell. Despite all the suffering and torment he'd endured in his short life, he'd never been placed in a cage, and the wildness he'd assumed living on the streets simmered violently inside him, for they had taken the very last thing away from him: his freedom.

He paced the cage angrily and, in his blindness, walked into the walls and bars of the cage more than once. He snarled at them – they mocked him – and the bile in his stomach burned for one last chance at the throats of his captors.

He did not know where he was, though he was certain of the fate awaiting him. Although his body was imprisoned, he found his mind could still roam. It roamed somewhere far away, not so much a place, but a time, when he shared an old blanket with Angus in the corner of his master's kitchen, and the reliable ticking of the kitchen clock, coupled with Angus' tumultuous breathing, lulled him softly to sleep.

But the unmistakable smell of death pulled him back to the cage. It was a presence here, as real as the hands that had seized him and slipped this constricting noose about his muzzle. It was the very same scent that had laid hold of the stranger's house, tainted the rooms and furniture, and infected the very man himself. Buddy realized it now: the stranger who blinded him was dying a very slow, painful death as his mind rotted inside his skull and the blood in his veins turned to a fine, red dust.

Buddy was dying, too. The darkness that stole away his sight was a seed sown by the stranger, and now it was spreading throughout his body like an incurable, malignant disease. But before he'd let it consume him, Buddy yearned for one last taste of blood.

Felix Mortimer unlatched the mongrel's cage and forcefully pulled the dog from inside, while the other dogs carried on raucously in their cages. They barked out an alarm. The humans had returned.

Buddy, already incensed, lashed out blindly at Mortimer. But the muzzle prevented him from opening his jaws. Undeterred, he growled at the man all the same.

"Pipe down, you mangy mutt," Mortimer retorted. "Or else you don't get none of this."

The 'this' Mortimer was referring to was a salve to place on the dog's numerous cuts and bite marks. He hated trying to treat a vicious dog, which this animal so clearly was.

Besides, he couldn't even understand why Brady would bother treating his wounds anyway. The dog had no eyes, it was obvious no one was going to adopt him.

Anyway, the shelter had a strict policy on sick and crippled animals. In order to free up space for healthy animals, sickies and cripples were euthanized immediately. So what was the Boss waiting for?

Hell, Mortimer couldn't wait to put down this monster and that white, little bugger he palled around with. *Especially the white one*. Maybe he'd only give the dog a bit of the deadly injection, that sodium pento- sodium pento- Hell, it had a long name he could never remember. The 'blue stuff,' he liked to call it. Always 100 mg's, the Boss told him, not a drop less. Maybe he'd only give him 50 mg's, just to see what happened. Maybe the dog would squirm around for a little bit, maybe whimper his little heart out. Mortimer would enjoy that.

God, he hated animals. So smelly and dumb, they'd eat their own filth if you didn't pick it up. He couldn't understand all these animal rights groups. Hell, just the word 'animal rights' seemed dumb. What rights does a stupid animal deserve?

Don't eat chicken, don't eat beef, don't wear fur, don't hunt. If you love the animals so much, you should go live with them. That was Mortimer's philosophy.

Let all those weirdoes hug the whales and save the trees and free the monkeys from the laboratories. Not Mortimer. His relatives never lived in trees. And he didn't come from no germs on a meteor, either. He was an

American, fourth generation born and raised, and was digesting red meat while other kids couldn't even keep down their mashed peas.

And this here animal was a pain in his arse and why the hell should he care if his bites healed when they were only going to put him to sleep, anyway?

"Ah, hell," Mortimer said. "I does me job, that's what I do. The Boss tells me to put ointment on a dog's bites, I put ointment on the dog's bites. Even if the Boss does strike me sometimes as a weirdo."

He grabbed onto the mongrel's haunch. "Hold still so I can put some of this here cream on your arse," he said to Buddy.

Buddy sniffed at the man's bandaged arm and replied with a growl.

At his office in the nearby courthouse, Brady sat at his desk, contemplating the remains of a mushroom and onion pizza. He was alone, for the secretary had left for the evening, though the silence in the room was so heavy it felt like another someone with him anyway.

He thought of the blind mongrel they'd captured this evening, bloodied and exhausted from the war he'd witnessed.

It seemed to Brady they were dealing with two different groups of animals here. It appeared the sightless dog and his companion were not traveling with the feral pack that had attacked the festival. The two animals had fought valiantly when greatly outnumbered, not to mention the obvious disadvantages of the terrier's small size and the mongrel's blindness.

And how had the dog become blind? Surely he wasn't born that way, and Brady doubted another dog had done that to him. Brady knew all too well the abuses that man afflicted on his pets, having investigated hundreds of animal cruelty cases in the county, and he was sure this pitiful animal was another victim. He treated animal cruelty cases very seriously, for he knew the abuse of an animal often led to abuses on women and children, and sometimes even murder.

Brady sighed. He wished he were with Mindy now, for the dirty reality of his work was getting the best of him tonight. He was well aware of the shelter's policy on sick and crippled animals, and he knew Mortimer was well aware of it, too. It disturbed him sometimes the way Mortimer pressed him on the matter of putting down an animal. "His two weeks are up, Boss... they certainly are, that's for sure. I'll go fetch the needles and do it quick, 'cause I knows you don't like it," he'd say to Brady. "It's a messy little job, that's for sure... though *I* don't mind it a bit, Boss. They just animals, not peoples like us." Then off he'd run like an eager child into the dreary, windowless room painted in government-issue green, pulling the unfortunate creature behind him. "Hold still, you bugger," he'd hear Mortimer say.

Brady shivered. Maybe it was a blessing that Mortimer was that way, for it was so hard to find workers willing to put down an animal. Mortimer went about his work with a certain amount of zeal, that was certain. Hell, he was even the first to call the sheriff and excitedly tell him they'd caught the blind dog.

The sheriff raced right down to the shelter, a newspaper photographer in tow, just to get a first look at the offender.

"Make sure you can see he's got no eyes," the sheriff told the photographer. "I want to make sure everyone knows we got him." He and Mortimer posed proudly on opposite sides of the cage, while the mongrel unknowingly faced out toward the camera.

Brady opted not to be in the picture, despite the persistence of the sheriff. Brady knew the photograph and accompanying story would surely be the first step in repairing the borough's now-scarred tourist industry. Nonetheless, he felt uneasy about posing next to the caged animal as if he were a trophy or a five-point buck.

Sick of the entire day and mindful of the images that would surely haunt his dreams that night, Brady locked up the office and reluctantly made his way to the shelter to help Mortimer close up, too.

The cool night air, along with the sound of leaves scooting along the sidewalk, restored Brady's state of mind, if just a little. Masked children raced by him and scampered up the steps to a nearby house adorned with an illuminated jack o'lantern. "Trick-or-treat," they greeted the resident.

Brady turned up the collar of his navy peacoat and pressed on another block to the animal shelter.

"Hullo, Boss," Mortimer said to Brady, as he closed the door behind him. "I was just locking up, I was." A twinkle sparked in Mortimer's eyes. "You want I should put the blind bugger down?"

"Go home, Felix. It's late," Brady replied.

"I mean it would be no trouble if I were to –"

"It's late, Felix," Brady insisted. "Go home."

"You want me to go home, I go home. I do it first thing tomorrow for you, then. Good night."

"'Night," Brady returned, closing the door as Mortimer's form fused with the darkness outside.

Brady walked down the aisle of cages, the old floorboards beneath him creaking from his weight. He was greeted by a chorus of barks and wagging tails, and bright, inquisitive eyes eager to demonstrate what a nice pet they'd make. As he'd pass each cage, its occupant would amiably press his wet nose to the bars and campaign for a moment of Brady's attention in anticipation of a kindly, "Hi, fella," or a chance to merely lick Brady's fingers.

Brady stopped at the cage of a female beagle mix, sixteen months old, her name, Sadie, scrawled in Mortimer's handwriting across a tear of masking tape affixed above the cage door.

"Hello, Sadie," he said to her. Her eyes glistened in response and her tail wagged an energetic reply. "How's Sadie? How's Sadie tonight?" he continued. The other dogs in the cages around her barked loudly at the sound of Brady's voice.

But the beagle remained silent, sitting timidly at the rear of the cage, fearful of the man looking inside.

"Don't be afraid, Sadie. I'm not going to hurt –" Brady's eyes fell instinctively on the date of arrival which was always placed at the bottom right corner of the cage. It read, "October 17." Two weeks to the day. Brady grew silent and continued on.

He reached the blind mongrel's cage, which Mortimer had conveniently located near the euthanasia room, so he wouldn't have to pull the dog very far.

Although he had barren eye sockets, it still was apparent to Brady the mongrel was sleeping, for his tremendous body ascended and descended with the force and grace of an ocean tide. His large, tired head with his maligned ear and disheveled fur rested on his front paws. Brady's eyes scanned across his many bite marks and desolate patches of missing fur, and he puzzled at the gnarled tip of the animal's bushy tail.

Tomorrow, he'd have to put this dog to death, an animal that endured the loss of his eyes and yet still managed to fend for himself and stay alive all this time. Twelve hours from now, he'd fill the syringe with 100 milligrams of sodium pentobarbital, what was referred to in his business as a noninhalant pharmacologic euthanizing agent. He'd convince himself it was for the animal's own good, and then he'd put Sadie asleep, too.

He looked around the room. frightened eyes stared back at him from their captivity. *Why, Brady?* they seemed to ask. *Why? What have we done, Brady? What have we done to merit this? What have we done to end up here?*

Their depravation and loneliness struck Brady for the first time, and he was suddenly aware of the world he was caretaker to. His legs felt weak and his collar grew tight around his throat. The floor melted away and Brady felt himself fall backward against the cages. Slowly, he slid to the floor, his back resting on the cage fronts.

The blind mongrel stirred slightly, shifted his body weight, and turned on his side.

"What are we doing here?" Brady sobbed, aloud. "Oh, sweet Christ, what have *I* done?"

Behind him, Sadie licked Brady's ear from inside her cage as the rest of the shelter turned oddly silent.

XXIX. How the Jack Ensnared the Alpha

Those which bestir themselves in dreams, when the gentler part of the soul slumbers and the control of reason is withdrawn; then the wild beast in us, full-fed with meat or drink, becomes rampant and shakes off sleep to go in quest of what will gratify its own instincts.

– Plato, *The Republic*

The wind turned suddenly cold on this Halloween night as autumn made its first appearance of the season. An uninspired breeze made its way through the gorge, but it was stale and lifeless. It shook the remaining leaves from the trees until their branches resembled ghastly, skeletal fingers clutching at the sky, pleading with a merciless god for rain. The wind then pushed its way past the Jack and rustled the matted hair atop his head. He scrambled for footing among the loose rock.

The Jack sniffed his way through the dark wood. The scent of the Alpha was strong here, seeping into the very ground like poison.

He pressed on. He was exhausted from his turn with the ferals and the sleep he gave into beneath the sparse cover of a withering bramble bush did little to restore his energy.

He dreamed of Buddy and the ferals, and the dark cloud that suddenly became the Alpha. He saw the icy water of the strip-mining pit, and the black rock of the mountains, and the little girl by the river. Then a shade of gray he recognized to be blood, splashed up from over the stone wall and swallowed them all up: Buddy, the ferals, the Alpha, the little girl, and himself. It was over, and he was relieved. He wouldn't have to concern himself any longer with things like food and shelter and wild dogs.

He awoke to the beast's laughter inside him, scratching at the walls of his belly. It jeered him for dreaming such foolishness. The Jack drew angry and snarled.

Let me out, the beast pleaded. *I have such wonderful secrets to share.*

No!

You're afraid of him, but I'm not afraid. I'll teach you...I am the wildness you've held enslaved within; I am the wildness you've been trained to ignore.

No!

You want to be me like me, you need to be like me–

No! I'm not like you, the Jack cried inside his head. *I'm a house dog, not like you at all. Different.*

Different, but the same. You can't keep me locked up. I am the points of your fangs, the keen of your eyes. I am the beast they have programmed you to forget.

The Jack whimpered. The Alpha was near, he could sense it. How could he defeat such an animal alone?

Not alone, the beast within hissed. It paced his innards and whispered in his ear things only the Jack was sure he could hear or understand. Things of death and dying, of killing and pounding of flesh, of murderous thoughts and snapping jaws, of the delicious taste of blood.

He could feel the primordial code of an ancient race unlocked within. Deep inside, a door burst open, shackles broke, the wild beast was free.

I am the one who commands you to dig, to rip and destroy, to pursue and to prey, it howled. *You've been taught not to hear my call... It is my time now.*

The Jack seized. He lurched forward and his eyes rolled white for a moment. When they returned forward, wildness altered their appearance. The beast was in control now.

He pitched his head toward the sky in the direction he was sure the moon lay hidden beneath the clouds. A peculiar howl, lacking compassion and fear, leaped from him and sliced through the night air. His collar loosened around his throat and slipped off his neck. It fell to the ground near his paws. He kicked it away. It was finished.

His nose told him the Alpha was very near.

The Alpha paced the floor of the den while his female nursed their litter. Five tiny, yelping pups struggled against one another for a right to their mother's teat. The Alpha singled out the smallest, and therefore weakest of the pups, which humans know as the runt, and separated him from the other four. He hoisted the pup by the scruff of his neck, carried him outside, and proceeded to eat him. As he finished, a flash of white caught his alert eye but for a moment, though long enough to distract him from his vile meal. It disappeared like a ghost in the wood but soon reappeared several feet away.

The white dog – But how? And why hadn't his pack returned to him?

A fine mist rose up from the land and hung just above the scarred, strip-mined earth. Had the white dog conjured it – no, there must be an explanation. No dog, not even one as mighty as himself, had power over the elements. But the white dog materialized again before him, for only an instant, and then was gone. *What trick is this?* And how had he –

Fangs lashed out at him and drew blood on his right haunch. The Alpha cried out, but caught himself. He turned too late to see his attacker. Was there more than one dog? He peeled back his muzzle. His pink gums and sharp teeth were stained crimson with his pup's blood.

The howl of the white dog seemed to call his name.

"Lazarus!" it cried from his blind side and put a savage bite on his throat.

The Alpha gnashed his teeth and leaped into the mist. He was sure he'd seen the white dog a mere second before. But it was gone again. The Alpha bounded into a shallow puddle, lost his footing and soiled his coat. Angrily, he pulled himself to his feet and shook the loose water from his fur.

"Lazarus!" The white dog seized upon his tail and took the tip cleanly away.

The Alpha whimpered. He circled several times before he managed to reach his tail with his tongue. He lowered himself to the ground and nursed his injury. The taste of his own blood was bitter in his mouth.

What madness had gripped him? Surely this was the same white dog he'd encountered before. There was nothing special about that dog, nothing that could move the terrier to seek him out alone and challenge him near his own den. No dog, not even the terrier's large, blind friend could match his strength, let alone strike fear in him like this – this ghost dog had succeeded in doing by himself.

That dog, like most dogs he'd encountered, reeked of men and their houses and of their wastefulness. Their underused muscles and senses were nowhere near as keen as his own. But this ghost dog… No, there was no such animal. He was the mightiest and the bravest and no dog shall dare challenge him.

He stood. The mist cleared in front of him just enough for him to recognize the shape of the white dog standing ten dog lengths away. The dog's eyes shone red in the darkness, burning, unafraid. The Alpha did his best to repress his fear. He lowered his head and bolted for the dog. But the white dog ran, too, and the Alpha chased him. He must kill this dog, he thought. He must kill him, or he might as well keep running. Insolence cannot go unpunished, and this dog and his cohort had tried him for too long.

Into the mist he followed.

The Jack ran gleefully through the forest. The Alpha's blood was thick on his muzzle.

Ha! he barked out. The wild thing inside laughed, too. The beast within was rollicking good company and very knowledgeable in the ways of war. It told him when to attack and when to retreat, and it taught him how to use the mist to his advantage.

The Jack's legs felt strong and his paws easily moved the earth beneath him. His senses were especially sharp, so much so, he could see the Alpha struggling behind him without even looking back.

The beast within told the Jack to lead the Alpha toward the town.

The Alpha growled. He could see the terrier's white tail bobbing before him but no matter how fast he ran, he was unable to gain on him.

What insanity plagued him? What ill infected the world this night and turned it upside down? What had become of his pack?

The lights of the town split the darkness ahead of him. The whistle of the train rattled the night like the lonely call of a dying animal, the last of its breed.

The Alpha was the last of his breed, the last of the Hogstooth legacy, the last chapter in the history of an accursed brood. The old man came to him now. "Lazarus," he whispered in the Alpha's ear. "It's over."

He dismissed it as the wind. The white dog's trickery seemed limitless.

The Jack veered onto the macadam of Chestnut Street.

The last of the night's trick-or-treaters roamed the sidewalks, kicking through piles of fallen leaves, hoisting their plunder over their shoulders in plastic sacks.

The Jack raced past a group of children crowding up the steps of the final lit porch and the beast within told him to go toward the river. The Jack complied. The beast's plan was nearly complete.

The Alpha's claws scratched roughly against the asphalt. *Yes*, he thought, *sharpen yourself, my children. I will allow you your fair share of ripping tonight.*

"Ferals!" a child screamed and pointed at the Alpha. The remainder of the group cried out in chorus: "Ferals! Ferals!" as they had been taught in school.

Porch lights turned on in response.

Startled by the commotion, the Alpha slowed his pursuit. His gaze fell upon the children. Grotesque faces with bulbous noses and unusually large teeth stared back at him. Their faces! The Alpha whimpered. What had happened to the children of the town?

He halted, changed direction and ran toward the opposite side of the street. More masked children emerged from a nearby home and screamed upon seeing the Alpha. Bewildered, he lost sight of the white dog, forgot him even, and raced down the center of the street.

Wait, the beast within commanded. *The damned fool is running in the opposite direction!*

The Jack circled back and streaked down the street after the Alpha. He barked and growled behind the black dog who seemingly was running in fear for his life.

The same group of children cried out "feral!" again, but the beast within silenced them with a snarl.

The Alpha turned the corner and was away from the horrid children. *What has hap –*

Wait, he thought. *The white dog's foolery once more.*

He swore at himself, scratched at the blacktop, and howled.

Damn him! Damn him and his tricks!

It's time, my children... it's time.

The Jack turned the corner wide and narrowly avoided the claws of the Alpha's front paw. He heard the black dog snarl. *Not good*, the beast within told him, *not good at all*. The Alpha circled him. The look of bewilderment was gone. The swagger had returned.

Be quick! You don't have the mist to protect you. The Alpha lunged at him, but the Jack slipped his attack. The Jack countered with a slight nip of the feral's shoulder, but paid for it with the Alpha's claws across his snout. A fresh cut opened above his nose.

The plan, the beast within hissed, *remember the plan!*

The Jack shook off the throbbing in his muzzle. He turned and ran for the river.

Ha! the Alpha howled. Has all your magic been used up?

He bounded down the street after the white dog, careful not to look at any of the children. The white dog was running for his life now, as his kind so often do. Whatever spell he had been under was gone now, and the world seem right once more.

He chased the white dog through the mostly quiet streets as the smells and sounds of the river grew stronger. The river? He was leading him there? Good. There would be nowhere left to run to there.

The form of the white dog became clearer as the Alpha closed the distance between them.

The Jack ran past the dirt road that led to the cave. He looked longingly in its direction. *Not yet*, the beast within told him, *there will be time for rest soon enough. Now take the bridge, the one you and the blind one had used before.*

The Jack did as was asked of him, crossing over the inky, black water raging just below. The Alpha was right behind him now. Perhaps his beast within was controlling him, too.

Here! Just as I remember it... just as you remember it, for I am you. Turn here. The Jack reached the end of the bridge and turned down a narrow path, thick with dried weeds, and charged down the embankment. The whistle of the last train excursion of the evening sounded off in the distance. Its tracks ran beneath the bridge.

Yes! Good boy... good dog. Not long now.

The Jack continued his descent to the water below.

The Alpha dismounted the bridge in one effortless leap. He could feel it now, the wake from the white dog right in his face. Where will you go, ghost dog?

The dog's tail was practically touching his nose, but the Alpha resisted the urge – for now. In a moment, they would be at the base of the gorge where only the river and a man's narrow pathway ran. The white dog would be forced to either stay on the path or go into the water.

The Alpha was well aware of the strong current of the river and knew the waters would easily carry the smaller white dog away. He also knew there were large rocks, just under the surface, for he had seen small animals smashed against them.

The Alpha grimaced. He was certain the terrier would steer clear of the water. That left the path. Without room on either side to maneuver, the white dog's impressive quickness was useless. With his long stride, the Alpha was convinced he could easily run the terrier down.

He could hardly contain his joy.

He's right behind you, the beast within told the Jack.

He reached the base of the embankment and leaped over the railroad tracks.

Go to the water! the beast within seemed to cry.

He's going for the river! The white dog was more foolish than he had believed. *Certainly, he'll be killed if he goes in, but... no ripping then, no squealing or blood, either. Damn him! He will not deprive me!* The Alpha leaped over the man's pathway, right behind the terrier, who halted at the river's edge.

Now my children... now. The Alpha stretched every centimeter of his muscular body and lunged for the ghost dog.

Down! the beast within cried out.

The Jack crouched, ducking just underneath the extended front paws of the Alpha. He watched as the feral glided right into the dark waters below.

The train whistle signaled the excursion's return in the distance. *Go now,* the beast within told the Jack. *Go toward the cry of the man-made creature.*

The Jack charged for the oncoming train.

The Alpha paddled against the swift current. It took all his might to reach the shore. He clawed his way up through the loose dirt of the river bank, until he was once again on the man's pathway.

Damn him! Damn that white dog! Damn –

There he was, off in the distance... running along the man's pathway. Fool! So easy to run him down... so easy.

The Alpha cursed and ran along the railroad tracks after the ghost dog.

The Jack continued for the speeding train.

Stop here! Right here... Here we will wait, the beast within told him. *Pick up one of your front paws.*

But why?

Do it! The Jack complied. *Now limp.* The Jack limped along the train tracks as the locomotive raced quickly toward him.

The white dog is hurt? The white dog is hurt! Oh, what sweet joy! The Alpha could hardly contain himself.

The Jack looked toward the Alpha. He was only seconds away. *Now sit!* the beast within commanded. The Jack sat on a splintered tie. The train was also bearing down on him, its light scanning the night like a solitary, unblinking eye.

Don't worry about that creature yet... remember the plan. It suddenly occurred to the Jack he did not know the plan nor was he ever aware of one.

He looked up at the sky and wailed.

The train whistle screamed out at its approach to the town. It rumbled loudly along the tracks and its light reached far ahead.

But the Alpha paid no attention to it. He dismissed the train as another trick of the white dog. The white dog, who was sitting on the man's pathway waiting for him like a fool.

He was not far now.

The Jack carefully watched the fast approaching Alpha and fretted over the train behind him.

Wait... Wait... Wait, just a bit more, the beast within told him. *Wait... Wait...*

The Alpha was right atop the white dog now. *Just a few more feet, my children, just–*

The train's whistle sounded once more.

"Lazarus!" it seemed to cry out. "Lazarus!"

No, the Alpha thought. *It's just the white dog's trickery...*

"Lazarus!" the old man called out to him.

The Alpha looked beyond the space where the white dog was sitting. A bright light washed over him.

Now! the beast within commanded.

The Alpha's eyes focused on the place where the white dog had been sitting moments earlier. He was gone.

He managed a disheartening growl. The raucous, one-eyed beast was only seconds away. It kept advancing toward him, fearlessly. Had it no respect? Did it not know who he was? He'd show the beast its reward for such impudence.

The Alpha ran toward the train, snarling.

My jaws will make quick work of you –

As the Alpha charged the train, his teeth glowing yellow-white in its light, it suddenly occurred to him he'd been tricked – again. But that thought, along with the memories of a harsh, violent life, was extinguished by tons of iron and steel. The mechanical beast raged over him. The train made his magnificent, muscular body into an ugly shadow stretched across the tracks.

Good boy... Good dog, the beast within commended the Jack as he lay alongside the railroad tracks, his tiny chest heaving. The train cars blurred by him, rumbling and screeching along the iron tracks, but the sheer force of the locomotive barely fazed him. Finally, the last of the cars, a classical, red caboose, scooted past, signaling an end to the parade of noise.

The voice of the beast and all its ancient wisdom quieted to a whisper, and from a whisper to an echo – an echo which lingered a moment in the Jack's ear before gradually being replaced by his troubled panting. Then the wildness, like a dream, faded away and the beast within, exhausted, returned to its cage, grateful for its taste of freedom.

A peculiar swarm of flies descended on the carcass.

Rest… rest.

But the Jack's rest was fleeting. This night, this journey, was not over yet. He'd defeated his enemy, every last one of them, but an emptiness touched his soul and dampened any elation. Buddy was in the town, he could sense it. He could feel his friend's fear mixed with the coolness of the dew in the air. The men had taken him.

The Jack struggled to his feet. He forced a growl and chased the flies away.

The flies rose up into the night air, momentarily casting a shadow of a winged creature over the autumn moon, and then disbursed into the darkness.

The remains of the Alpha were gone.

A pair of barren eye sockets burned in the Jack's mind.

He raced for the town.

XXX. Buddy's Fate

Behind his gun, the Jackal started to swear, softly, venomously. He had never missed a stationary target at 150 yards in his life before.
– Frederick Forsyth, *The Day of the Jackal*

Brady's skull hurt, and his clothes smelled of liquor. He leaned forward onto his desk at the shelter and rested his head in his hands. Mortimer had beaten him to the shelter this morning and met him at the door.

"You want I should put the blind bugger down now?" he asked.

Brady pushed past him and made for the office, ignoring the pleas of the caged dogs who sought only a moment of his attention.

"I get him ready, Boss. Okay?" Mortimer called after him.

Brady didn't respond. For although a night of hard drinking by himself brought amazing clarity to Brady's troubled mind, it also made him regard Mortimer with even more distaste.

Brady was an animal control officer and his duties were as his position's name implied: to control the animal population. That was accomplished by putting down animals who were deemed "unadoptable," to make room for animals with a better chance of finding a home. A blind mongrel certainly fell into that category, especially one who drew as much outrage from the public as this animal. Besides, an animal without its sight surely was a risk to itself. He'd be doing it a favor if he put it down. Surely, he would.

"Go ahead, Felix," Brady called out, reluctantly. "But remove that damned muzzle first." The dog was owed that much respect, he reasoned.

"Right away, Boss. Right away."

It had been a long, weary morning for the Jack. Wanting to rest, to sleep, he pressed on for the historic district and the county animal shelter where an irresistible force, like the urge to bark, was drawing him near. His friend was there, the Jack could feel it, just like he had known where to find the Alpha's den. But his sense of Buddy – his memory of him – was fading. He could not recall the sound of his bark, the scent of his fur, or the outline his tremendous form cut against the burnt sky. He could not remember–

What did this mean? Was his friend dying? Or worse, was he– The Jack drove this memory away like a rogue cat from the backyard. He was still alive, he had to be, the Jack assured himself. Or the events of the past few days, the ferals, the foxes, and the Alpha, was all for nothing. No, Buddy was still alive, the Jack had to believe, and he would be alive when the Jack found him and led him from the town. The dimming memory of his friend impelled the Jack through the empty streets of Mt. Canaan to a place where Buddy's essence was strongest.

The Jack found himself outside the locked doors of the impenetrable prison that is the county shelter. He stood up on his hind legs and did his best impression of the fat, old raccoon. Pushing at the doors, scratching at them, the Jack tried desperately to gain entry. But the doors stood defiantly against any such intrusion. The only way a dog could enter the shelter was in a cage or the wrong end of a control stick.

He threw his head back and howled, a mournful, desperate cry that was answered by a chorus of equally mournful, desperate howls from inside the old stone building. The peculiar song, which conveyed a vanquished message of lost hope, flowed out into the cold night air like a sad lullaby and coaxed the Jack into a spell of dreamless sleep.

And there on the front step of the animal shelter, a place where most stray animals would certainly try to avoid, the Jack slept until the next morning brought Felix Mortimer in his county-issued vehicle. The sound of the vehicle's door closing shook the small dog awake and sent him off and running for the only safe haven he knew: Josephine's garden.

Josephine awoke that morning to a dreadful cry that nearly shook her from the bed. She instinctively reached for Jim but her hand only found the cool sheets where her husband had lain hours before. Her eyes strained at the clock. It was a moment before she recalled it was Saturday morning and Jim had promised bright and early he would go to a neighboring town and buy the necessary parts to fix the gate.

She lay her head back on the pillow. Perhaps she was dreaming. But that notion was quickly dismissed when she heard the cry again.

Why, it sounded like... like... a dog? Why, just like... the Jack? She sprang to her feet, ripped her flannel housecoat from the hook on the back of the door, and slipped into it has she hurried down the steps. The anguish in his cries – something was wrong.

Josephine darted into the kitchen, threw back the door to the garden and found the Jack sitting on the stone pathway.

There was blood on his muzzle and across his nose, and his fur was dripping with filth.

"My Lord, Jack... what happened?" She dropped to her knees and pulled the dog close to her. "Where's Buddy?"

The Jack pulled away from her and barked toward the street.

"What's wrong, Jack? Has something happened to Buddy?"

The Jack barked all the louder, and more urgently. He ran to the street, stopped and looked back.

"Do you want me to follow?" she asked.

The Jack answered with another bark, which made Josephine believe he most certainly did want her to come.

"Okay, Jack. Take me to Buddy," she said, chasing after the dog and looking foolish in her pajamas and housecoat.

Buddy hardly slept at all in his cage. The steel crosshatch beneath him was cold and hard and not at all comfortable like the layer of dried leaves in the cave he shared with the Jack.

The Jack – he wondered how the little guy had fared against the pack. He was a brave fellow, he certainly was, and Buddy hoped against hope, the Jack had somehow survived. He knew the terrier was a resourceful creature, brimming with cunning and intelligence, and if he managed to outwit the ferals, he could live a long life in the wilds. Anyway, he'd be better off without the burden of caring for a blind mongrel.

Buddy sighed. He sensed what time remained of his life was not much at all, for the smell of death and abandoned hope crowded him on all sides. But he made a promise to himself during that long and sleepless night; when the evil hands lay upon him that final time, his fangs would be ready.

He had endured all the cruelty he possibly could, and not another second of it would he tolerate. He would match aggression with aggression, and tooth against fist. And when that moment death came for him, he would go, knowing he fought valiantly, making the Jack proud he kept him alive all this time.

Mortimer gleefully seized the syringe and blue-colored liquid from the cabinet. He looked down at the bottle in his hands. 'Eutha 6,' it read on the label. In much smaller print were the words, 'sodium pentobarbital.' That's the stuff. Brady had once told him it stops all neural transmission in the animal's body. Mortimer didn't know what that meant. All he cared was it killed 'em.

He could hardly contain himself.

In a few minutes he'd inject the miserable animal with the blue liquid, slowly, very slowly, perhaps in his hind leg so it had further to travel to reach the dog's brain, and then he'd step back and watch him struggle. Yes, struggle… struggle in confusion with the foreign invader racing through his bloodstream. Mortimer hoped it burned all the way. And in that final moment, right before that wonderful blue liquid laid siege to the animal's brain, killing it, a look of realization would manifest on the dog's face, a realization that he was dying, and that Mortimer was responsible for it.

Bon voyage, Mortimer thought. That's what he'd always say as the animal's legs buckled beneath him and the creature lurched one last time. Bon voyage. Good riddance to you, you stinking bugger. To hell with you and all animals. He cursed his station in life.

Cops, mailmen, even garbage men, had it better than him. Why the hell was it his misfortune to be born without smarts, at least the kind of smarts you needed to make something of yourself. No, his fate was to care for miserable, stinking creatures that no one else goddamned wanted anyway. So what if he took pleasure in the one sole perk the job provided: putting down these filthy animals he was condemned to look after. *So be it*, Mortimer thought.

"Come and get your medicine, you filthy bugger," he said as he approached the mongrel's cage.

In the darkness of the kennel, the mongrel growled.

Brady remained at his desk and poured through a mountain of bills, working out the shelter's expenses on a calculator. Repeatedly, Brady's finger leaned on the "clear" button as Mortimer's disgustingly cheerful voice threw barbs and insults at the animal, and interrupted Brady's thoughts.

"Come on, you stinking bugger. Out of the cage with you," he heard Mortimer coaxing the mongrel from the kennel. "Let's go now, you filthy beast. On with you."

Fire him, Brady thought. *Fire him right now. The animals do not deserve* that *kind of abuse before they're put down. Fire him. No… no matter how vile he is, he serves a useful purpose here. Yes Brady, he most certainly does… he does your dirty work for you. No, that's not true… I'm very busy. It's very hard work controlling a county's animal population. There's that word again, Brady. Controlling. It's a nice, clean word, like managing or management. It doesn't imply the nastiness you're actually employed to do. You're in the business of killing, Brady. You're a killer. Oh, sure you rarely get your hands dirty anymore now that you have ol' Felix around…*

I'm very busy, Brady told himself again. *Sure you are, Brady. Sure you are.*

"Damn you, filthy bugger, let's go," Brady heard Mortimer say. And then in a lower voice, "We'll get your friend, too. We certainly will."

Brady slammed his hand down on the desktop so hard all the objects resting on it jumped at least two inches in the air. *Damn him!* He exploded into the kennel area.

"Mortimer!" Brady cried. He looked at his slow-witted employee who was pulling with all his might on the end of a leash fastened to the mongrel's collar.

"Yeah, Boss?"

Brady exhaled and composed himself. "Be done with it already, okay?"

"This bugger ain't exactly light, you know?"

"Of course," Brady replied, picking up on the hint. "Of course." He positioned himself behind Mortimer and helped him tug the mongrel from its cage.

It took all their strength to move the giant dog, but they eventually did, despite its snarling protests.

"He's a mean one, Boss. I told you so."

They were inside the euthanasia room.

"Let's get him up on the table, Felix. And get a muzzle on him, too."

"You want I should put it on 'em again?"

"Unless you want a bandage on your other arm."

"Sure thing." Mortimer hurried off to fetch a muzzle.

Brady studied the blind animal, his nose pointed off in the distance, his chest breathing heavily. He wondered what the creature was thinking, if he burned inside with hatred for these two men who were about to put an end to what must certainly had been a miserable and tragic life. Brady wanted to tell the dog that not all men are bad, that it was just the luck of the draw he was thrust into such a life.

He lowered his hand to the animal's matted fur and stroked him. The mongrel returned his kindness with a fearsome growl that shook his entire body. Brady instantly withdrew his hand in fear.

"You can see –" Brady said, astonished. "You can see – better than any of us." He pictured himself forty years in the future, broken and worn down by a lifetime of killing animals. What kind of karma was he creating for himself? "You can see," he repeated. "Better than me, anyway."

The mongrel turned his head back toward the direction of Brady's sympathetic voice. He seemed almost to look up at him.

"Forgive us – forgive me."

"You say something, Boss?" Felix asked, returning to the room.

"Get that on him and let's get him on the table already," Brady replied, looking away.

"You tell me to take the muzzle off him, I takes the muzzle off him. You tell me to put the muzzle on him, I puts the muzzle on him. Ol' Felix does what he's told. He certainly does."

Buddy sensed the wretched man in front of him. He recognized the smell of tobacco on his hands. His hands… Buddy bared his fangs and lashed out at where he perceived the man's hands to be. His teeth found the soft, loose flesh between the thumb and forefinger of Mortimer's right hand. Buddy tasted the man's blood on his tongue.

"Oh! You damned bugger you!" Felix cried out, dropping the muzzle and clutching his injured hand. "Oh, dammit! Oh, dammit, anyway!"

Buddy lunged at the sound of the man's voice. His front paws impacted with the man's wiry torso and sent him to the floor. While the man lay crumpled, Buddy attacked some more. His teeth easily tore through the man's clothes, which were ripe with perspiration, and he found quivering skin hiding just underneath.

"Oh Christ, he's killing me… he's killing me!" Mortimer cried.

Brady stood in disbelief as the mongrel pinned Mortimer to the ground. *Every dog has his day*, thought Brady. Oddly, he felt no urgency to rescue Mortimer or to stop the dog's savage onslaught.

"Do something, Boss! He's aiming to kill me, he is!" Mortimer screamed.

The dog most likely did intend to kill him, Brady concluded. I should probably do something… in a minute or so.

Mortimer drew both arms up to his long face and tried to shield himself from the mongrel. "He wants me throat! The damned monster's after me throat!"

"Bon voyage," Brady commented.

"What's that, Boss? You there?"

"Uh, I said, 'I'm going for my gun,' Felix. You hang in there, okay?"

With a large paw, the mongrel battered Mortimer's head. His claws cut into the back of the man's hand, and instantly drew blood.

"Hurry the hell up, please! He's killin' me here!"

Brady casually exited the euthanasia room. What was wrong with him? Did he actually intend to allow the dog to kill Felix? *Oh, damn it!* Brady rushed for his sidearm in the office.

"What the hell's going on here?" Brady heard a voice cry out over the growling of the dog. It was the sheriff. "Brady!"

Sidearm in hand, Brady hurriedly returned to Mortimer and the mongrel, only to find the sheriff's firearm trained on the large dog.

"You hold still now, Felix," the Sheriff cautioned, his finger tight around the trigger.

In expectation of what was about to transpire, Brady looked away.

XXXI. Judgment of the Strays

"Oh, it's you," said he. "What are you bothering for? All the cobras are dead; and if they weren't, I'm here."

– Rudyard Kipling, *Rikki-tikki-tavi*

In the warm morning sun, when only a hint of the previous night's chill remained skulking in the shadows of the downtown buildings, the Jack was drawn to the county shelter once more. This time however, he had an ally. Someone who could open doors – literally. The Jack barked a command to hurry up.

"I'm coming… I'm coming, Jack," Josephine panted.

It had been sometime since she had run, at least this fast, and she wished she had taken the time to put on her sneakers instead of these darned slippers. But the alarm in the dog's cries could not be mistaken; his blind friend was in some sort of trouble. So Josephine was not at all surprised when the Jack Russell terrier abruptly halted at the front doors of the animal shelter.

"Is Buddy in there?" she asked the Jack.

The Jack danced in a rigid circle and barked at the closed doors.

"That's good enough for me," Josephine replied.

She tugged open one of the two steel doors, and the Jack darted inside.

"Brady!" a voice boomed. Josephine knew it was the sheriff. The incensed growling of a dog and the falsetto cries of an obviously frightened man echoed in the hall. She saw Byron Brady race from one room into another.

"Byron!" she called to him, but he did not hear her.

Josephine watched the Jack skate along the slippery floors and veer into the room after Brady. She passed a row of caged dogs carrying on raucously inside their kennels.

"Byron –"

A gunshot sounded – then a wail.

"Jack!" Josephine screamed, and then she ran into the room after Brady, too.

"Oh sweet God," Felix Mortimer bellowed, lying on the floor, clutching his leg. "I'm hit… I'm hit!"

The Jack, with Buddy hitched to the scruff of his neck, crowded past Josephine, nearly knocking her to the floor.

"After them!" the sheriff commanded and bowled into Josephine, sending her into Brady's arms.

The Jack found the doors. They were still ajar, and he led Buddy out into the street, to freedom.

"Josie?" Byron said, holding her up.

"What's going on, Byron?" she asked.

"Brady!" the sheriff yelled. "They're getting away!"

Brady stood Josephine upright. "I can't talk right now…" He steadied her and then chased after the sheriff who was already outside.

"Oh, I need me a doctor… I need me a doctor!" Mortimer moaned, still holding his leg and writhing on the floor. His uniform was bloodied and torn, though in Josephine's opinion, he did not appear to be seriously injured.

"Oh please, Mizz McGillis… I've been shot…"

Josephine stared out toward the open doors where Brady and the sheriff had left in pursuit of the dogs.

"Oh, stop your damned whining, Felix. It's just a flesh wound," she said, and then slipped out the doors, too.

The Jack led Buddy along Broadway, where the day's tourists were steadily filling the streets and shops. The Jack barked and growled just like his beast within would have wanted, and cleared a path for him and his blind comrade to run. He knew the men were behind them and he was sure they carried those noisemakers, too.

Buddy ran along the Jack, not quite sure how he had found his friend and the outside, but grateful nonetheless. The little guy had come through, he certainly did. But he, too, knew the men would be following them and they were responsible for the explosive noise.

Buddy had felt the heat of the gunshot, felt it whizz past him and impact into the man's leg. And he also knew if that explosive noise were to happen again, it could surely put an end to both him and his pal.

Buddy ran all the harder to keep up with the Jack.

Sara was playing a form of tag called "Blackie," with Justin and her new friends outside Josie's shop on Race Street. Its name had derived from a similar game the young boys had played after a hard day in the mines, nearly a century ago. The filthiest of the boys, the one covered from head to toe with coal dirt – "the blackest," was "it."

Crouching behind a parked car, silent as a mouse, Sara had to laugh. Just last year, she'd declared herself "too old" to play such childish games. *My God, she was nearly twelve!* She watched Justin pass by. There was something so persuasive about him – he made it feel okay to be different. When he suggested they play "Blackie," it suddenly seemed fun.

Justin was "Blackie." Just the thought of him, the mere mention of his name, made her weak. The anticipation of his hand tagging her, touching her bare arm, caused her whole body to tingle in a most peculiar way.

She rested her back against the car, her heart beating loudly in her ears. The cold of the metal penetrated the thin layer of her cotton t-shirt and felt nice on her skin. It was a good hiding spot, as good as any, for it was the third time Justin passed and had not discovered her. Also, she could see Josie's shop window from this vantage point and the reflections of any approaching children.

"Hey everyone," a child suddenly called out. "They're trying to shoot some ferals on Broadway!"

Sara strained to listen. Was it a ploy to surrender her cover?

"It's the big, blind one that was in the newspaper this morning!"

Sara's heart stopped. The feelings of puppy love temporarily faded. The blind one…

"My friends!" she cried, and bolted from her hiding place.

"Sara?! Where are you going?" Justin asked.

"My friends… they're going to kill my friends," she replied, rushing by him.

"Who?"

But Sara didn't answer. She bounded down the set of cement steps behind Antonio's, two at a time.

"Sara's friends are in trouble," she heard Justin shout. "C'mon!" And Justin and the other children followed after her.

Mindy McGovern was on Broadway that morning, humming songs she'd listened to the night before, her mind filled with thoughts of Brady.

Brady serenading her with a mandolin outside her window… Brady rowing her across the still surface of a placid pond… Brady running along Broadway waving a pistol… *Wait a second. That was real!*

That really was Brady running on Broadway. What was he doing with a gun?

Mindy pulled off her shoes and ran after Brady in her stocking feet.

Jim had finally gotten the right latch and hinges for the gate. He couldn't wait to see the look on Josie's face when she awakens to discover the gate's been fixed. *Funny*, Jim thought, looking at his watch. *She should be up by now*.

He set the gate flat in the garden and fastened the set of new hinges to the wooden door with a Philips screwdriver. Jim marveled at the way the holes in the wood aligned perfectly with the allotted holes in the hinges. Why, if he'd known this was going to be that easy, he wouldn't have put it off nearly so long.

He reached behind himself for the latch. Two masses of growling, matted, fur brushed under his nose and streaked past him.

"Holy crap!" Jim exclaimed, and jumped to his feet. "Ferals!"

The dogs found the shelter of Josephine's rosebushes and cowered beneath them, panting heavily.

Should he go and fetch Josie? A large hand fell on his shoulder.

"Get... back," the sheriff snarled, breathlessly. He struggled for a moment to regain his wind. A .35 revolver was held at his side. Wheezing, he raised the gun and leveled it at the dogs lying amongst the roses.

"Not in my garden," Jim said.

He slapped the gun from the sheriff's chubby hand. It skittered harmlessly along the stone walkway.

"McGillis!" the sheriff said, his eyes burning. "That's obstruction of justice, it most certainly is."

The two men glared at each other.

"What's going on?" Brady asked, reaching the garden.

Neither man answered.

Brady spied the fugitive dogs nestled along the fence line. The Jack Russell terrier looked up at him while the mongrel seemed to 'look' off in the distance, his massive tongue working hard to cool himself.

"Shoot them, Brady," the sheriff commanded.

"Don't you dare, Byron Brady," Mindy McGovern warned, running up the McGillis walkway.

Behind her, Josephine waddled her way into the garden, her hands on her hips, her cheeks flushed. She said nothing. She was having trouble breathing.

"In here," Sara shouted, and led an army of children into the garden. "They're still alive!" She pointed to the dogs. The Jack's ears perked at the sight of Sara.

"Shoot them, Brady," the sheriff repeated. "You shoot them, or I will." His eyes narrowed. "And I'm not as good a shot as I used to be." He smiled fiendishly. "Ol Felix can attest to that. I may not kill them on the first try."

Brady's mind raced. It was true. He was probably a better shot than the sheriff. Brady most definitely could put the dogs down with one shot each.

He slowly raised his pistol so the stock was aimed squarely between the mongrel's empty eye sockets. He knew the sheriff didn't place much value on the lives of a couple of stray dogs. He was a lousy shot, too. He'd make a mess of things if it were left up to him. Brady imagined a nightmarish scene of the sheriff chasing the dogs around the garden, directing shot after shot into the dogs' hides until they finally succumbed.

What would my father do? Brady wondered. He concluded his father would most certainly have used a gun. In fact, he'd witnessed his father do it. If you were a good shot, it was quick, easy, and effective. This situation had gone on long enough. It had to be resolved, for the animals' sake.

"Get the kids away from here," he said.

"Byron... please," Mindy pleaded.

"Mindy... it's my job. I'm an animal control officer."

"But –"

"Let me do my job." His own voice seemed weak, uncertain.

Brady noticed the Jack staring back at him. His gaze was unwavering. The animal was covered with filth and blood. The last time Brady saw him, he was leading most of the feral pack deep into the woods. How did he survive? What terrible things did those eyes see? What did he look like through those eyes?

It was admirable the way these two dogs had stayed alive... *Whoa, Brady. They're just dogs. You're giving them human characteristics*, he told himself. *But haven't you always been a believer in animism – the belief that all living things have a soul? What about your own soul, Brady? What have you done to it? Stop – can't let it get personal. If you make an exception for these two dogs, you have to spare the lives of every animal in that shelter. Are you prepared to do that? A better question: do you have the power? It's just not possible.*

"Go away," he said aloud, not looking at any of them. "Walk away and let me do my job."

"Don't kill them, Mr. Brady... they're my friends."

Brady recognized Sara's voice. How could he make her understand? What would she think of him now?

All the children began shouting, "Don't kill the dogs! Save them! Don't kill them, Mr. Brady!" Brady even heard Mindy's voice in the mix.

"Shoot them, Brady, damn you!" the sheriff roared. "You shoot these monsters, or you look for another job, you hear?"

"Enough!" Josephine screamed above all the other voices. Brady had never heard her raise her voice so loudly before. An uneasy silence fell over the garden. She walked up to Brady's side, but Brady refused to look at her.

He kept his eyes on the two dogs.

"I've known you since you were a little boy, Byron Brady," she said quietly to him. "Since the time you fell off your skateboard in front of my house. Remember?" He remembered. "You were crying." She smiled warmly, and he saw that warm smile from the corner of his eye. "You'd skinned your knee and I brought you in and dressed the cut." He felt her hand touch his forearm, the arm in which the gun was held. "We became friends that day, you and I, life-long friends. I know you so well. In fact, I've known three generations of Brady men, and you're the best of them. You can't fool me. You can't shoot these dogs in cold blood… and you won't."

Brady swallowed hard. It wasn't fair. She wasn't playing fair.

"Be your own man… be your own *Brady*. Do the right thing, Byron." She turned and walked away from him. "He's going to do the right thing," she announced, confidently.

"Yes, he is going to do the right thing," the sheriff remarked. "He's going to keep his job. Isn't that right, Brady? One hundred years of service to this county… can't argue with that. Brady men are going to have another one hundred years of service, ain't that right?" The sheriff scratched his belly through his shirt. "I know you a long time, too. Don't I, Brady? Sure do. I remember when you were no more than knee-high, clinging to your daddy's trouser leg down at the courthouse. Remember? You wanted to be an animal control officer just like your daddy. All your life, Brady, you've prepared for this moment, to protect and to serve this fine community. Now look at you: afraid to shoot a couple of worthless strays. What would your father think of you now?" The sheriff's words stung Brady's heart. "The right thing? Oh, he'll do the right thing, that's for sure." The sheriff laughed.

The Jack continued to stare at Brady. There was no fear in his eyes. He knew, and in some strange way, Brady knew the dog knew, too. He was never going to shoot these dogs. He didn't have it in him. He never really had it in him at all. He'd been fooling himself all this time. Maybe it was time to break from tradition… maybe it was time for this Brady to strike out on his own. It just didn't feel right anymore: shooting; euthanizing; killing. Brady laughed, too.

He turned to the sheriff and said, "There'll be no killing today, sheriff. Or anymore." He lowered the pistol and let it drop to his feet.

"Wh-what?" the sheriff stammered.

A chorus of cheers rang out from Josephine's tiny, secret garden, which considering the number of people, didn't seem nearly so secret now.

"I'm done, sheriff… through."

"Oh, you're through all right, Brady," the sheriff growled. "I'll make sure of it."

"I love you, Byron Brady," Mindy cried, falling into his arms. "I love you."

Brady kissed her.

"Get the hell outta my way, you damned kids," Mortimer said, dragging his injured leg behind him. He shoved his way through the gathering until he reached the center of the garden.

"Leave me to bleed to death, will you," he hissed. "I have half a mind to put a bullet in the whole lot of you."

"Good ol' Felix!" the sheriff exclaimed. "Felix will shoot the dogs, won't you, Felix?"

A confused look manifested on Mortimer's tired face. He scratched his head. "Well… I, sure I will. If that's what you want?"

The sheriff laughed. "How does chief animal control officer Mortimer sound?"

Mortimer ran a bloodied hand through his greasy, greying hair. "Bugger… that sounds pretty damn good, me thinks."

"There they are, Felix." The sheriff pointed to the dogs. "Two shots away from a higher tax bracket, eh Felix?"

"Now yer talkin'." Mortimer hurriedly pulled his county-issued pistol from his hip and steadied it on his bandaged hand.

He drew a bead on the Jack. Although he hated the mongrel, he hated the small, white dog even more. "I told you, you stinking bugger," he said. "I told you ol' Felix would get you in the end."

The Jack stared back at him blankly. It was one of those noisemakers the man pointed at him, he was certain.

He was so tired. Everything seemed set against him and his friend. Why fight anymore? He looked to his beast within, but he was all used up.

Cordite reached Buddy's nose. That smell… the explosive noise he had encountered at the pound. The heat and force of the gunshot replayed in his mind. He felt the Jack tense up next to him. It was coming for the Jack.

Buddy had had enough. This friend had already done too much for him. It was time he did something for his friend.

Buddy stood and moved in front of the Jack. How much could it hurt? It couldn't hurt worse than losing his friend. Buddy pointed his nose in the direction of the smell.

Brady noticed it first. The blind dog was sniffing at the cordite. *He's going to take the bullet for his friend. What an amazing animal – he's going to take the bullet!*

Mortimer's ghastly hand shook. Finally, he was going to get some damned recognition. The blind one moved in front of the little one. *Two shots... So what if the big one wants to get his first. Ol' Felix will get 'em both. He certainly will.*

Mortimer took a deep breath and tensed his hand inside the bandages. He had the center of the mongrel's chest in his sights. *Bon voyage*, he thought. He had the – he had the center of Brady's knee-cap! *Brady!*

Sara held her hand to her heart. Brady was shielding the dogs. She knew it! She knew that Byron Brady was a good man!

Sara ran into the line of fire and raced toward Brady.

A shot rang out.

"Sara!" Josephine and Mindy cried in unison. Both women instinctively chased after the child.

"Cripes!" Mortimer howled. His hands shook even more. He nearly shot the girl. He couldn't get a good shot with all these buggers running around.

Sara hugged Brady, whose eyes burned at Mortimer. Josephine and Mindy threw their arms around Brady and hugged him, too.

"Come on," Justin shouted, and all the children joined Brady and the rest in front of the dogs, creating a wall around them.

Josephine glared at Jim, who was still standing on the side.

"Coming, Josie," he replied sheepishly, and added his considerable size to their defense.

"Damn you, buggers!" Felix screamed. "Let me do this here job!"

"Put that gun away, Felix," Josephine scolded. "Before someone gets hurt. Namely – you."

"This is obstruction of justice," the sheriff cried. "I'm citing everyone present with obstruction of justice!"

"What about trespassing, sheriff?" Josephine countered. "I don't remember inviting you in."

The sheriff turned red.

"Sheriff," Josephine continued. "They're just dogs… just dogs." She pointed to Buddy. "This one can't even see. What could be so dangerous about these two dogs?"

"Well, they're, ah… they're ferals."

"Ferals? Ferals are wild dogs." She pointed to the Jack. "Does this Jack Russell terrier look like a wild dog to you?"

"Well, he... er, he bit ol' Felix is what he did. And what about the tourists? We can't have dogs roaming our streets and attacking tourists."

"Sheriff, come on. Do these two actually look like they were running with that pack of ferals? I mean, for God's sake, this one can't even see."

"That one there's a killer, Josie. If I hadn't a come in to the shelter when I did, why, ol' Felix –"

"Would have one less bullet hole in him," Josie replied.

The sheriff flushed. "Now you listen here, Josie –"

"No, sheriff. You listen. You're not shooting these dogs in my yard, or anywhere else. Now leave, please."

"Josie, these two are dangerous and it would be damned irresponsible of me, the top lawman in this here county, to just up and leave two killers in this yard with all these fine children about."

"Killers? sheriff, you need to look at these dogs, I mean really look at them, and see them for what they really are: just dogs."

"Now, Josie, I've looked at them enough, and I still say they're killers."

"Sheriff, they just want what we all want: a place where they can feel safe, a place where they can belong."

"They belongs in a hole in the ground is where those two buggers belong, they do," Mortimer remarked.

Josephine scowled.

"Josie," the sheriff said, "you're harboring killers here. Now you don't want to be known around town as someone who harbors killers, do you?"

"Killers, sheriff? Really! Does this young Jack look like a killer to you?"

"Ah, Josie…"

"I said, 'look!'"

The sheriff looked at the Jack. "I've seen enough…" Quite suddenly and unexpectedly, his face softened. Sixty years of wrinkles and sun-dried skin faded away, and with it, a lifetime of concerns. The sheriff looked like a young lad of twelve again. His gaze drifted to a faraway place. His eyes glistened with adolescence and hope, and his entire future lay ahead of him. "My God," he exclaimed. "Teddy. He looks just like Teddy."

"Teddy?" Josephine replied. She shot Brady a look of disbelief. In response, he shrugged.

"Teddy," the sheriff whispered, quietly. "My Teddy."

"Who's Teddy, sheriff?" Josephine asked.

"Theodore J. Arnett… My Teddy. He was a gift from my Da when I was twelve, the cutest little Jack Russell terrier you've ever seen. He knew a half-dozen tricks and he came when you called him." The sheriff's eyes were watery. "Then one day, the ice truck was making a delivery – we were too poor to own a freezer then – and ol' Teddy, he loved to chase cars… And that truck was moving pretty good down Broadway, but poor Teddy, he –" But the sheriff couldn't finish. He collapsed to the ground. "My Teddy," he repeated, staring at the Jack.

"He's a killer, that bugger is!" Mortimer erupted.

"Felix," Josephine said, "shut the hell up!" She turned back to the sheriff. "It's okay, sheriff," she said, removing his hat.

"Look at me, Josie. A grown man…"

Josephine stroked his threadbare, sobbing head. "There's no shame in it, sheriff." She looked at Brady and smiled. "You're human after all."

Josephine winked at Sara. "Let's make this legal, sheriff. How much for two dog licenses?"

"Why," he sniffled, "twenty dollars, Josie."

"I'll take two, sheriff. These two 'buggers' are my dogs now."

She turned back to Mortimer. "Now get out of my yard."

Mortimer looked to the sheriff.

The lines shifted near the lawman's eyes, and he managed a weak smile. "The dogs are Josie's now," he said. "Go on home."

"You tells me to shoot the dogs, I shoot the dogs. You tells me don't shoot the dogs, I don't shoot the dogs. Ol' Felix does what he's told, he certainly does. But Dogammit, makes up me mind!" Under his breath, he muttered, "Bleedin' hearts, the whole stinking lot of you. To hell with you."

Mortimer limped reluctantly out of the garden.

"I guess I'll be following ol' Felix, make sure he gets home okay," the sheriff said softly.

Josephine nodded.

He turned. "Josie, I –"

"We know, sheriff." She smiled. "We know."

The sheriff put his head down and walked away.

"Do you really mean it, Josie? Are you really going to keep them?" Sara asked, excitedly.

"Yes, sweetheart. I mean it." Josephine turned to Jim. "Fix that gate already, will you? Before we find an elephant hiding beneath our rosebushes."

Later, after the last of the people had left the garden and the gate was firmly in place, Buddy walked the perimeter of the yard, sniffing at the fence line.

He could get used to this, he thought. The world was too big a place for a dog with no eyes. But a garden, that suited him just fine.

The Jack peeked out through the slats of the gate – so many strange scents and things out there. *I wonder what lies behind that row of houses, and up over the other side of that mountain and – but wait*. That's what got him into trouble in the first place. He looked back at Buddy, who didn't need him to navigate around the confined space, and was contentedly roaming about. *No, this feels good*, he thought.

This feels like home.

XXXII. Buddy & the Jack at Rest

This animal, our good familiar dog, simple and unsurprising as may to-day appear to us what he has done, in thus perceptibly drawing nearer to a world in which he was not born and for which he was not destined, has nevertheless performed one of the most unusual and improbable acts that we can find in the general history of life.

– Maurice Maeterlinck, *On the Death of a Little Dog*, from the *Double Garden*

It took some time for Buddy and the Jack to become re-accustomed to home life, but not nearly so long as one might think. True, the dogs did acquire a certain wildness while living the stray life; however, their roots were as pets, and both dogs remembered how to act like one.

Buddy adapted a bit faster than the Jack, inasmuch as he was older and more experienced. Actually, the blind mongrel fell quite easily into the rhythms of the McGillis home: breakfast at seven, nap at ten, play at one, nap at three, dinner at five, nap at seven, snack at eight, bed at ten. And though he was quite put off with humans in the beginning, as could be expected, he eventually came around.

For Jospehine was a persistent soul, and no one living in her household was excused from her random hugs. So Buddy learned to appreciate a warm embrace, a scratch behind his ears, and especially a rub on his belly.

With the Jack, there were some other problems. It seems before he left his home in Lansford, he was never properly housebroken. This meant the poor Jack could not differentiate between the bushes in Josephine's garden and her authentic Victorian pieces in her parlor, nor could he tell the difference between a patch of grass and an expensive Persian rug. But, through a delicate balance of training, patience, and a rolled newspaper applied to his fluffy, white bottom, the Jack quickly became an educated canine.

With the aid of a simple, routine surgical procedure, which removed the remainder of roaming from the Jack and animosity from Buddy, the two became respectable members of pet society. When not engaged in play, or seeking out some form of affection from either Josephine or Jim, the two could often be found stretched out by the stone hearth, lazily reposed, dreaming of their next meal.

There were changes in others' lives, too. Brady was true to his word, and never returned to his office at the courthouse. In fact, no Brady man ever held the position of animal control officer in the county again.

But what was a man like Brady to do? His entire life had been centered around the care and management of animals. Certainly there were opportunities for a young man like himself if he moved away.

But Brady liked Mt. Canaan, and the people who lived there. Besides, Mindy McGovern was there, and he couldn't leave her. Amazingly, Sara had the answer.

"Why don't you open your own animal shelter," she asked one day, as he lamented his future.

"My own animal shelter?" he said aloud. He did have some money put away.

"Yes, one where no animals are ever put down," she said.

"A 'no-kill' animal shelter?" Brady liked the idea. It was going to take a lot of money and a lot of land to see this idea come to fruition though.

Mindy McGovern liked the idea, too. In fact, she had many useful ideas that helped make the shelter become a reality.

The facility would be a not-for-profit organization that would rely highly on the generosity of animal lovers across the region. Nearly every business along Broadway would display an empty, plastic bottled water container that solicited donations from shoppers, and there would be adopt-a-pet day at the local shopping mall every third Saturday of the month.

For Brady, it was a dream-come-true. A wealthy benefactor and animal lover donated 6.5 acres atop Mt. Canaan where the land had once been strip-mined, robbed of its resources, and then filled back in. It was worthless to the coalmine owner who donated the land, but to Brady, Mindy and Sara, as well as the dozens of animals it housed, it could easily have been heaven. Their hard work and determination greatly reduced the stray animal population in Anthracite County and in effect, all but eliminated the need for an animal control office in the community.

And through the years, Brady prided himself in the fact that no animal was ever turned away, or destroyed, or felt the backside of a man's hand.

The sign on the shelter's front door summed up his philosophy best:

"Wanted: Unwanted Animals"

XXXIII. A Last Word About the Ferals

How ill this taper burns! Ha! Who comes here?
I think it is the weakness of mine eyes
That shapes this monstrous apparition.
It comes upon me. Art thou any thing?
Art thou some god, some angel, or some devil,
That mak'st my blood cold, and my hair to stare?
– William Shakespeare, from *Julius Caesar*

Of course, the feral pack was never seen again. True, any strange dog observed in the town was quickly branded a "feral," though no stray ever aligned itself with another to form a similar confederacy. Nonetheless, superstition and rumors persisted. The Cwn Annwn still prowled.

A fisherman saw it on the river. Some children claimed to have seen it down by the floodwall. The conductor of Mt. Canaan's only steam locomotive, *Ol' Number Nine-Seven-Two*, reported seeing it along the train tracks. Brady himself thought he might have witnessed it on a rainy, fog-ridden evening, running across the viaduct, ears alert.

A sleek, muscular dog, as dark as midnight, eyes an eerie, yellow glow, paws silent; a cold wind felt across the cheek.

Elsie Pendleton claimed it returned to her garden, this time passing through her fence instead of over it. She said it peed on her perennials. Felix Mortimer reported seeing it, too. It chased him in his '68 Dodge Dart from Molly Macguire's Pub and caused him to crash into a tree. He failed the sobriety test and was locked up for ninety days. Mindy McGovern thought she saw it, too. A black, phantom dog lurking near the school. But poor Mindy didn't have her glasses on and what she took for the Cwn Annwn turned out to be Lady Haversham's new toy poodle.

All agreed the dog was transparent, and all reported it vanished into thin air. Even Brady failed to see it in his rear-view mirror after he'd passed it, just seconds before. Though details were added to make the tale more engaging by the fireside, the creature's behavior was described the same:

Searching...

Perhaps for the pack that never returned to him; or for his next victim to lead to Annwn; or maybe, just maybe for the little, white dog who'd deceived him on an All Hallows Eve when the children of the town turned ghastly and a strange mist covered the land.

Perhaps.

XXXIV. A Journey Through Light

It seemed to Hazel that he would not be needing his body any more, so he left it lying on the edge of the ditch, but stopped for a moment to watch his rabbits and to try to get used to the extraordinary feeling that strength and speed were flowing inexhaustibly out of him into their sleek young bodies and healthy senses.

– Richard Adams, *Watership Down*

One frosty, winter morning, after many years and many more adventures, far too many to recount here, the Jack, who was becoming a bit long in the tooth, awakened from his restless slumber feeling a slight chill. A strange darkness pervaded the kitchen where the dogs slept, and the windowpanes were glazed over with a sparkling coating of crystallized ice. No morning sun danced upon them, and a most persistent dampness invaded the old dog's bones.

As was his usual custom, he snuggled closer to his life-long friend, Buddy, whose enormous size was always useful to warm one's self on a morning such as this; however, no warmth was to be found this day.

For Buddy, who in recent months had also lost his hearing, though still managed to get around thanks to the dependable Jack, had none to give. Because on this unforgivably cold morning when the birds outside chose not to sing but instead to seek the comfort of a warm nest, an unwelcome stranger had passed through the Jack's own corner of the world.

Sometime during the night, while the Jack had chased away bad dreams and phantom dogs, Death himself had crept beneath his very nose and stolen away the only friend the terrier had ever known.

After a lifetime of adversity beset with equal physical disadvantages, most of which the mongrel had triumphed over, a tired Buddy forfeited the remainder of his life (as if any more was due him), and succumbed to the inevitable darkness that awaits us all.

The poor Jack, who knew nothing of a subject such as death, simply wondered why his usually warm friend had become suddenly cold. With a gentle nudge, the Jack prodded his dear friend with his muzzle. But the only response the Jack received was the complete and utter nothingness that is death. There was nothing more.

The mongrel was dead.

Inasmuch as dogs have no such words as farewell and good-bye, none were said. An empty, lonesome wail consumed the Jack and he felt himself die a little, too. He lowered his head and rested his chin on Buddy's still chest.

Josephine, who'd passed away a restless night of her own, where she tossed and turned and nearly ran poor Jim off his own side of the bed, awoke that morning and immediately sensed something was wrong. The Jack had not scratched at the door.

For many years, she'd been awakened by the spunky Jack who had yet to allow her to sleep past seven. However, on this morning, at a half past eight, no such sign was forthcoming.

,Concerned, Josephine bolted from the bed, covered her generous frame with a flannel bathrobe and went to investigate.

For a moment, she'd thought she was still asleep, for she'd stepped certainly into a nightmare. There lay the Jack awkwardly over Buddy, staring out past her at nothing.

Buddy, whose head lay itself at a most peculiar angle, suggested one thing and one thing only: never again would she see the intrepid mongrel nosing about the flowers in her garden or barking at the sound of fallen leaves. No longer would she find him curled up on Sara's big, comfy chair in her shop or sitting on Jim's lap, the only lap big enough to accommodate him. She thought of his affinity for Antonio's pizza crust and her legs grew weak.

Her first instinct was to run to Buddy and scoop him up in her arms, this dog who earned the right to trust no one but trusted her all the same. But she knew he was gone, "to be at the feet of God," she heard herself whisper.

Another needed her now, one whose heart though valiant and strong, ached for his fallen comrade. She dropped to her knees and pulled the Jack close.

Without resistance, the Jack rested upon her bosom and sighed.

Jim buried Buddy in the far corner of the garden, beneath the very rosebushes where Josephine had discovered Buddy and the Jack hiding many years before.

All Buddy's friends were there to see him off: Josephine and Jim; the college-bound Sara and her mother; even Byron and Mindy Brady, who brought along their son Jakob. And of course, the Jack, who couldn't quite understand what all the fuss was about.

His friend was gone, and no amount of fuss was going to change that. But he sat quietly and observed the memorial, anyway. After Josephine and Sara had said a few words, and the last of the dirt was placed upon the mound, the Jack sniffed at the grave and then plopped lazily atop it. And that's where he could often be found, when there wasn't snow piled about, just in case the old mongrel needed him.

Over the next several years, the Jack continued with what life he had left and mostly slept by the crackling fire, often dreaming of a colossal mongrel with the strength of ten dogs and the heart of twenty. And when he'd awake, he'd sometimes find himself wondering if the big dog ever really existed at all, or if he was just a queer dream.

Epilogue

But in some canine Paradise
Your wraith, I know, rebukes the moon,
And quarters every plain and hill,
Seeking its master.

* * * *

As for me
This prayer at least the gods fulfill
That when I pass the flood and see
Old Charon by Stygian coast
Take toll of all the shades who land,
Your little, faithful barking ghost
May leap to lick my phantom hand.
– St. John Lucus, *To a Dog*

In a bright meadow not far from the patriarchal watch of an old willow tree, an enormous mongrel lay sunning himself in the midst of burgeoning red, blue, and violet lilies, tulips, and Gladioli. The flowers waved only slightly in the gentle breeze.

The dog rolled onto his back and twisted his torso from side to side, extended his legs into the air, stretched his limbs and pawed lazily at a monarch butterfly passing by. He stared up into the sapphire sky that was interrupted only by an occasional wispy cloud. He barked at the clouds, which often formed recognizable shapes, and in response, they scooted along until nothing else infringed upon the blue sky for as far as the dog could see.

Pleased with himself, he lay on his side and closed his eyes. He could not recall how long he had been here or where he had been before – just darkness – then light – and this meadow.

He'd investigated every inch of tall grass since his arrival, sniffed out every small creature. He'd played with a tortoise, had been stung on the nose by a bee (it didn't hurt much), and slept beneath a canopy of stars. He knew there was more to this place than just this meadow, sure of it, in fact. Great mountaintops, tipped with snow, jutted out in the distance, and he once traced the flight of a hawk with his eyes until it became so small, it seemed the sky had swallowed it up. But he resisted the urge to roam, to explore, for now... He was waiting, for who or what, wasn't clear. But a very certain feeling, a voice inside his head, distinctly ordered him to wait, and he learned in this world, it's in your best interest to pay attention to such signs. So contentedly he did, reposing in the hypnotic swirl of the grass. It wasn't hard work, and he was becoming quite good at it. Today, if there were such a measure of time as a day here, the mongrel's wait would be over.

Off on the edge of the meadow, where a dark, impenetrable forest made up of tall trees and oblique shadows was the defining line between light and dark, a cacophonous bark emerged from within and was carried along the mild breeze.

Alerted, the mongrel sat up, ears pricked, and scanned the entire meadow for the owner of the strange bark. Inevitably, his gaze was drawn to the meadow's border and the looming forest where an endless row of gnarled, leaning trees formed a tunnel-like passage where he'd often observed strangers appear before. But his senses told him none of those strangers were meant for him, and his feeling of waiting had persisted.

But now, his body rippling with anticipation, he leaped to his feet. Inexplicably, he found himself racing toward the strange, twisted trees. Within the forest, another shrill bark was cast out.

As he reached the limits of the meadow where the forest's dark shadows lay across the grass like a pair of sentries' crossed spears, the dog halted and called into the wood. His thundering bark poured into the forest leaking into every crack, and filled up every pocket of silence.

In response, yet another bark made its way through the trees and into the light. Excitedly, the dog pursued his tail once around and howled.

Slowly, a white form materialized before him at the foot of the trees, and separated itself from the shadows that dwelt within. Stoically, a somewhat small, white terrier emerged from the trees and passed from darkness into the light. He was all white, save a brown patch of fur on his right ear that extended well below his right eye. A cotton swab, which served as his tail, stood straight from his hindquarters and wagged frenetically. The large dog had never laid eyes on this one before, he was sure.

Cautiously, the white dog approached, his eyes working to acclimate themselves to the brightness of the meadow. They sniffed at each other, which is a dog's custom, and decided neither meant any hostility toward the other.

The mongrel filled his nose with the stranger's scent, his own tail working furiously. Quite unexpectedly, the white dog bit at the underside of the mongrel's chin.

The mongrel was taken back. *What is this?* he thought.

He–He was playing! I get it now. My God, after all this time... The mongrel froze. Something was so familiar about all this... But he didn't have time to ponder it more. The white dog was atop him, bouncing, pouncing, *grrring*, licking, yapping. The canine ritual of play engulfed the mongrel, sparking faded, disjointed memories of a town, a garden, a forgotten friend; a life.

Like two long lost lovers, reunited at last, they fell upon one another, barking, nipping, playing, and tumbled joyously end over end into the field of waving flowers.

In time, they'd make their way to those majestic mountains and the secrets that lay hidden beyond. The sun would remain high in the sky for as long as they wished.

A warm, soft breeze carelessly passed over the tall, uncut grass. A hummingbird hovered above a dandelion and sampled its sweet nectar. A young sparrow left the confines of its nest and took flight for the first time.

Above, the white, woolly clouds returned once more.

THE END

Although *Buddy & the Jack* is a work of fiction, Buddy's ailment unfortunately is not. Many blind dogs find themselves in animal shelters each year. For most of them, there is no "Jack" to rescue them. Hundreds of unwanted blind, but otherwise healthy dogs are euthanized every year. But it doesn't have to be that way.

Unlike people, sight is not the sense on which dogs rely most. It's not even second. According to leading veterinarians, a dog relies mainly on his sense of smell and his hearing, which is hundreds of times more acute than our own. In addition, dogs possess a unique skill called cognitive mapping that enables them to "see" the geography of a particular place, such as your home, by remembering the pattern in which they have previously traveled. This enables them to cope more easily with blindness than their human counterparts.

Furthermore, there are medical procedures that in some cases can restore partial or total sight to the blind dog, depending on their cause of blindness. Unfortunately, as one could expect, these procedures can prove costly to the dog owner. Thankfully, there is a fund set up to help owners of blind dogs afford the expensive surgeries their dogs need. If you would like to contribute to this noble cause, please write to:

IMOM (In Memory of Magic), Inc.
PO Box 282
Cheltenham, MD 20623

To find out how to adopt a blind dog, please visit:

http://www.blinddogs.com/

A percentage of the sales from this book will be contributed to the above fund.

Yours in compassion,
W. Bryan Smith

Printed in the United States
4783